SIX DAYS TO SUNDAY

Books by
Bernard Brunner

THE FACE OF NIGHT

URANIUM!

THE GOLDEN CHILDREN

SIX DAYS TO SUNDAY

SIX DAYS TO SUNDAY

a novel by Bernard Brunner

McGRAW-HILL COMPANY
New York   St. Louis   San Francisco
Toronto

Book design by Robert L. Mitchell.

123456789BPBP798765

Library of Congress Cataloging in Publication Data

Brunner, Bernard.
    Six days to Sunday.

    I. Title.
PZ4.B8897Qar   [PS3552.R8]   813'.5'4   75-4812
ISBN 0-07-008579-X

SIX DAYS TO SUNDAY

ROSTER

Carson Le Motte—General Manager

COACHING STAFF

Jim Lowry—head coach
Gabe Simson—defensive line coach
Bob Ellis—coach of the wide receivers
Tim Dewey—backfield coach

Ted Davis—trainer
Dan Fallon—public relations

STAG DEFENSE

No.	Name	Pos.	Ht.	Wt.	Age	Exp.	College
23	Elijah Johnson	RCB	5'11"	180	35	10	USC
37	Louis "Green Wolf" Greene	RS	6'	195	27	5	Florida State
43	Perry "Jellybean" Taylor	LS	6'2"	185	25	3	Weber State
52	Fred Dickie	MLB	6'3"	240	30	8	Purdue
67	George Schmidt	DT	6'5"	270	34	12	U. of Idaho
68	Roger Garrett	DT	6'4"	245	27	5	Memphis State
77	Allan "Daddy" Wilson	DE	6'7"	235	30	8	Southern U.
88	Alexander "Poppo" Popovich	DE	6'2"	245	28	6	U. of Illinois

SPECIAL UNITS

No.	Name	Pos.	Ht.	Wt.	Age	Exp.	College
31	Howard "Gooch" Kozak	S	6'2"	220	26	4	Washington State
33	Ron "Bebo" Mancuso	S	6'1"	230	28	7	Wisconsin

STAG OFFENSE

No.	Name	Pos.	Ht.	Wt.	Age	Exp.	College
11	Earl "Chip" Hughes	QB	6'	185	30	9	Syracuse
14	Thomas "Apples" Grover	QB	6'4"	235	23	1	Nebraska
17	Karl Olson	QB	6'2"	195	25	4	New Mexico
25	Bill "Short Stuff" Saylor	SB	5'10"	205	26	5	Kansas
32	Walter "Dude" Shea	K	6'	175	30	10	Brigham Young
33	Albert Harris	SB	6'3"	220	31	7	Baylor
57	Mike "57 Flavors" Heinz	C	6'2"	235	32	9	U. of Georgia
61	Peter "Rook" Donaldson	C	6'4"	240	22	1	Minnesota
63	Mark Youngblood	LG	6'5"	260	30	6	Grambling
66	Larry "Toof" Merwin	LT	6'3"	240	28	5	UCLA
70	Harold "Li-bary" Mulenberg	RG	6'4"	245	23	2	Augustana
74	John "Lips" Mangialardi	RG	6'6"	255	27	4	Ohio State
78	Harold "Harry the Hawk" Hawkins	RT	6'2"	235	28	5	Texas A & M
81	Weldon "Bird" Jones	WR	6'1"	195	29	8	U. of Tennessee
87	Ronald "Jay" Jaworski	TE	6'2"	230	30	7	U. of Pittsburgh
89	Levi Tucker	WR	6'5"	209	25	5	Tennessee State

THE GROUP

Dori Frazier—the Queen Bee
Jackie—Locker Room Annie and grower of plants and pets
Shirley—special units
Maybelle—reserve mattress for the team

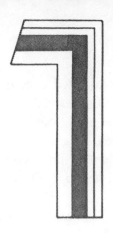

The crumbled old stadium on the lakefront was a pit of roaring light. Banks of light blazed. Spotlights glared down from the cement pillars on top of both stands.

Deep on the smoky bottom, lines of men bucked into each other, plunged and strained, grunting, churning heavily. Receivers and defensive backs flew out from the exploding play. The Chicago Stag quarterback dodged and skittered backward and was beaten down before he could cock his arm to throw.

Wobbling to his feet, he tugged his shoulder pads back into place. A bowlegged giant came toward him, his smashed mouth drooling curses.

"Jaworski," he said, "stop kicking ass and run those patterns." The big tight end had gotten a fist in the mouth, and he was running all his routes directly over 250 pounds of prone linebacker. "Or get off the field."

The maddened eyes flared at him, then dropped in submission. Unsteadily Chip Hughes knelt down in the huddle. His head was still full of drumming light from the blast he'd taken. "Okay," he said to the barred faces panting down at him, "same play right back, sixty-two dart, Y-ten and out. On two. Bird, open the throttle all the way."

This time Jaworski hauled in the pass and bashed downfield for sixteen yards. The glaze and glare swirled with happy noise. The public-address voice mumbled hugely, and the sticks moved forward on the sidelines— phosphorescent orange markers ten feet tall, painted with a round blank face and a spike body.

Play moved back and forth on the field. The markers pitched along with it, barbaric, ancient.

In the fourth quarter the Stags got a field goal, and the scoreboard blazed VIKINGS 14, STAGS 10. Lights danced, rippled all over the board and collected into the head of a stag, a capering beast of light. But wide in the southern sky above it, the clock glowed nine minutes left, and around it a circle of lights blinked out one after another.

With 5:31 to play the Vikings were forced to punt. The Stag offense trotted on, green-and-gold men moving tiredly now. Chip Hughes sauntered up to the line of scrimmage, looking over the defense, reading it swiftly as he chanted signals. The lines crashed together. Shouts of obscenity. Grunting collisions. Eyes rolling in a torn slobbery face and a linebacker screaming, "Blue! Blue!" But the honey-colored face of the Stags' left guard was smiling in its cage as he stepped back to pass block. "Now we gonna dance, baby," he said. His legs driving power-fully, he sledged his forearms into the helmeted charge of the Viking tackle, again and again and again, thrusting up from his bull-muscled haunches. He'd forgotten what game it was, the score, everything. Beautiful, it was beautiful.

Slugging, heaving his man backward, he was only vaguely and gradually aware that Chip had put the ball in the air, that the play was moving away downfield. Then there was a gasp from the high thundering stands, and grape-colored jerseys were bouncing up and down, pointing his way. "Musta been a fumble after the catch," he said to himself and ambled toward the sidelines. The cat he was working against was one swift being, but he didn't use his hands good.

"Wipe it out," Chip said to Bird, whacking him on the butt. "Good catch, good catch." The defense came lumbering by, their shoulder pads rocking wearily. "Get me back the goddam seed," he yelled at them. "Get it for me, George."

A soiled club of a fist went up, answering. But time was running out, and the stadium horns fell into windy laments. Mushy-legged, the offensive guard playing opposite George Schmidt wiped the blood off on his jersey and set himself in his stance. His whole body whimpered as it waited to be hit again. There was just no way to stop the man, no way. He came charging over, around and through you, and when he really wanted a play, holy fuck, the moves he put on you. Stopping him was like trying to catch light. "He's rapin you," Coach kept screaming from the sidelines. In a glaze of helpless fatigue he lunged forward at the snap of the ball. The gold helmet did a crazy dance, dipped and floated like a fiery wheel. Upended on the turf, he saw Schmidt chase down a fumble and cover it.

George's sweet busted face was transfigured, shining

with a big jack-o'-lantern smile. The whole defensive team was hugging him, cuffing him and roughing his hair. "Way to go," Chip said to him, running onto the field. Emotionally but formally, George slapped hands with him.

The clock was moving, though—2:35, 2:34—and the ball was on the Stag sixteen-yard line. As he strutted up behind his center and reached under him for the ball, Chip suddenly felt cold and lonely and trapped. Could Super Mouse get out of this one? The 43,450 fans were yelling for it. All they wanted, he thought bitterly, was just a little old miracle, just John Unitas at his prime with Baltimore.

Grimly he took a pop at it. The only possible call was a pass, so he dropped back as if to throw and slipped the ball off his hip to Short Stuff, his running back, who rammed into the center of the spreading line for thirteen yards. Then he pumped a quick pass to Birdie, down and out, for nine more. The fire was lit. The mild, tame voices were roaring now, chanting in the underwater light: "Go! Go! Go!"

He rolled to the outside, faked with his shoulder, and turned the end for six more yards before he was wrestled down. He was actor and bullfighter, bruised dancer, magician. With each play the rhythm built up and up, a frenzied drumming in the stands. Sammy the Stag threw his hooves around; the stadium horns were braying. The pompom girls joined arms and kicked like Barbie-doll priestesses at the sky. "Go! Go! Go!" The chant came in great waves, discharges spilling over the field.

Chip Hughes scarcely heard it. For him the drive had become something entirely different and interior. It was execution, it was selecting plays, it was knowing his receivers and all their moves, the Viking zone defense, and that the weak-side safety was hurt and the cornerback was giving the inside to Tucker, his other wide receiver—and using all of it in a kind of chess game in his head.

He sent Short Stuff off tackle for seven yards and a first down on the Viking 40. Then he lobbed a pass over everybody, just to keep the defense honest. When it pulled in tight again he broke the pocket and zigzagged like a frantic mouse, feinting through tackles while his receivers skimmed downfield in different patterns, cutting and slanting off, streaking, curling in. Nobody was open. He scrambled some more while they ran busted patterns —deliberately multiplying the chaos to create that split second where there would be a gap between a receiver and the defense. Then instantly he drilled the ball to precisely that tiny theoretical area. As he released it he was buried by half a ton of massive bodies, bludgeoning forearms, face masks, shoes. But all that was somewhere else. The breathless logic was linking together inside him. The game itself was happening inside him, dark and glass-pure in the howling light.

Seconds were lopping off on the clock: 39, 38. He had fourth down and a foot on the Viking 29. The book call was a dive play for the first down, a time out, and then as many passes as he could squeeze in. Instead, he laid the rent money on the line. "Tuck," he said in the huddle, "take that free safety out of it. Suck him with you." And threw deep, putting everything he had on the ball. Bird, on a hitch and go, broke past the cornerback and sprinted under the long high floater at the goal line—

The dark chessmen fell down in his head. The roaring collapsed, went limp and sick as the Viking free safety cut in from the side, leaped high and snagged the ball and came careening back upfield. He was flattened by three Stags, but it didn't matter. Wine-colored Vikings were springing around deliriously.

The gun went off. Weak boos dribbled out of the emptying seats.

Slogging off the field behind the team, he gave the Hughes salute, a middle finger jabbing upward. The boos thickened like a whirl of snowflakes. He stopped and pretended to play the violin, bowed, and trotted off in a blizzard of booing.

Up in a box of neon light attached to the Grecian pillars portable typewriters were tapping: "Vikings down Stags . . . fourth consecutive defeat" . . . "worst start in club history." A squatting mimeograph coughed logs of fourth-quarter play. Three dull-faced women sat at Western Union Telex machines. Vengefully Al Whitman, resident bard of the *Times-Examiner*, was pecking away: "In the glory days of two years ago, Chip Hughes took the Stags to within one point of a division title. Now days of blight have fallen on the land. At the end of the game the fans were booing the onetime golden boy whose wand seems to be running out of stardust."

"Pus arm," muttered big John Mangialardi in the dressing room. "That's what he's got, a stinking pus arm."

"Take it cool, Lips," one of his buddies told him.

Stamping his feet and grumbling, Lips peeled down to heavy muscle slathered with dirt and sweat. His genitals swung between his legs. "The little hot dog," he muttered. "I can piss further 'n he can throw." He didn't dare say it out loud, though, not yet, and that crammed the frustration tighter inside him. Suddenly he was a 255-pound tantrum with red hair and thick blubby lips, kicking and shouting, "We couldn't 've lost to them jagoffs!"

He was wild, but he was putting on a show too, and he got so busy with his fit that he almost bumped against Fred Dickie. His heart flopped over inside him as if he'd seen a mouse. He shrank backward. Dickie didn't move. He was crouched in front of his locker, naked, his head plunged down from his brute back. He dropped a mouthful of spitty blood onto the cement floor. After some games it took him an hour before he came out of it enough to shower. If anybody even brushed against him then, he came whirling off that chair with his fists slugging and his eyes all burning and crazy.

"Man oh man, I am stone beat." Wearily a player flopped his shoulder pads up on top of the locker. They lay there like a heap of empty seed pods. He laid his fingers on the bleeding pain of his nose and mumbled, "I think it's busted."

The locker room was clogged with wet and stinking jerseys, tee shirts, socks, snarls of tape. The clubhouse boy worked along the aisles, picking up after the players and dumping the messes into hampers. A dim shape kept tagging after him on crutches, poling and swinging himself along. It was a veteran who was out for the season with torn knee ligaments, and the guys just looked away from him now that he was injured. He was nothing to them; he was alone, lost, freezing outside the great warm body of the team. Frantically he clutched at the punchy little man with the armful of sopping towels. "It hurts like a sonofabitch, Jocko."

"Yuh."

"Even my prostrate hurts. I ain't getting any tail anymore. Adele went back home with the kids, but I can't make myself leave, you know? It hurts like it's gonna kill me."

Painfully, Chip Hughes reached for his sports coat and pants hanging from a pipe under the ceiling. As quickly as possible he got out of there, shrugging past the reporters in the annex. "I thought," he said, "we came in a good strong second."

Most of the players left hurriedly too, glum and bruised and limping. But not Alexander Popovich, the big defensive end. He was standing in the boggy aisle with his arms spread out, naked, hairy, gigantic, singing in Croatian. "God fucked my mother today," he sang in a deep bellow.

Sourly the other players looked at him. One of the blacks, a little cornerback, said, "That's enough jive outa you, man."

Poppo beamed at the handful of black muscle and bone, picked it up and put it gently in a laundry hamper. "I am sad too, only in my way," he said to him. The blacks didn't like it. He smiled some more.

But then the yammering quieted as Daddy Wilson came walking by toward the shower. To the blacks on the team he was "master of *all* situations" and "the ultimate." Tall and purple-dark, he walked with the majesty and silence of a sacred king. At the end of the aisle he came upon George Schmidt, lying on a bench. The great old veteran had done it all. He'd even come up with that clutch recovery to give Chip one last crack. Tears were running in his plowed-up face.

"George, you are for real," Daddy said. And Poppo grunted in Croatian.

The half-empty mouth formed the words with difficulty: "It tears my balls to lose like that, guys."

Daddy laid his hand on the bruised and sorrowing chest. Then in silence he and Poppo helped George to his feet. George went on with his post-game ritual, hobbling into the training room to cut off the tape. The coaches came by in a grim pack, with the General Manager trotting at their heels and yapping, "You told me we had the bodies this year. Well, where is it, I ask you?"

Following them into their locker room, he railed, "We have to do something. We can't just sit on our big and hairy."

For a second they just looked at him, as bleak as their bare little room and their clothes hung in West Point order in open wire cages. Then one of them in the back said, "We're not getting our share of the breaks, Mr. Le Motte."

"No more excuses!" he fumed. "Don't talk to me any more about bad bounces. That's all Shinola. Our potential is division leader right now."

His breath was dry, shaking. Those heartless light eyes under the bills of the caps—already he was perspiring and ill from the strain.

"This is a state of emergency," he insisted. "We're losing fans, the papers are all going over to the Bears. I want you to know that everybody's noggin is on the chopping block, mine included. We need to join heads here. Jim, you're boss man. What do you think?"

In a montone Jim Lowry recited a haphazard litany of impressions: He thought the defense played a good fierce game, but the offense didn't make the big play, and—

"Yes, yes, but I mean—look, we can't deal for a

quarterback. Olson has a shoulder separation, Hughes isn't winning, and Grover has only one season under his belt. So what do you think?"

"I don't know, Mr. Le Motte."

"You, Bob? Dewey?" he asked, looking at the assistant coaches. From each he received politeness and curt replies. The coaches might have their little differences, but they were a ferocious elite set hard against him. He felt himself becoming weightless, transparent, unreal.

Almost in tears, he turned to Gabe Simson, the gross defensive coach, sitting in piled-up masses of flesh and holding some of his paunch with one hand like a 310-pound Buddha. Hoping, yearning, he said, "Well, Gabe?"

The jowly face didn't move. The General Manager was close to panic. His entire image was simply on the verge! Was Gabe going to snub him, not answer him at all after being so strong on the subject? The bottom part of Gabe's head, like the bottom part of his body, hung in great sleepy folds. Immense, half turned away, he was like a bloated god who might or might not listen to prayers.

Underneath the stands the hard-core devotees were waiting in the dirty gloom—mostly kids with programs, a few broads and Locker Room Annies, white and black. The shadows all around bulged with rows of muscular pillars. The cement floor was broken, and whitewash was peeling from the flesh-colored walls. "I'm going to get six autographs. That's my *quest*," a pimply girl kept saying.

Lips Mangialardi and four other players came shouldering out of the locker room. "Don't bug me," he growled at the imploring flutter of programs. Half joking and half paying him homage, his people wedged the fans back like bodyguards. "Outa the way. Give him room."

They went out a side exit toward the parking lot. Car horns barked, and the clogged lights of the traffic jerked and slowed, stopped. An old old woman who peddled souvenirs was packing up, stuffing green-and-gold Stag dolls back into their little cardboard coffins. She dropped one. The helmeted head popped off and wobbled away, and all the baby-pink faces rocked into motion, bobbed up and down in a puddle of light.

As she shambled after the weakly orbiting head, Lips took one of the dolls and deftly slid it into his coat pocket. This made him feel better, and he began putting it to the rookie reserve center. "Rook," he said solemnly, "you played a helluva game."

They all joined in, nailing the compliments in with relish. "Way to go. Beautiful game, baby."

"He did the hat trick tonight," Lips observed. "He got in for three plays."

Guffawing, swatting each other and horsing around, they trooped toward their cars.

"Hey, Lips, what's the game plan for tonight?"

"Yeah, how many squaws you got lined up?"

Gabe Simson padded naked down the hall toward the players' shower—a fleshy monster, a satyr gone to seed, but put together so perfectly that he seemed almost small in spite of his breasts and gut. Mountainous and light, graceful, he seemed to float down the row of stuffed hampers.

"Hey, Coach!" Dragging a gray-haired mop, Jocko

poked his lumpy face out of the locker room. The aisle gaped behind him, empty except for Fred Dickie. "Coach? Hey, that was a bitch to lose, huh?"

"Well," Gabe said mildly, "the sun's gonna come up tomorrow anyhow. Where's my dough?"

"Oh! Yuh." Jocko handed over the fifteen dollars he owed him, and Gabe tucked the bills between his buttocks to keep them dry while he shaved. They sprouted from the crease like green leaves.

"How could we of lost?" Jocko lamented. "Somebody musta put a good witchcraft on us."

"Witchcraft my tiddy. We been playing pitty-pat football. You got to stick it in their gismo in this league." Of all the coaches he took defeat the hardest, but today Jocko didn't get a grumble out of him. He went back to work, and Gabe, droning like a beehive in his chest, peered into the mirror and sliced at the white foam on his cheeks. In a minute he heard a commotion, then a crash in the locker room—and there was Jocko, face down in spilling mop water. Dickie must have given him a real shot. Like plenty of former linemen, Jocko was sort of punchy, but it took one hell of a lick even to deck him. Fred Dickie was strictly bad news after a game. That roughhouse in the bowling alley, for one, and the time he got to that broad and about killed her. Ever since then his attorney waited outside the locker room and took him home. Grinning, Gabe considered calling the legal eagle in now.

Instead, he took the money out of his rump, laid his razor on it, and paddled across the hall. Dickie was bent over on his chair again, his thick back jutting out into the aisle. Without warning he spun around and lashed at Gabe too. Gabe stepped almost daintily inside the punch and flicked out with both hands. Dickie was swept back, flung against the wall.

His stump head hit the green tile, and he flipped over on the floor, blood springing from the gap in his scalp. He pushed himself over on his elbows. The crazy flare was guttering in his eyes, but he climbed to his feet and lobbed a ponderous red punch.

"Come to me, Dickie." Gabe smiled and belted him a few times—carefully, so he wouldn't bust his neck on the locker or anything. One last good jolt and the battering hand hung down, the heavy roots of his legs came loose, and he went over on his back.

Gabe stood over him, breathing like a furnace. His body was roaring with excitement, with the old feel of hitting in the line. Half-forgotten games blazed up through the cindery years of retirement, match-ups, head-on-head with the thundering defensive tackles of his time, Karras, Art Donahoe . . .

He wouldn't have minded another go-round, but Dickie had had it.

"You're a good one, though," he said. "You're not so hot against the pass and you're too stupid to call defensive signals. But you can mow people down and you got that plus, Dickie. You're a mean fucker. Now Schmidt, he can do it all, he could be an immortal, but he ain't mean enough."

The little eyes blinked at him. The head was bleeding like an ancient sacrifice stump. Groping clumsily, Dickie heaved himself onto all fours and came at Gabe again, crawling. His gory face swung between his staggering arms.

"Mean and wild too," Gabe said with respect. "That's my flavor." Lightly, affectionately, he cuffed him down and this time he stayed there. "You're a special breed, you are. You love them head-on traffic accidents. Like old Burrell with the Eagles. He got knocked the coldest cocksucker I ever seen. We laid him on the sidelines and the next thing I see he's crawlin onto the field. Still out cold, too! That's my flavor."

Tenderly he raised Dickie up in his arms and hauled him half over his shoulder. "Guess what, Dickie boy," he puffed. "How'd you like to have a new quarterback for the Cardinal game? No lie. How's that for a present?" Grappling and skidding around in a bloody punch-drunk waltz, he got him into the showers. "We're gonna go with our power, Dickie. No more pitty-pat. We're gonna blow out with the big arm and our muscle. . . ."

Chip was going to sit down!
Exactly how the word got out was a
mystery, but by 11:30 P.M. it was
moving swiftly in the psychic
bloodstream of the team.

"I'm still incredulous," Short
Stuff said. "It takes five years to grow
a quarterback. You know?"

"It's incredulous to me too,"
Dude said. "It's a mind-fucker, a real
mind-fucker."

"Yeah."

Dude swung the car into his
driveway, and they went tramping
into Short Stuff's house. These two
not only ran together and battled each
other at pool, bowling, golf, and every
other game they could find, but they
had bought houses side by side. Turn
and turn about, they ate supper after
home games at each other's place,
with their wives joining forces in
putting out the meal. Tonight it was
another funeral feast. Slumped in the

bright rattle of the TV, they forked in the food: steaks, baked potatoes, chili, salad, beer.

"I hate when you lose," Dude's wife said. "You come home so crabby."

After a while Stuff said, "I'm still incredulous. I really am."

"Yeah . . . Well, the kid can run with the ball and throw it a mile. You gotta give him that."

"So what?" Stuff said, angrily loyal to his quarterback. "It takes more 'n that. I bet you he don't last the first half against the Cardinals."

"How much? Make it easy on yourself."

Short Stuff breathed loudly. His wide, heavy head was fused to his shoulders by muscle, and he had to swivel his whole torso around to turn his face. "I bet you a nickel," he said. Now it was serious. They both got to their feet. If he'd said ten, fifty, even a hundred dollars, it would only have meant money, but this was a matter of honor, of manhood, a blood pledge. Eyes boiling, they shook hands on it by grabbing each other's erect thumb and locking.

It had begun to rain, a thin October drizzle that wet the bland yellow light sloping out of the windows. Birdie Jones was standing by himself on his front lawn. Over and over he was catching that pass. It couldn't have been intercepted. No way. His wife called to him, "You come inside right now, hear?" Instead of obeying he just looked at her with his pale squirrel-shooter's eyes. "You'll catch your death," she screeched, but she closed the door.

Lean, expressionless, he turned on his heel, walked to the bags of leaves in the gutter by his car and kicked them to pieces. He did it with a measured, deliberate violence.

The soft green bellies vomited, split open and gushed breakfast-cereal leaves. He ripped the slick plastic apart with his hands and scattered the dry shreds all over in the darkness. Then he walked back inside.

Most of the black players were cooling it in Daddy Wilson's pad. Except Levi Tucker, who sat in a corner, brooding. "I styled on that motherfucker good. That free safety, he jus too dumb *stupid* to come with a fake." Gradually he became aware of the voices discussing the switch to Grover. "My brother, we are in it up to our eyeballs now. . . . Shi-it, let them white cats fight it out for theirself."

"Shut your fuckin mouth," he screamed, jumping to his feet. "Jus shut up! Chip's my *man!*"

Daddy was stretched out on his zebra-skin sofa, drinking J&B Scotch from a large chromium goblet and souling along with the stereo. Slowly he stood up in his velvet smoking jacket. "It's a lightning bolt," he pronounced. "But some bolts hits and some bolts miss." Then, as drunk as a god, he carefully did not stagger to the bathroom.

Blat! Lips Mangialardi delivered a mighty fart of jubilation, a thunderclap, a stadium-horn blast of triumph. "Grover starting over Chip! Good deal!" he gloated. Standing in his beer-doused underwear, he spread his hulking arms in glory and prophecy. His head was a splatter of red wet hair. "Watch us build a winning streak now. We'll wipe the Cardinals."

"Yeah, and then the Lions," Jaworski said. His mouth was still bleeding from the game, and he hawked a red slop into the ashtray.

"Gut-check time," Lips announced. Taking hold of Jaworski's arm, he bunched up his fist and said, "Go!"

Jay's face, eroded with old acne scars, rolled back with prodigious effort. He strained, he groaned like a woman in labor—nothing. As everybody whooped he gave his arm to the numbing smash. Gleefully Lips went the rounds administering the test: fart on command or get it in the biceps.

"Now *you.* Y-o-u," Jay growled, turning on him and grabbing his arm. Effortlessly Lips exploded another clap from his meaty rumps—invincible, the god of farts, laughing. Swaying his head in gloomy wonder, Jay held out his arm for another clout.

"But you know," Gooch said, "I still figger it's only a rumor about Grover."

"Yeah," Bebo said. "Apples ain't movin up from bustin heads to no first-string quarterback."

"No way," Gooch said glumly. He and Bebo were tough and reckless, two of the wild bunch on the kickoff and punt-return teams. The kid was their man. He'd actually volunteered for the suicide squad, "just to be doing something" while he was learning to quarterback. But Coach didn't let you mash fenders if he had any real plans for you.

"He's got balls, though," Bebo said, brightening. "He hits that wedge, whammo!"

"The kid's got the balls and he's got the arm," Lips said. "Okay, he's hurting for experience, but I still say he can't miss. And with him pitching instead of that tin-arm sonofabitch—man oh man. I say the next party we invite him to join the herd. Hand me that pizza, Gooch, my appetite has just gone way up." Lolling on Shirley's white

Naugahyde couch, he chomped on a triangular flap of pizza and flushed it down with a can of beer. He mashed the empty in his fist and tossed it behind her plastic philodendron.

A faint squawk of protest came from the bedroom.

"The Rook ain't exactly keeping her busy," Lips said, peeling open another can. "Work hard in there, Rook," he called.

"I don't blame him," Gooch mumbled. "That stuff is terrible! What a pig! I mean she's a dog." Savagely he raked the hair on his overdeveloped chest.

"Yeah, where's that other chick at?" Jay grumbled. Two of the females had failed to show and another had cut out, leaving Shirley to handle the action. Even Lips's Polaroid shots of the epic feats in there had fallen flat. Bebo made animal noises out of an old Tarzan movie— "oo-oowawa"—but halfheartedly. When he was in the mood he could sound like a square mile of jungle. After a while he and Gooch started arm wrestling again. "Shit," Bebo said as his arm went down.

Bored and surly, Jay drifted from the Book-of-the-Month Club books down to the women's mags and settled, finally, among the third-grade textbooks that Shirley taught in school. Lips turned toward him with a heavy smile. "Hey, Jay," he said, "didn't you pass that course at Pitt already?"

"Shut your ass," Jaworski snarled. "The University of Pittsburgh is the best school in the country. The b-e-s-t."

"I was just puttin you on," Lips said. "Read me the part about Dick and Jane again, okay?"

Jay was humiliated. But not for long. The Rook

came out of the bedroom, a big-muscled Gerber baby pumping his arm over his head and crowing, "Chalk it up!"

Immediately Jay put him down. "Peter, Peter," he chanted, "he's our leader. Peter, Peter, eats our peter."

This one never failed to get a laugh, and the Rook wilted in their guffaws. Sauntering over to him, Lips snorted a challenge with his ass and said, "Gut-check time."

Without hope, the Rook cramped up his face like a student pretending to try to remember an answer. And *Brrt!* for the first time in history he produced a sound, a little cry, a small dumb hosanna. His large, clean, inexpressive face divided in a beatific smile. "I done it!"

"Way to go!" "Way to fart, Rook!" they all congratulated him, hooting at Lips. Instinctively he shifted gears and grinned, offered his arm for the rookie to slug. He was Big Stud with them, but he was aware that you had to make a lot of right moves to run it. You had to half know, half feel when to go with them and how far, when to sit on them, when to cut somebody down and when you better not because this time he'd take a brick to you.

And pretty soon he got it all back and more in the Beer Olympics. Between shots at Shirley, the game was to put away a six-pack in six spilling gulps and then do twenty pushups. His cropped head bobbing up and down, his enormous cartoon arms flexing and powering upright, Bebo made forty without vomiting and flopped over on his back, a winner. Bending over him with the wastebasket, Lips held out a Polaroid shot of him rowing furiously on top of Shirley. "That still don't make you throw up? God damn, Bebo, you have got some stomach. Watch this," Lips said then. Superbly he turned up the stamping music and swilled down a six-pack. Beer dribbled down from his fleshy mouth, creamed over his chest and gut. He hit the floor on both hands and heaved up and down, up and down, up and down, his belly slopping and lurching with beer like a gasoline truck on a highway: 76, 77, 78.

"What the fuck!" Jay said, covering his eyes. At the end they were yelling the count and beating on furniture, 98, 99, 100. He surged to his feet, streaming beer and sweat, and topped it off with a blockbusting fart. They were cheering.

Grinning, Lips took the Stag doll from his coat pocket and planted it in the vinyl philodendron, where it perched among the imitation buds and leaves, a cute little deity smiling with a football tucked under its arm. "Baby," he said, "we are in high gear."

"Road Hog!" The Country-and-Western classic streamed out of the jukebox, almost lost in a glossy new arrangement. Posing her long delicate arms, the redhead dancing with Fuzzy just flicked her hip, tall and swaying in a pantsuit of silky orange. "Beep! Beep!" the juke horned sweetly and she'd snaked her knees and belly twice so fast it was out of sight. The ex-lineman bucked and galloped, humped in the air like a wild ox, like a beefy angel taking off, while lightly, almost invisibly, Dori altered the balances in her elbowing body and fitted them to his mighty contortions.

"I'm draggin ass," he puffed hopefully.

He was a big old boy from the Lions, always living it up like he was still in the big time. Sliding up at him, she said, "Great moves in there, Fuzz." He beamed between the pelts of curly hair on his cheeks. They were in Freyr's, *the* jock watering hole in the city, tucked away in a disintegrating hotel where the most fanatical fans would never look. The walls were gleaming with photographs. Large men in jackets took up the center of the floor: jocks and former jocks and hangers-on, loitering in a loud swarm, laughing, nuzzling their females and soaking their weighty bodies with alcohol.

They were all watching Dori Frazier. The halfdarkness was sprinkled with little lights, and all the glows seemed to run into the sweet orange flame of her body, moving there as if motion were light. "That'll blow your mind," they said to each other. "Hey, man, fine. Is that fine!" And the highest praise of all: "Now that is *eating* material."

She chose not to hear that one.

Her face was creamy plump and her red hair sculptured into curls and tendrils that tipped against the high cheekbones of her Cherokee grandmother. There were four tiny moles, four dark spots around her firm little mouth. She was smiling as she danced, but she was thinking, Where could Chip have gone? He must be really hurting.

"Any calls for me, Freddie?" she asked the bartender when "Road Hog" faded out.

"Just that pitcher again. The one you met here last week. Now he wants you to go to L. A. with him."

"Oh God! If I could just get the ticket money from every third-stringer who wants to take me somewhere I'd be rich. And if I had that much vacation time I wouldn't have a job. Thanks for running interference, Freddie."

Wondering if she should phone Chip's pad again,

she went back to her stool at the end of the bar. There in a line by her purse were eight Bloody Marys. "Hmm," she said, smiling, "somebody here is trying to make me. Which one of you is it?"

Big laughs bounced down at her. The men knew she was waiting for Chip and that they didn't have a chance, but she was too good to give up on, so they hung in there, mountainous boys petting her with their looks. They were so beautiful. She loved the beautiful power of them, their feral grace, their bellowing high spirits and their talking silences, even the blasts of magnificent obscenity. The San Francisco scout was really putting out. His ruthless cat-eyes were boyish, open, warm, and he was reading the jokes off the cocktail napkin, hoping to please her. It was like taking a long bath, warm and scented and bubbly, the luscious water licking you softly, wrapping around you like sleep.

"Another round of sunshine here," boomed Fuzzy, but she couldn't stay under this time. Damn it, what a raw deal Chip was getting, a 60 percent completion average and they put a sack over his head anyway. George and Poppo were out hunting for him, but George was better at quail and deer. And Poppo—that crazy Croatian might be doing anything.

Reluctantly she climbed out of the tub of sexy feeling, refused to dance. Her beautiful serpent eyes changed. Inside the greeny-gold powder and sunburst lashes they went dark with conjectures, alternatives.

At one-thirty the guys came dragging mournfully in. "He ain't anywhere," Poppo said.

George nodded. "He ain't anywhere, Dori." His injured eye was like a split plum now, blue and oozing. He was limping badly, too, and shivering in a cotton sport shirt. Tenderly she sat him down on her own stool and rubbed his back.

"Where's your coat, screwball?"

George dangled his head sheepishly and Poppo chuckled. "He's sad like me, he set it on fire. It took him two cans of lighter fluid."

"Don't fuss at me, Dori," George said. "Not tonight." This Sunday-school teacher from South Dakota was a strange one. Every time they lost a game, he busted or threw away something, a hat he prized or a suit maybe. It wasn't done in fury and it wasn't exactly to punish himself or to appease the hostile fates. It was a completely incoherent rite.

"If you don't win pretty soon," she teased him, "you'll be bare-ass, George."

He rubbed at his stopped-up eye. "I'd set fire to my car . . . if Chip . . ." His hands spoke for him, great battered hunks imploring, "Dori, what are we gonna do?"

"Stay cool," she told him. "Let's see what Dori can dig up." It wasn't exactly an ego builder, but she went dawdling along the bar to ask about her missing date.

"Chip?" Maybelle was a girl with fat legs and a sweet broad face who worshipped sports figures and laid what she adored. She leaned her head against the big shoulder beside her. "Ain't he prettier than Joe Namath?" she said, and giggled.

"Joe ain't in it," Dori said. "Especially around the knees."

Skipping a girl who was feuding with her, she nudged old Jill's corseted back.

"Don't ask me," Jill muttered. "I'm O for forty."

She was a cold ghost tumbled over her empty glass. Dori had Freddie stoke her up with some of the Bloody Marys. "Chip?" she said, coming weakly to life. "He's with Jackie, I heard. Yeah, he's with Jackie."

"With Jackie? That whore?" Dori joked, but her breath was stumbling. Jackie, the dumb fluff who came nearest to being her best girlfriend! The bitch! She must have gone in heat like those chihuahuas and cats of hers. No, no, it was stupid to think Chip would change beds just out of despair. Not Chip. Nothing made sense.

Fuzzy and the others had given up the quest for the night, so there was more space around her stool. Poppo was grubbing up Stagburgers and George was staring at the Lava-Lite next to the whiskey bottles. He was lost in it, hypnotized. His mouth hung open. "Huh?" he said when she snapped her fingers. "Oh, Dori! What's . . . gonna happen?"

Something, maybe the helpless power of him, drove a splinter into her heart. "Beats me," she said. "Move over where I can watch that thing too."

"Hey there." It was Mr. Sophisticated in his cashmere coat and dark silk scarf. Just the way he carried himself was Big Time, the sort they spotlight and introduce in nightclubs. He was standing behind her with Jackie, dark and quick, his bald forehead cut with mocking lines. "What program is it?" he asked.

"It's a super-spectacular. A combination talk show and egg-laying contest."

They both laughed, and inside she could feel herself tremble to him, shiver like fragile glass tapped with a silver knife. The feeling was there even when they made love, which was weird because he wasn't exactly the Astrodome scoreboard in bed. And yet it was so pretty and dark and intricate. George was battering Chip with great cuffs of relief and devotion. Poppo was moved too. The big wild lineman stopped stuffing fries into his blunt face and said affectionately, "You crud, you."

"We couldn't get aholt of you," George said. "I was sure chewing my tongue, Chip. Where you been?"

"We wasn't doing nothing," Jackie said, tossing a nervous look at Dori. "Honest! You know I'd ask you first. For permission."

"Lies, every word of it," Chip said in the laughter. "She tried to rape me, but I stayed true to you, Dori, and my wife and my two adorable children, little Ray-Ray and Peggy."

George and Poppo squirmed. You didn't talk about things like that. But chuckling, Dori asked, "And to that airline hostess too?" She was watching Chip closely. He'd been drinking, but his coat and his expensively cut hair were as smooth as ever. It was the way his small cold teeth smiled in his sharp face. He was in bad shape. Really uptight.

"You called a beautiful game today," she told him, taking his arm. "Fourth down and a foot and you pass deep—that was far out. And the audibles at the line of scrimmage, that was great." And his fellow professionals dipped their heads and said, "Yeah. Yeah."

Irritably he shrugged them away. He took a pinch of her silk pants and slithered it between his fingers. "I thought I told you to wear something simple."

"I did," she said and then nuzzled his ear. "I'm not wearing panties." Spurred by his little smile, she said,

"Tell me something, you beautiful crazy bastard. Okay, you're the free spirit, the freaky one, but my God! When you get intercepted you know you're supposed to bow your head and kick a little grass. Playing a violin! It's blasphemy, Chip. It's un-American."

"It was a glass violin," he said. "I didn't think anybody could see me."

This was bad; she wasn't reaching him at all. Not angrily but absently, he was rubbing the scar like a neat mend on his cheek. Loyally George said, "They oughtn't to booed you, Chip."

Poppo came in strong too, and the three of them worked to reassure him. "It can't stick, changing over to the kid. It don't make any difference if he's another Roman Gabriel if the team ain't with him. And it's your team, Chip."

They were all very careful not to mention Mangialardi and his herd. Chip grinned at them, that small wintry grin; his quick eyes flicked sideways. "Don't you fret about Lips," he said and patted the pocket of his topcoat. "The ass of Mr. Mangialardi is mine."

They gaped at him.

"You promised!" Jackie burst out. He put a finger on her lips but she whispered frantically to him, something about Cesare Borgia and Cynthia.

"Ssh!" he said and turned her around, gave her a small push toward George. "This is for you, roomie, a token of my affection. Jackie, he ain't the fastest gun in the West, but he sure 'n hell is the largest."

"Aw, Chip. You know I don't . . . after a loss . . ."

Poppo said, "Hey, come on back. Where you off to?" and Dori began, "Don't you think—"

"Nag, nag, nag," he said. "Ta-ta, folks. Got an errand to run." And moving a bit stiffly from the pounding he'd taken in the game, he strutted out the door.

Instantly Dori seized Jackie and demanded, "What *about* Cesare Borgia?"

"I promised not to tell," she said in a peeping little voice. "Oh well, since I'm gonna tell sooner or later I might as well do it now. I offered him Cesare and one of the Siamese kittens, but he wouldn't take nobody but Cynthia."

Dori nibbled on a fingernail. Her eyes and the long narrow lines of her nose sharpened in her smooth face. Cynthia was the white mouse. That beat her. He had to be going over to butt heads with Mangialardi—and big John didn't just bust your legs; he sucked out the marrow. Still, Chip had that look of icy control, and his bag of tricks was very deep indeed. George and Poppo were veering around her, about to stampede. "Sit down," she told them. "We'll give him half an hour to make his play, whatever it is."

"Piss on that noise," Poppo said, but they were used to taking orders from coaches—and from her. At contract time she'd bluffed ten thousand dollars more out of Le Motte for George, and she'd bailed Poppo out of some godawful scrapes. And they weren't the only ones. It seemed as if a dozen players were under her wing for advice, bail money or comfort when they were benched. Right now she was holding a whole wad of checks until after the post-game binge. "He can take Lips," she said tensely.

"Lips! A pig fucks his sister," Poppo said. "Let's get our ass over there and back him up."

George said, "Sure thing. He oughtn't to gone over there at all."

"I'm scared he's gonna hurt Cynthia," Jackie was wailing.

"Lips lays a hand on Chip and I'll put him in the hospital," Poppo said cheerfully. "Let's move out."

"No fights," George said. "Less'n we just have to. We need Mangialardi for the Cardinals."

"No *nothing* yet," Dori crackled. "Get back on your butts." What bothered her most was that George was worried, and he knew. His whole life was the team, and deep underneath, under thought and speech, he *knew* things that even she didn't. Panic whirled in her like dense smoke, but she said, "If you're bored I'll strip while I recite 'The Cremation of Sam McGee.' "

He was driving, Chip thought wryly, like a one-car funeral. More and more the idea seemed not just risky but suicidal. The dark late streets gliding by were seared and smeared with neon lights. The steering wheel was greasy with his sweat, but a quarterback had to have the offensive team solidly with him, and that meant keeping Mangialardi in line. Already he had Jaworski, and the rookie center would be a starter next year. If he didn't put Lips down, Grover would come on with Lips talking it up for him and pulling the whole team his way.

He wished he was at Freyr's with Dori and the guys, trading a few verbal punches and resting his hand on the back of her neck. She was some kind of woman under all that polish he'd put on her. And smart. Man, could he use some of that smart now!

He drew up for a stoplight. A jack-in-the-box, a

candy-striped giant fifty feet tall, twirled in the sky and swooped its leering baby face down at him. Was he dragged. Dead beat. And his guts were pinching the way they did the night before a game. Keep Lips in line, Christ! Six foot six and 255 pounds of mean mother-fucker. And not stupid. Just smart enough to be the perfect animal, tough to handle, merciless. When one of his own pack was injured, Lips, for a joke, had presented him with a trophy inscribed, "Most valuable cripple." To go over there at all looked like a confession of weakness, and if Lips sniffed weakness, if you made up to him or just acted friendly, above all if he thought you needed something from him—then it was good night, Mr. Hughes, sometime All-State at quarterback, second-team All-American, misunderstood husband and father, boy magician, chess whiz, and endangered species.

What he had to have, first, was a damned good reason for coming over, an opening move. Anything physical was out. Lips was too big and tough to whip, and to cripple him, to get him in the nuts with a kick, was absolutely taboo; the whole team would hate his guts. No, he'd have to finesse him, psych him out, and that was going to take some combination, beginning with the tiny warm creature stirring in the woolly womb of his pocket.

He was walking down the hall to Shirley's apartment. Man, this was *hairy*. The sounds grew and thickened around him—amplified guitars and a gibbering voice, a drum beating and beating in his head, slugging in his body, and without knowing it he had come to a stop.

And he could see Vandercamp at the end of the hamburger line, a nifty gimmick Coach had for players who fucked up or dogged it. The sweats and stinks of the ancient high-school gym. A broken mouthpiece on the polished floor. Coach strolled off into his office, the bastard. The players loomed in two rows like big boulders. Trembling, he walked into the first smash in the stomach. Down the aisle of grinning jocks, getting a tap from a buddy, then a whack with a flat hand as hard as a slab of oak, staggering, reeling toward the stupid sunface of Vanderkamp, the 250-pound deaf-mute tackle. Sometimes, for no reason at all, he'd just pat you, but always, always there was the awful fright that still came lurching into your sleep and pawed you awake with your guts squeezing and a pain like a sharp stake driven into your chest . . .

He knocked and voices bawled, "If you're female, come in." Keeping his hand in his right pocket, he sauntered into the revels. And was all but ignored. Lips, enthroned on the couch in a swirl of raunchy music and beer smells, cans, gory pizza discs and tangled clothes, was conducting his version of the fumble drill. "Ball!" he barked like a coach and tossed a cookie between two of his beefy disciples, who were hunkered down face to face. They dived headlong for it, crashing together, throwing forearms and rolling over, clawing. Gooch came up munching the wafer triumphantly. Swaying back and forth, he sprayed crumbs all over Jay, who was still kneeling groggily on the rug.

"Hey, hey!" Lips finally took notice of his visitor. "If it ain't our back-up quarterback." The insolent blubber of his face bulged with a smile. Reclining in a drenched tee shirt and baggy sweat pants clinched at the belly and ankles, he inquired, "Anything special you want here?"

The others stared at him now, their moron arms dangling. They were all charged up, and they were all ready to go with Lips.

Chip felt his testicles shrink. "I just thought I'd try some of your pussy. Mine's got the harem crud or something."

Lips bought it—with hair-raising quickness. "Help yourself, benchie. You're next."

Chip had to get to him fast. Now. Casually, bluffing over the live nerve of panic drawing tighter and tighter in his neck, he eased himself between ponderous groups of muscle. The space between him and Lips was stuffed with bodies. The music pounded. "Hey," Lips said to him. "You'll be tryin out for a new position next season. Better get in on the fumble drill. You against the rook."

"Yeah," they chorused. "Him and Rook. Eat up, Rook."

"Not me," Chip said as the rookie came up to him and set himself. "I'm retiring at the end of this season. Going back and finish hairdresser college." And he turned his back like a bullfighter and strolled away from the bewildered rookie.

"Gonna hang it up, huh?" Lips said. The instant had passed. If he had said "Ball!" right away, the rook would have splattered Chip all over the wall. Without interest he pitched a couple of cookies into the lunging scrambles, then stood up and stretched himself gigantically. His separated yellow teeth came leering out. "So the Queen is outa commission, huh, Chip? Snooty bitch thinks her cunt's worth a million dollars. Okay, let's see if your dick is weak as your arm."

Chip went cold and empty. Who could get a hard-on as dead stone tired and scared as he was? The bedroom door was opening and they were pushing in to have a look at the virility games. Bebo was straddling the old sow, plowing exuberantly. Shirley was as dazed and trampled as a temple prostitute at the end of a feast day, but her bruised mouth sucked at his shoulder, whimpering. The guys stood around the bed, stomping and whooping it up. "Go! Go! Go!" His hairy buttocks bobbing up and down, Bebo grunted like a sports car with each stroke.

"Let's go," Lips said to Chip. "Get the threads off. Or just take it out." And to illustrate he tore a hole in his sweat pants and flipped out a burly fish of a penis.

Chip's mind went to its knees. There was a powder-box doll in the mirror, a Gift Shoppe antique statue goggling stupidly at him. The TV set flashed busily and buzzed away in the corner and the chant went on in the dizzy light, "Go! Go! Go!"

Jaworski took off his shorts. "Me next," he said, his prod rising in front of him, heavy and thick and blunt. To Chip it looked like salvation, the U.S. Cavalry appearing at the top of the hill with swords and bugles shining.

Until Lips said, "Tough shit, Jay. It's Chip's turn." After some bitching Jay sullenly put his shorts back on and Lips, gurgling a laugh, bent down to the flopping bodies on the bed. "Chipper is next, Shirley. How's that for great?"

"Somebody give me a sip of Coke," she said.

"Shit!" Chip heard himself saying. His head was a drumming glare and he was calling the play from memory, or out of some sort of mental instinct, pulling it out of his ear. "You mean with that skanky stuff? Me? You guys actually ball horrible stuff like that? I help it across the street."

"What did you expect, asshole? This is Shirley's pad, ain't it?"

"I expected an airline hostess grounded for bad breath, at least. Maybe a waitress with a hernia." As his head cleared he realized what a sweet break he'd caught finding just Shirley in there. Loftily he went out of the room. Behind him Shirley was screaming and the guys were silent—really cut down.

Lips rallied first. "You're just pimping out," he snarled. "Fucking spaghetti arm, spaghetti dick."

Shirley draggled out behind him, a TWA blanket clutched like a hammock under her long pouchy breasts. "Whatta you mean, skanky? Who invited you anyway? Stuck-up Dori throw you out?"

Chip had wriggled free again. He could simply get off the merry-go-round and walk out the front door, but he had to stay and go on the offensive, really take it to Lips.

"Baby," he said to him, "you played like shit tonight, but you play better 'n you fuck. Big mover, huh? Don't miss, huh? Next week I'll bring *you* a grandma."

Lips bellowed over Shirley's howl, "Me! Play like shit! I beat the hell out of my man all night." He was breathing fire now. "You little fucker, let's go, one on one."

Inside Chip a little puppy rolled over and exposed its plump tummy and pissed on itself. Hoarsely he said, "No, let's wrestle. Come on, big man, you and me."

Shirley was pleading, "No fights." Tears runneled down her belly and dropped into the bog of wet hair between her thighs.

"Shut up, cunt." Lips seemed to puff up, to unfold himself in larger and larger contours of murderous intention. The onlookers, excited by the blood smell, formed a ring around them, a pit for the combat.

"Take off your coat, why don't you?" Jay said to Chip.

"Shit! I don't need to take my coat off for this light work." Stooping, he put out his hands and circled.

"Take him apart, Lips!"

"Kick ass, Big John."

His brute shoulders and arms spread wide, Lips came in on him, charging high and straight, stupendous. Instead of dodging or snaking out his hands to get a hold, Chip stood straight up and gave himself to the thunderous shock, riding with the hit. It was really easier than taking it from a red-dogging linebacker to gain that extra fraction of a second to throw. And as he went down in a dump of beer cans his quick hand slipped the mouse into Lips's sweat pants.

"It's a mouse," he gasped into Lips's ear.

Lips felt the tickling squirm along his leg. Frantically he ripped at the cord tied around his gut and plunged his hand down at the wriggle, clutched at it, missed. Then he lost control and began to scream mindlessly, grabbing only feebly at the little thing tunneling around under the cloth. All of a sudden he humped over, vomited reddish spews of beer and pizza. While he gagged and strangled, his pack laughed at him.

"Yeah," Gooch said. "A mouse always gets to him like that. I forgot."

"You sonofa"—Mangialardi retched—"bitch."

"Her name," Chip said, lying on his elbows in the trash, "is Cynthia."

Wearily he slumped backward in the beer cans, lying next to the battered plastic tree and the Stag doll.

He was still The Man, the King. Once more, when it was life or death, he had made big magic. Lips was doubling and bucking forward as if his body were being swept with invisible whips.

A gray shriek squirted out of his pants and Bebo snagged it. They began throwing it at each other, then to each other, playing catch with it until it was just a scrap of bloody white fur. "We use to do this with gophers when I was a kid," Bebo said.

Chip pulled himself to his feet and, strutting toward the door, tossed them the Stag doll. "Play with this, gentlemen."

George and Poppo and Dori were hurrying into the lobby. He went right past them. He was charred under the eyes with exhaustion. Now that the pressure of the long cruel day was over, the cramps were coming back, hard. He was sagging. He was kneeling in the gray light snowing down from an arc lamp, a small wintry echo of the puking lineman upstairs.

"You all right, honey?" Dori asked, laying her arm on his hitching shoulders.

Chip nodded, retching. "It was a giggle, baby. No problems."

The blond kid in the computer
room got up and stretched himself
against the blinking lights of the
central processing unit. It was 2:30
A.M. "If you could 've waited till
morning," he said to the head coach
of the Stags, "the courier woulda
brought it over."

"Sorry."

Sleepily the kid put the program
title onto an endless scroll of paper,
then fed Jim Lowry's stack of
punched cards into the reader. Lowry
watched in the stunned awe a
computer always gave him. There was
an eerie sheen of polished metal and a
deep humming in the air, dials stared
like fire eyes in the squatting cabinets,
and in the middle, flashing ghostly
sparks, was the panel of the processing
unit.

Lowry took the sheaf of
precious sheets back to his office
at the stadium and from them

made up a tentative list of thirty plays to use against the Cardinals. This was work he enjoyed, solitary, scrupulous. Dark horn-rimmed glasses, tinted brown, gave him a monkish look. His figures showed that against the tough Cardinal zone defense the plays with the highest effectiveness rating were swing passes into the flat, passes to the man coming out of the backfield, draws and inside traps.

Exactly on the hour he called Grover again. Because of the Monday-night game it would be a short week, and he wanted to start working with the boy right away.

No answer. He must still be out partying.

He went back to the film of Sunday's game against Dallas, which the Cardinals had won 35–13. Switching on the projector, he began to recheck for secondary factors, adding to the thick pack of charts he already had: Dallas in a strong side right with the flankers split wide, the Cardinals in a 4–3 zone . . .

The years in a minor seminary had left their mark, and as he bent over the projector there was a broken priest in the long narrow stoop of his body. Drab, scratching the flaky sores on his legs, he tripped the switch and stopped the glowing swarm on the screen. Grimly he ran the play back, ran it through in slow motion and then ran it through once more, like a relentless conscience probing for sin.

It was terrible. He had knuckled under to Le Motte, let Gabe sabotage him and as good as take over the team. He should have resigned. It was rash, it was complete and 100 percent folly to start a raw kid with so little preparation. With not even a full week of practice!

He had failed in the seminary and it was happening again, happening as inevitably as damnation. They couldn't win with Grover, and if the Stags kept on losing he would be fired to appease the fans. On the other hand, if by some ungodly chance the kid did get them some wins, Simson would look like a prophet; he would get all the credit *and* the head coaching job next season.

Gabe. His muscle, the whip, the snorter who lit a fire under the team and lifted them to a peak for a game. But oh God how he hated him! Obese and laughing, foul-mouthed, he was Baal in the flesh. After twenty-five years the Bible History picture was still in his mind, hideous: Baal, a whip in his right hand, lightning and ears of corn in his left. The outhouse of his childhood on a Minnesota farm, the stench of it in summer, the fat flies whizzing over the piles of turds underneath.

He hated Gabe like that, and he could destroy him with Le Motte by Sunday night. All he had to do was go through the motions and let the kid really foul up.

Forlorn, he watched the poor temptation wither as it sprouted. Already a feeling of guilt shuddered inside him. Since he hadn't resigned he was in conscience bound to do his darnedest with the kid. To prove it, he tried again to reach him on the phone. *But*—but there was a limit. If Grover, in his judgment, was not able to handle it, they could all go fly a kite and he would give Hughes the call against the Cardinals. On this he took his oath.

What sectors of the Cardinal zone were the weakest? He'd lost track. It was 4:40, 5:10. Fighting to stay awake, he gaped at the clots jamming together and tugging, forming and breaking up, play after play after play. He was in a dim and sleepy hell, falling, disintegrating in the sleepy fire of the screen . . .

Fourteen hours later he still hadn't contacted Grover. The new Stag quarterback was sprawled in the second row of a Loop theater, watching *Ben Hur* again, really soaking it in. Horses swerved out of the far turn, growing on the track, teams of them pounding toward him and bursting up in a gigantic splash of muscle, foam and kicked dirt. Charlton Heston was a grimy, yelling face in the chariot strapped to the driving haunches of his team.

Last night after the game he and his buddy had caught the flick and it was fine, really fine, as good as that one about the Grail. Li-bary had dropped out after six hours today, but he had a real thing for this one. There was a guy down with all the skin pulled off his face. Scooping into the buttery, salty, warm puffs of popcorn, he slid further back on his tail, serene and whole in the trumpets and the togas and the golden glare.

"You! Grover!" He felt his shoulder gripped and jerked back and forth. It was Coach! He jumped to his feet, erect in the pouring color and sound. "Sir?" he gulped.

"Where were you last night? You didn't answer your phone."

"Huh?"

"Never mind," Coach snapped. "You've wasted very precious time for both of us. I had to call that boy who runs with you."

"But hey, Coach. I just went to the movie. Then I went home. I guess I didn't hear the phone."

"Forget it." All around, pale lighted faces were shushing them. "Let's go." He herded Grover out to the ornate old lobby. "Okay," he said, "listen. You're going to start on Sunday if you can get ready."

"Me? You gotta be kidding, Coach. Is Hughes injured?"

"No, Hughes is not injured."

Awe lit up the young face nesting in shags of yellow hair. "Wow," he breathed. Certainly as far as physical equipment went no quaterback in pro football could touch him; he was 6-4 and 235, and he grew up from his powerful legs in springy lifts of muscle, stacking up to shoulders that overloaded his green Stag jacket. He was digging in his sideburns, still trying to take in the news. "Wow," he said again.

Impatiently Lowry said, "Here's the ready list. Go home and hit that playbook. Hard. By tomorrow morning I want you letter perfect on these plays."

"Yes, sir."

With a chilly nod Lowry dismissed him. Grover loped away, a golden lout padding through the lobby as if he were barefoot. This was the Chosen One, the hope of the Stags. Lowry sighed.

After a quick hamburger and the evening call to his wife, he went back to work with the offensive coaches. "Okay," he said wearily. "Let's go over the variations in that Cardinal defense."

Occasionally from the next office he could hear the rumble of Gabe and his people setting up defenses. How Gabe got the results he did was a mystery. He was in there, rolling film and just staring at it. His idea of analyzing was to mutter, "That seventy-one, look at that pisser. He ain't got it straight ahead." And his reaction to the computer was equally crude: "You and that brainbox, Jim. You worship that fucking thing."

The door swung open and Gabe lumbered in, Xeroxed pages flapping in his hand. "What's this shit, Jim?"

Indignantly Lowry switched off the projector. "If you'll look at the top line it says 'game plan' right there."

"Game plan! Game plan my sore dick. Where's the long ball? The deep stuff? We got a great arm out there and you're playing ring around the rosary."

"Yeah?" Angry blood scorched Lowry's face. Inside him a voice was shrieking, Ring around the *rosie*, stupid! and The game plan is my responsibility, mine! But instead he said patiently, "You don't pass deep against a zone, Gabe. You know better."

"Shit. We got two great receivers, two real burners, and a cannon arm. All we gotta do is isolate either one, man on man. They got the moves and the kid's got the howitzer."

"I don't agree. Your best percentage is the short pass. You catch the linebackers flying back into their areas and hit short in front of them."

"You mean Hughes again."

"Well, what's wrong with a sixty-percent completion average?"

"Plenty. To win in this league it takes ball control. And that means a big running game and a big arm when you got to put it up."

"Listen, I agree with you, ball control is vital. But Hughes gets it for us. Ten to fifteen plays to score sometimes. He uses up the clock as good as anybody in the league."

"Yeah, yeah, but he lives by the nickel-and-dime pass, and every time you put it up in the air for grabs it's that much more chance against you. Plus it takes his flutter ball a half hour to get there."

"He's not intercepted that much. On the average he—"

"Average, shit. Nothing works with him. They stack

in tight on us and shut off the run *and* the nickel pass. That's why we're losing our ass."

"Listen, it's not that simple. We don't *have* a running game. Shorty is all we've got. Harris doesn't have it any more and Curly's out with that knee—"

"Next year we'll draft us some more horses, but right now use the kid, goddamit. Put in some quarterback draws, run some options. The kid's a strong boy. It'll take three people to drag him down."

Lowry had to admit the justice of this. God, it was bitter salt to eat, but he realized he'd designed a game plan for Hughes instead of for Grover. With cold suffering patience he took it back to the drawing board. Quarterback sweeps off a rollout . . . it would take him and his assistants half the night. He clawed at the sores on his ankles. The tiny gray shriek went on and on inside him: But Chip Hughes was just perfect for the Cardinals! The computer said so; the charts and the assistant coaches said so. Chip could pick that zone to pieces. The only hope was that in spite of his best coaching, Grover would flop in the practices.

At 8:30 the next morning the players began to straggle in, vacant and sluggish, hung over, disgruntled. In the trainer's room Ted Davis and his assistants were patting and slapping handfuls of stiff muscle. George dangled his aching leg in the whirlpool and squinted at his mail. Players dawdled around in socks and jock straps, pulling themselves into gray sweatsuits. The reek of barbecued ribs left in a locker oozed into the smells of old sweat, dank concrete and decomposing socks. Short Stuff hobbled back from the towel room, his thick legs dark with bruises. "It's incredulous about Chip," he was bitching. "I mean it's unreal."

Poppo stretched his neck cautiously, experimentally, and waggled his head from side to side. "Maybe it *ain't* gonna come off," he said.

Boos and groans pelted him: "Check it out, Poppo. You could be wrong."

Just then Big John Mangialardi loitered in. Loud hoohaws broke out. "Hey, watch it, Lips! There's a mouse!"

"Squeak! Squeak!"

"Hey, Mouse! Let's hear it for Mouse!"

He went scowling to his locker and pulled off his clothes, raked by sniggers and tiny mouse shrieks. Goddamit, Hughes had spread it around before he went to quarterback meeting. And if he told them to shut up he was an asshole and they'd eat him alive. The team was down and taking it out on him; their brawny faces flared with pleasure. Even his own guys opened up on him; even Jocko, the clubhouse boy, was meowing and hooting like a crazy man. Pretty soon the jigs joined the party: "Ooooh!" Jellybean cried in a falsetto voice. "I jus see a mouse in my locker. Save me! Oh help!" And he jumped over his chair, prancing his clever brown legs seared with white scars. Lips glowered helplessly. He could only pray that the nickname "Mouse" wouldn't stick and the team would forget the whole thing again, fast.

All at once there was an odd change in the air, then the soft thup of gym shoes on cement. Mangialardi looked up. Tom Grover had come lolloping in. He pawed around in his locker and came up with his playbook. "I forgot my playbook," he said to everybody in general.

He was ignored. And Lips, in enough trouble as it was, had to turn his back on him like the others.

Crushed, Tommy scuffed back to the office. It was a dumb-ass thing to have said, he saw that now. He'd sort of known the team would be with Hughes, but he hadn't expected—it really rattled his drawers. At Nebraska it had been a stroll all the way, big man on the freshman team, written up in the national magazines as a potential All-American before he ever played a varsity game, and he'd always gotten along good with the guys. But here— they thought he wasn't shit. Making it here was like, wow, climbing straight up Pike's Peak.

"You have to be married to that playbook," Coach said to him.

"Yes, sir."

"There's a very great deal to put in your head in a short time. You can study the plays we added tonight. This morning, let's see, we'll work on the sixty-two-snake-Y-corner . . ."

The gray remote face rattled plays at him. Groping, struggling with his whole soul and body, he wrestled the numbers, letters, words like "wheel" and "pow" and "sawhorse." And all the time Hughes, his idol Chip Hughes, lounged in his chair looking bored and twirling a small elegant cigar. It really messed up his mind. Coach was asking him a question.

"Sir?"

"I said, you *do* know what a rip is."

"Uh, a rip is a rollout, I think."

"What's a Y-man?"

Tom looked at him with his mouth open, scared.

"A Y-man is a tight end, Grover," Coach said with terrible patience. "X is your split end and Z is your flanker—take notes for heaven's sakes! A sixty-two-snake-Y-corner isn't going to mean much if you don't know Y is your tight end."

Crouched over the playbook, his ballpoint poking out of his big fist, Tom stubbed notes on a page. He was scared shitless.

The kid had a mind like a parking space. Chip grinned to himself as the meeting ground to a stop. And with Lips defused for a while and the team solidly his, he could afford to sit out this dance. All he had to do was play it cool, stand there and look like John Unitas while Jack Armstrong, the All-American boy, fucked up for Hudson High.

Still, it hurt to be out of it even temporarily. When he warmed up with his receivers he always threw first to Bird, his favorite target. It was a bitch to see him at the head of the line, his long shanks pulled tight to spring off while the others bobbed up and down and jigged their hands like puppets on a wire, and to see Grover in *his* spot with the ball.

The kid drew his arm back like a javelin thrower. Birdie broke down field and made his turn and the ball had smacked off his chest, a spinning blur in the bright sunshine. Jesus. If there was such a thing as physical IQ the kid was another Einstein.

Chip turned away and flipped passes to a graying twelve-year veteran on the taxi squad. It took more than an arm, he said to himself, but his heart worked painfully in his chest and the blocking sleds jutted up from the turf like scattered engine parts, bones, pieces of a carcass. The tackling dummy hung like a corpse from its steel scaffold.

Grover cut loose again. This one was ten feet over Tucker's head, but Jesus H. Christ it was a rocket, and off at the end of the field Gabe Simson exploded a windy snort of satisfaction. "Okay," he said to the linemen standing like monoliths around him, "you're gonna play the best team, personnel-wise, in the league. George, your guy is a basher. He don't do nothin tricky but he's a basher. Wilson, with yours you got a man that's like a tree. He raises up on pass blocking and he's like a tree. . . ."

After the introductions he put in some wrinkles for Sunday: "We're gonna smack a little different. George, you're here, reading that guard. Wilson's up and you're back. Now look, you go like this . . ." He acted it out for them first, stepping as lightly as a blimp touching down and side-slipping in the wind. Then he walked them through it again and again, one at a time, beating, pounding the moves and the new routes into their flesh and blood, into their spines. "Poppo." He grabbed a handful of Poppo's sweatshirt and steered him through it. "He'll never trap you from two feet. . . . Roger, if that guy full A-blocks on you, don't just stand there with your dick out. . . . No, no, it's gotta be automatic. Like an instinct, Rog. If you have to think about it he'll kill you. Snap, it's gotta be right there. Okay, now all of you together. Go!" he rumbled, and they fired off in a ponderous row. "Go!" he said again. Taking off his baseball cap, he wiped the sweat ring on his fleshy head.

The klaxon sounded, and the scattered parts of the team assembled to work on plays. Lowry and his offensive coaches stood in the huddle, correcting, explaining. "On the Z-out, Grover, just go to Jones and don't bother with your secondary receivers for now. Drop straight back ten yards, all right?" Tommy nodded, straining to take it all in. "And stay in the pocket."

Hayheaded, his U of N tee shirt bumpy with muscle, Grover set behind the center and barked, "Hut!" Split wide to the right, Bird hurled himself downfield, full throttle, and cut toward the sideline, looking back for the ball. The kid was standing there like a fucking statue. "Unload!" the coaches were yelling at him. "Unload it!" The ball whistled two yards behind Birdie. His face expressionless, he trotted back to the line of scrimmage. The coaches were having fits, carrying on about the fourteen-yard patterns in the control zone, timing, three-and-a half seconds to put the ball in the air. The team lined up, listless, surly. "Talk it up! Talk it up!" Coach Ellis hollered. His handclaps popped like damp firecrackers.

Again Bird sprinted all out and slashed to the outside, driving himself the way he drove a car, gunning forward, swerving and hitting the brakes with a furious stamp that scorched the tread off the tires. The ball zinged over his head. Panting, tearing off bites of air and swallowing, he came jogging back. In his opinion Coach was taking his hogs to a damn poor market with this kid, but he was pure disgusted with the guys who were dogging it. And yet when he thought about it being the kid instead of Chip throwing to him first, he mourned for the little ritual. He felt like—there was a red splatter in the screaming air of the sawmill and his cousin Billy Joe was staring at the spurting gap where two fingers had been. "Hut!" the kid barked. Bird raced downfield and raked sideways, stretching out in the air and clawing for the ball as it shot past his hands.

He turned and came back, ripping at the turf with

his cleats. Coach Ellis' Easter Island face jutted in stony planes under his cap. "Goddamit, Jones. You could 've had that ball."

Bird looked at him with his sharp little eyes. He wanted to say, I'm drawin my payday to ketch em on the field, Coach. Not up in the box seats.

Discontent crackled like a brush fire as the team suited up for afternoon practice. Short Stuff threw down his helmet. "Ain't enough to have two sessions the first day, we gotta bust heads. No team in the league scrimmages in the season."

"Man, I am wasted *now*," Lips joined in eagerly. And pretended not to hear the mouse squeaks.

Tucker scowled. "I don't dig this kinda coaching. We on a losin streak, so they come up with a bush quarterback. Just beautiful."

"All this overtime," Poppo said. "And that Nebraska Cornhusker ain't gonna make it anyhow. Coach has got to be out of his mind."

"Coach, huh," said Daddy Wilson. He was still completely naked, a carved black pillar at the end of the aisle. "Lowry never played with *his* helmet off. Lowry ain't the one."

George said, "Aw, come off of it, Daddy."

"Shit, brother," scoffed one of the blacks.

Daddy raised a glossy soothsayer's arm. "I got a *feeling* about this changeover, gentlemen. And when I get a feeling it's better than Chip inventing tactics in the huddle. Just *who* is the culprit? *Why* is the hoe cakes burning? Le Motte is why. Sweet Carson Le Motte."

"Hey, yeah!" Dude said. "Chip is Lowry's man."

A linebacker guffawed. "Yeah! Mr. Swish has got

his finger on the panic button." The whole team picked it up. George couldn't stop them. Only Dickie, blank and silent, a toothpick clamped in his mouth, stood in front of his locker, strapping himself into his shoulder pads. The others were raising particular hell. "Got his finger where?"

"I read you! He's a real ass-doer, right?" The center Heinz was in ecstasy. "A *femme fatale!* He's got the itchies for the kid."

"Wait!" Daddy said. "I'm not *sayin* he's sweet and I'm not *sayin* he's gay. He just wants to chew on that Cornhusker pee-pee."

All the resentment, the frustration of four defeats, all the brutish anger of the team burst in a hailstorm of homosexual jokes, insults, mincing walks, wiggles. As they were being taped they worked over Davis the trainer, a sober family man with four children, leering at him and heaping lewd praise on his technique: "Daisy, your rubdowns *do* something for me." During the practice Youngblood came cantering off the field for a rest and another of the black players simpered, "Kin I have the next dance, baby? A 260-pound belle of the ball, Youngblood daintily flapped a stub of taped fingers. "You kin have the next one any ole time, darlin."

The horseplay turned more and more rowdy. Coming out of the shower after practice, Poppo suddenly bellowed, "A pretty girl is like a melodee!" Whacking asses with his towel, he sashayed like a stripper toward his locker, grinding and bumping his gut and stroking his massive bearded chest seductively. When he ran out of words he mixed in belches of Croatian obscenity: "*Ochish-te moy kurats,*" he rumbled, ogling lasciviously as he pulled *on* his shorts. "Shake it!" "Go get it, baby doll," they shouted. Grover padded in and gawked. Hands slapped a vicious, lurching unrhythm. Poppo wobbled like a sexy mastodon. With a horrible downward smirk he zipped *up* his fly and slithered *into* his shirt.

"Carson gonna buy you a drink, honey?" Jellybean asked him.

"I'm peroxidin my hair," Poppo cooed, "and goin out for quarterback."

The coaching staff was generally discouraged—except for Gabe Simson, who seemed to be half asleep. "We put a few things together, but we're drivin on flat tires," Ellis said, shaking his craggy head. Lowry wasn't so sure. In one day he'd managed to stuff seven plays into the kid's head. Not only that, he was releasing faster and more accurately.

Disheartened, Chip trudged out to the parking lot, told George to drive and slumped down in the seat. The red-and-yellow trees in the park were emptying, and the cars sucked dry waves of leaves behind them.

"Maybe Coach won't stay with the kid," George said.

"Yeah?"

"Well, anyhow . . . please don't look so down in the dumps. . . . Not yet anyhow."

"I am not down in the dumps, George," Chip said sourly. "I'm having a nervous breakdown and working on my farewell address, but I am *not* down in the dumps."

"Fee fi fo fum," Dori chanted, "I smell the blood of an Englishmun. Be he alive or be he dead, I'll grind his bones to make my bread." Hamming up the old victim-rhyme, she pointed back and forth at Jackie and herself. "Red, green, blue, I pick you!" she cried, fixing Jackie with the fatal word.

"No fair. Do it eenie, meenie, mynie, mo!"

"Tough, kid. You lost. You got to do Grover. Now put on that little number with the fringe and those Greek earrings and—"

"Well, I won't do it," Jackie pouted. "You cheated! You're always conning me into doing stuff for you and I never get nothing back." She slopped down in front of the television with her two small boys. She was wearing a USMC fatigue shirt washed to a soft grass color, and her glossy legs were lapped with colored light from the TV. A chihuahua scrambled up and worked itself between her thighs. "You're just a love, yes you are," she crooned to it, snuggling it in her soft arms and kissing it on the mouth.

Dori balanced herself on a roly-poly balloon chair and considered her next move. "Beat it, Moses," she hissed and shooed a dog away from her ankles. Sometimes Jackie's place really turned her off. Stained glass and rotting cat food, overfed chihuahuas snoozing and screwing under the coffee table, yapping fights and horoscope posters and even statues of animals. A pregnant Siamese cat dozed like an earth mother on a partly refinished trunk. The goddam place was a zoo and a shrine to pets and an arty junkshop all in one.

Jackie was playing hard to get. Why? She squabbled with her kids about the Mr. CornKing commercial, got a draw and haughtily sent them off to bed, bitching about how dumb they were. "Dori, you're so intelligent, do you ever watch that afternoon program 'I Married a Genius'?"

"I work for a living, remember? Look, Jackie, do you realize what it means? Chip called me and he's in bad trouble. Grover is coming on like the great Chicago fire!"

"No thanks. Anyway, how do you corrupt somebody if you can't get their boots off?" She raised one objection after another. Wasn't he engaged? Who was going to introduce them?

"Keep it simple," Dori said. "Go over to his table and lift your dress."

"Oh look!" Jackie cried. "It's the finals of Miss Teen-Age Illinois! I'm rooting for Miss Libertybelle. She's the cute one fourth from the end there."

"Miss Liberty*ville*," Dori corrected her. "The Liberty Bell is in Philadelphia and has this great big crack in it. You can remember by that."

"Oh. She won the talent contest yesterday. She done this thing with a torch."

"With a torch! My God, what can you do with a torch? Wait, don't tell me. She's a teen-age fire swallower, right?"

"No, silly. She held it in different positions like, you know, out to one side and over her head. To music!"

Dori looked at that child face tipping out of long hair and decided on bribery. While she put in her eight hours at the office, Jackie scraped along on child-support payments, gifts from jocks and a mysterious tavern owner named either Jack or Giles and by trading in doubtful antiques.

"Hey, little girl," Dori said at the next commercial, "exactly how much do you owe the vet?"

Jackie said she didn't know. Or care.

"Which means he's not gay. Well, I want mine in

cash if you won't do it. You owe me thirty-five dollars, not to mention that wig you borrowed and lost. Plus three 'anything you want in the worlds.' "

"*Two* anythings," Jackie retorted. "That last bet don't count. His breath smelt like horseradish and I couldn't relate to him."

Dori broke into laughter and wallowed her balloon chair up and down. "You're a blast, honey. I mean you are a panic."

"No, it's the God's honest truth."

Dori switched off the TV. "There's not much time, Goldilocks. After practice Grover eats his sixty-three hamburgers at that McDonald's and then he's gone."

"I don't give a pee. I personally don't see anything attractive about him. Now will you kindly turn that TV back on?"

"Not till you tell me why not. Quit raping that creature and give out! Are you in love? You've got a crush on that ground ape from the Cardinals!"

"I don't either. I don't even know why he keeps calling me. He can't even get a hard-on."

She kept blowing tickles of air on Pope Leo XIII's tummy, and when Dori took him away from her and told him to take a walk down by the Sistine Chapel, Jackie went into the sulks. "I miss Cynthia," she said accusingly. It was ten minutes before she blurted it out: "I want an anything and I know you won't give it to me, so what's the use?"

Dori swore she could have any anything she wanted, cross her heart and hope to die, but Jackie only ducked into her long oat-colored hair. "You'll just kill me if I tell you—oh, all right, you made me say it. Could I please date Chip?" Her face came peeking out. "Please? Just for a little while? Will you make him go out with me? Will you?"

She was so fresh and young. She was the divine helpless cunt, so naïve, so beautiful, reaching at things like a baby grabbing your hands.

But Chip! "Are you crazy? He's not all that great in bed, you know."

"I don't care."

But Chip! Chip was special and definitely not Jackie's type; he was class and sharp and complicated. He was just too much for Jackie, the crazy great one who, on a TV sports panel, said, "Coach Lombardi and I feel the same way. . . . He's dead? Ah, that explains it." The nut who bought a manure spreader and hooked it up to George's car. Who told the press after a tough loss, "My psychiatrist says I played very well." The weird one who helped her name Jackie's pets, who fed vodka to the lizard and said, "Hey, Jackie, what's-his-name just fainted in my arms." Just thinking about him brought back that tiny reverberation, like a little glass bell chiming inside her.

Not that she was jealous. She just couldn't imagine what the bloody hell was going on in what Jackie used for a mind. Or, for that matter, how she could get Chip to agree. She'd have to tell him he had to sell his fair white body to get his other bodies back.

"You must be crazy," she told Jackie. "But it's a deal. Chip for Grover and a second-round draft choice."

"Oh wow! Great! You promised, you promised and you can't take it back." Jackie jumped up to get dressed and whirled off her Marine Corps shirt. Naked, her arms spread wide, her breasts swinging and riding plumply, she twirled around and around. Her long skirt of hair lifted out, swept sideways over the tender folds of her mouth.

"Oh, this is like—wow!" she cried. "And don't ask me why. You can ask me a hundred thousand times and I won't tell."

But then she slowed and darkened and her hair was quiet on her arms. Her eyes darkened from inside. She was standing by the leaded window, and her body, all its round light, seemed to yearn at the dark whiteness in the checkered surface. "Thank you," she said in a small voice. "It's what I want the very very most." She put out her arms and laid her face under Dori's face. "You're super-sophisticated and all the guys look up to you, which they never do me. I know I'm not too smart, but you're always nice to me."

Dori wanted to kiss her. "For God's sake," she said, holding her for a second and then gently detaching herself. "You have about eight seconds to get dressed. Florence'll babysit. I called her already. Okay, now here's the game plan. Use him up, screw him dizzy, get him drunk. Anything to keep him away from that playbook."

"Hey, you're super-brilliant. I bet you were like this when you was a kid. I bet you could always solve any problem you wanted to."

"Oh, I don't know," Dori said somberly. Sure, she'd been a whiz as a little kid, a real plotter. Her daddy had wanted a boy and her mother was tickled to death with her pretty little redheaded girl. But she'd wangled them both against each other till she was Daddy's girl, learning to play baseball with him, taking his part against Mom when he'd come home drunk, helping him in the fields. Till one awful day while she was driving the tractor she saw blood running down her leg and showed him. He wouldn't talk about it; he told her to run on up to the house and ask Mom. She refused, and all that long hot day she drove the tractor having her first period. Not long after she had to go to high school in town. And then came the problem that being a whiz did *not* solve—finding out you were country and ranked just above the Nigras and nobody would talk to you. When she'd come North it was Chip, the slick one, who had taken a pretty redheaded hick and nudged her on to night school and then coached her on that first job interview. And not only that, but how to come on smooth at work and at the cocktail glass. Sometimes she hated Chip for his aloofness, but she'd learned from it too—how to use it, how it was a good idea to be a tiny bit distant because it was a kind of protection and sometimes did more for you than the most expensive clothes worn just so. She was damned if anybody was going to take his job away, but it would take a hell of a road block to stop the kid.

"You better get Grover to fall in love with you," she said.

"Hey, neat! Like with what's his name?"

"You mean Johnny Orff?"

"Yeah. Him and I were introduced and he scored thirty-one points. Then he laid there all night squeezing me till my ribs hurt and telling me how he *adored* me." Shimmying into her bikini panties, she yelled at her kids to for Christ's sake stop that and go to sleep in there. "The next game"—she giggled—"he scored like about two points or something."

"It was five, against the Lakers. Did you ever tear him to pieces! First his shot went and then his moves. He could only think of one thing at a time, and it was your pussy."

They giggled together. Then Jackie sat down at the mirror. Reverently she painted her face, daubed a blush onto her cheekbones, pausing to look at herself before she ripened her lips with Pink-Glo. With ceremonial gravity she began coloring her eyelids with thick green strokes.

On Friday came the test, a full contact scrimmage. Lowry had cut down the number of plays, abandoned audibles and generally worked his butt off. Farther than that he would not go. "Gabe," he said, "I want to tell you something."

Gabe hung up his coat before he gave him a meaty stare.

Lowry met it. "I've gone along with this harebrain scheme, but Grover has got to show it out there this afternoon or he's not starting. And you can call Le Motte and tell him that for all I care."

Taking in air noisily, Gabe peeled his shirt from the heavy sack-belly hanging out over his belt. Apparently the conversation was over. The stinking heap of guts—curse him, God curse him to hell. In agony Lowry changed clothes as fast as he could to avoid seeing that nightmare of bloated nakedness. Yesterday after practice —Gabe was the only coach who could shower with the players without losing prestige—yesterday he'd gone whistling down the hall, through the naked men, a balloon-monster of fat and muscle, and motioning for silence, tiptoed up behind one of his massive black linemen. "This is for you," he said, placing his penis in Roger's hand. A power on the field, Rog was a shy, humble man with a stutter. He nearly fainted. Squealing with shock, he floundered back against a laundry hamper. Everybody yawped and slugged each other in ecstasy. "Don't put it in his hand, put it in his ass!" "Yeah, that's where it belongs."

It was unbelievable. Not only was it not queer but it lessened the queer jokes about Le Motte and the kid that had been going around. On the surface it was to reward Roger for playing well—on the surface. Or was it unconscious? He was one of them in a way that made Lowry feel alien and miserably alone. Gabe had actually gained stature by lowering himself like that. He splashed into the shower and, honored by his presence, the players splashed around him like big meek dolphins, soaping their balls and stuffing the lather into each other's mouths to amuse him.

It was loathsome, appalling. He didn't give a hoot now how risky it would be to go back to Hughes—or how unfair. He hated Gabe, he hated him! With his whole soul he prayed for the kid to screw up so he could send him back down to the special units.

And screw up he did, royally. On the second play of the scrimmage he lost it all. He fucked up the count. The lines misfired with a crash of pads and helmets, and everything, every play he had crammed in, spilled back out again. Panic-blind, he staggered through one tackle after another, broke loose and galloped like a wild stallion around end.

"Hold it! Goddamit, hold it!" the coaches yelled at the tumbling chaos.

On the sidelines Hughes was laughing. "Where did he get that play? From *Knute Rockne, All American?*"

Blowing on his whistle, Lowry went striding onto the field to chew him out and pull him. Hughes tugged his shoulder pads, set to come in. Gabe stayed where he was with his defensive people, biting on a stem of grass, but Lowry could feel him back there, the piled-up folds of slumbrous flesh bursting out of the green jacket, the red slitty eyes in the heavy face. Lowry wavered, slowed down. It was as if there was a soundless drumming in the windy light. He stopped. Oh God, it was awful, it was like dying in a state of mortal sin. It wasn't even the danger of being fired; it was Gabe, Gabe Simson, the mountainous drumbeat of his will rolling over him, rolling him under.

"All right," Lowry said quietly. With defeated eyes he looked at the shamefaced kid slouching back with the ball. "We're put to the task, that's all. I'll send in the plays myself and you just execute."

"I freely admit it's our Valley
Forge," Carson Le Motte was telling
the reporters and broadcasters
assembled in the VIP Lounge.
Drugged with booze and roast beef,
they had been exposed to highlights
of the Stags' fifth consecutive loss,
then to some obituary remarks from
Lowry and some red-faced stuttering
from Grover. Now the Monday-
afternoon press luncheon was
dribbling to a close. "But don't think,"
said the GM, "that we're taking to the
lifeboats, guys. I'm confident, as are
all of the coaches, that we've found
the quarterback that will lead us out
of the wilderness."

Sagged deep in the upholstery
like a sack of leaky footballs, the PR
man for the Stags counted the mixed
metaphors. His hanging old eyes were
attached to Le Motte. When you are
sixty-two years old and you've
had two strokes, when you

aren't allowed to smoke any more, or drink, or even drive a car because you're a menace at the wheel, you don't have many pleasures left in life. Dan Fallon's was Le Motte.

Carson Le Motte III had gotten his start in television producing a bit of electronic stinkfinger called "Games for Little People." But he'd "always been rah-rah about football," and quickly he wriggled his way up to network director of sports. When he and his group bought the Stags, Carson took over as general manager. It was, he said, a challenge, one fraught with greatness, and to this challenge he brought the morbid sensitivity of a Hollywood producer, the showmanship of Bill Veeck and the sexual appetites of Miss Daytona Beach. His first project was to build "instant tradition."

He set up a tabernacle of trophies in the downtown suite of offices: gilt statuettes, plaques, medallions of uncertain heritage, the mummy of a leather football from the Thirties and a bust of Knute Rockne looking like the Heidelberg man. One entire wall became a pantheon of heroes. Since George Schmidt and Fred Dickie were the only Stags with a name, he pieced them out with cloudy blow-ups of Red Grange sweeping a forgotten end, Sid Luckman in a bulging leather helmet, Bronko Nagurski blowing tacklers out of his way and a couple of the Four Horsemen. Every time Dan looked up from his desk he enjoyed a kind of sour martyrdom at the hodgepodge of stolen immortals thundering on the wall.

But it took more than trappings, and as the Stags went down, down, down, Carson's congenital alarm became terror. "We've got to scrape off our barnacles," he chattered. "It's a decadent situation. I know you think it's heresy, but we're in the entertainment business and we can't sell losses." He trebled his tampering and trading, he pulled rugs out from under size fourteen feet, he called the coaches in for "creativity sessions." And still his tribulations increased. Now, pipe in hand, he faced the cynical reporters and said in his high-pitched voice, "I'm very bullish about it myself. Finding a first-class quarterback has been our Grail for several years, and in my opinion I think we've found him. Certainly Grover deserves another chance next week."

In a single quaver Carsie had reduced his great, new one-year plan to one more week, win or else, fellas. The mod pontiff was about to faint. He bobbed back and forth in front of the white movie screen, his oversized head dwindling down into small finicky feet. "I'm exteremely gung-ho about this," he said.

As soon as the services ended Carson went dashing after Whitman of the *Times-Examiner*. "Oh, Al," he twittered. "Oh, Al!"

What a thorn Whitman was in his side! His account of the Sunday fiasco had been terribly, terribly cruel: "The Stags," he had written, "showed up for the game like Frankenstein's monster with a new head and arm sewed on. The head didn't work and the arm was 4 for 14."

"Al," Carson said sorrowfully, "come on, now. That forty-six-yard pass for a TD was a beauty, don't you think? Tommy ran like a powerhouse and I thought he mixed up his plays very well."

Whitman looked at him like a dyspeptic leprechaun. "I thought Lowry was sending in all the plays."

"The knifer," Le Motte said as he moved away. "He

goes right for the jugular every time." Then he turned on Dan. "Whyn't you keep him in line? That's what you're being paid for."

Every few minutes Dan punctured him again. "What do you want to do about Dickie?" he asked. "He got away from his handlers again and stomped three guys in a bar. Seems he's for Reagan and Goldwater and the flag."

"How did he get the vote? Why doesn't that lawyer chain him to the radiator and throw marshmallows to him?"

Fallon brought out more bad news, feeding on the discharges of hysteria. "Oh yeah, Hughes wants to borrow five grand more. He got burned in the commodities market again."

"What! He already owes the club more than he'll ever make. Tell him no, absolutely and finally no. No! I hope he goes to debtor's prison. Do they still have them?"

By three o'clock the screams were a death rattle. Le Motte had been on the phone to one of the major stockholders, blithering about "physical football, it's the only way to the roses." Suddenly he cracked up. "Gabe has just bitten off more than I can chew! It's too big a risk. I'm not a riverboat gambler, I'm going back to Hughes. At least that way I'll make him earn the money he owes me."

Gabe Simson's schedule was a jumble during the season, so he usually had his late meal at the Beehive on his way home—to the smoked frame house where he was born, near the blast furnaces of the Bethlehem Steel Works. Heaping his mammoth body into one of the booths, he ordered a double porterhouse steak and American fries. The TV in the corner hummed with monotonous giggles from a rerun of *Neptune's Daughter*. Fat barbecued chickens tumbled over and over in a cage of light, sweating honey-colored drips from their crackly skin.

Waiting for the steak to broil, Gabe said, "Give me one of them chickens." The men with him, the equipment manager and the lame old geezer who kept time and sounded the horn in practices, were discussing ways to improve the blocking sleds.

"That don't do it," Gabe said. "You gotta make 'em grunt." Clutching one of his monstrous sacks of gut, he poured himself another mug of beer. Obliterated it in his hand.

Le Motte came tripping in. "Hi there, guys," he said, smoothing at his cravat. "Surprised I knew your hangout?" He drew up a chair and ordered a vodka martini, very dry. Gabe told the Greek waiter, while he was at it, to bring along a plate of olives and cheese, different kinds of cheese, and a wheel of that sesame-seed bread and some fried onion rings. And another pitcher of beer.

Carson fluttered tobacco into his pipe. He had handed over the head of Chip Hughes on a platter, and it wasn't easy to ask Gabe to please give it back. And it was so hard to think. Gabe was a concussion in the racket and the foody smells, crushing the breath out of him.

"Veal don't do it," Gabe was saying. "What you do is you stick chicken, lamb and beef on a skewer at the same time. That way the flavors link up. . . ."

Wretchedly Carson triggered his gold lighter. He sucked the flame into the cup of sleek wood, sucked again and finally kindled a perfumed little fire; it sent up a trickle of smoke and died.

Platters of food were cleaned off. Gabe rolled back behind his tun belly, besieged with flattering talk from his courtiers. Golf and the courses they had played.

Carson inserted himself eagerly. "Would you like to give Wilmette Country Club a go sometime, Gabe?"

"The way to play golf," Gabe rumbled, "is with a barrel of beer and a cart. Fuck the score. What you do is play the course without walking. Hit your shot and drink outa your keg."

Then he lapsed back into that huge inattention. The steaks arrived. Gabe looked off and away from the charred meat. Then without hurry he cut it into bleeding pieces and took them in. The fried potatoes and the salad went too, and he was sitting motionless over the bones. Carson had seen gargantuan eaters on the banquet circuit, stupendous eaters, in the tradition of Herman Hickman of Yale, he'd seen 300-pound ex-linemen cram in trays of lamb chops, whole roasts of pork. With Gabe it was different. It was more like setting an offering in front of a colossal statue. You looked again and it was gone, and the stone breasts and belly bulged in the reeking torchlight and the merciless stone eyes looked, as they always had, past everything.

Carson was in despair. He felt that if he looked in a mirror there would be nothing there at all, blank whiteness. "The fans and the press are in full cry, Gabe. But I'm gung-ho on Grover, never you fear."

Gabe beckoned to the waiter.

"Gabe? I'm sure he'll be our Messiah . . . if we stick with him. Right?"

"Mr. Le Motte, there's only one way to find out about a player. Throw 'em in a pit and cover 'em over. The ones that crawl out you keep."

"My God! You mean you're not sure about Grover? You sold me a concept, Gabe. I acted on your word."

The inhuman eyes looked at him. "I said we ain't gonna win that turkey with Hughes."

"Oh," Le Motte said, trembling, "I see. It's the test of fire. I remember now you said nobody could tell." Brokenhearted, he realized that Gabe hadn't even noticed his new cravat or anything. "Well, thanks much for your time, Gabe. Gentlemen, take care now."

What the fuck did he want? they asked Gabe.

"He wanted his cherry back was all," Gabe said. He told the waiter to bring him another one of those barbecued chickens. While it was coming he settled his gut between his legs and lit up a cigar. Let it go deep in his throat.

Reels winding and unwinding, sprockets gritting, the projector repeated Sunday's disaster on the little screen. Hairy faces gaped and squirmed. Bubble gum popped and big gloomy bodies in sweatsuits sagged down in the classroom chairs.

"No, no, no!" Lowry said. "Grover, you're breaking that pocket too quick." Reversing the film, he ran the play again, and again the kid back-pedaled and set himself, erect, his receivers squirting off into the secondary; again he wavered, ducked down and butted into tackles until he went under. "You see? You didn't pick up Tucker. He had that cornerback beat. You got to stay in there and look downfield."

Grover nodded, his head lowered. "Yes, sir," he said.

Coach Ellis growled, "You coulda at least gone to the outlet man."

"Yes, sir."

The Tuesday-morning post-mortem was in progress, offense in one room and the defense in another. Ignored by the coaches, Chip gnawed his jaunty little cigar into rags. He was rotting inside with frustration. Dumb ass, it was nothing but. Losing to the Cardinals was like drowning in the kiddie pool; he could have put the game away in the first quarter. And they were staying with the kid after a crud job like that!

"For Christ's sake," he muttered. "It's on-the-job training."

"It's incomprehensible," Short Stuff said. "You know?"

Sensibly the coaches decided not to hear that—or the groans and hawks and spews of profanity in the flickering darkness as Grover overthrew the open man, fumbled a drive away and fouled up the timing on simple handoffs. "The cocksucker can't even make a handoff," Short Stuff said out loud. "It's incomprehensible."

Hungrily Chip listened to the angry noises.

Only Mangialardi was feeling no pain. Big John had played the game of his life on Sunday, and now, arched back with his arms folded on his chest, his arrogant feet loitering in the aisle, he was watching the star of the movie: him. On the third play of the game he'd hooked that nigger tackle and all but taken his head off. In the next series of downs he face-masked him, then chopped the hell out of him when he came charging. After that it was strictly no contest; he peeled and ate him. Blissfully Lips soaked himself in the stream of plays. Ah, here it was, the strongside keeper in the second quarter. Whammo! He blew the nigger into the linebacker and the cornerback and wiped them all out, swept everything on that side of the field out of bounds—

"Unnh!" The sound from the other players was like the whomp of a bass drum. It was the highest possible tribute and Lips expanded in it. In the silence that followed he blasted out a fart like the last trumpet. Guffaws patted and slapped him admiringly. "Way to go, John," said Coach, old Tim Dewey from Green Bay.

"Wait'll we play the Giants," Lips said. "I'll destroy Heraman for you."

"Play 'em one at a time, John. We got this week to think about."

"Right, Coach." He grinned his mouth up into the red tips of his sideburns. He was alive again—but he was still wary of Chip, and instead of turning around and jamming him with a look, he sneaked up a foot and goosed Youngblood, the other offensive guard. The jig squealed and bucked up into the projector beam, flapping like a winged hippo and wallowing light all over the walls and ceiling. Chairs overturned. Coaches bawled. "Gonna pop you one, motherfucker," Youngblood panted, "you mess with me."

Chip barely looked up, dark inside with misery. It was his team; they were his bodies. And to be benched by a green kid. Man, his ego was bleeding. Okay, he wasn't a superstar, but by God he was the greatest non-great in the game, and on his good days he was number one.

And what the fuck, so he despised the fans, he loved the game. The strategy and counter-strategy as the defense switched on him and he changed the play at the line of scrimmage, the beautiful wheel-and-deal of a handoff smack into a setback's hands, the "hut!" and drop back with receivers shooting off in patterns and hitting the open man just before he went out of bounds—hell, the old pride of craft. Some quarterbacks could sit the bench for years, hold for place kicks and draw their pay. Not him; he didn't have that kind of a temperament. It was worse than the bone pile.

What's more, he knew who'd cut down his beanstalk. It was old Two-Ton. Not Lowry or Le Motte but Gabe Simson. Biggie was keeping Grover in the saddle, Biggie was making the guys put out 120 percent while the dropout tried to learn his trade.

Suddenly the screen seemed to flame up. Receivers sprayed off from the line like sparks from a welder's torch. His testicles cramped up as Grover let go a sixty-yard shot that just skidded off Bird's hands.

Man! If he didn't find some way to get to Gabe fast, to put him down with the players before those passes started connecting . . . But there was no way to do that, no way. Gabe bulled the team ruthlessly, but they worshipped him. Even George, even Old Faithful, thought the sun rose and set with Gabe.

They scrimmaged in the afternoon and came draggling in, slamming down equipment and griping, "This is for shit." Queer jokes about Le Motte and Grover boiled up. Poppo had spent all day Monday building a faggot trap, which he set up in his locker. Snapping the wire door up and down, he boomed, "Look at that! Look at that velvet lining! Is that beautiful or not?" His small face, perched on his burly neck like a child sitting on a stump, smiled proudly. He threw out his big arms. "Perfect!"

"That's some kind of a deal, Poppo."

"Beautiful!"

"How you gonna use it?"

"Hey, Poppo, that blows my mind. What kinda bait we gonna use?"

"You oughta put a sign 'Men's Room' on it. That'll fetch the queer."

"Nah, put 'Little Boys' Room.' "

Slurping big laughs, they pummeled each other, blacks and whites together. Pounded faces rocked back and forth. Jocko swung his drooling muzzle and danced up and down. Daddy Wilson held up his arm, a knotty Maypole in the circle of naked men. "Only one bait to draw him. And you *know* what that is."

"Yeah, Grover's dick!"

Chip whacked his towel for attention. "No, let's use Gabe's."

The laughter chopped off, dried up around him. All of a sudden *he* was in the pressure cooker. "Rog," he said to the big lineman, "look at that hand."

Rog was already dressed, decked out in candy-striped pink and green, a medallion flaming like a sun disc on his chest. "Huh?" he said.

"Gabe put his dick in that hand, Rog. You better wash it with soap, baby, because Carsie had ahold of that dick first."

"Aw," Roger stuttered, "G-Gabe's awright."

"He's got your picture in his wallet, too," Chip said, but it was a lost game. The muscular faces looked uncomfortable, shoulders seesawed with embarrassment, feet spatted away toward the shower.

It was the foot-long icicle up the gismo. He had fucked up, but royal. These boneheads could watch a film clip of Gabe and Carson Strangelove humping and they wouldn't believe it. Meat, that's what they were, hamburger. But he had to get them back, had to, or he was dead.

"Kiss me on Mayday, playday," sang three sirens on the jukebox in Freyr's. The waitress shook gracefully to the beat, moving out of the leafy alcove. "Hey, man, this is a drag," Jaworski complained. "Where's the wild life at?" He had come here after practice because he was sick of Shirley and the other stuff Lips served up, and so who was waggling her fingers gaily at him from the bar? Shirley. He scowled at her and massaged his throbbing elbow. Doc would have to drain it again.

Poppo was messing around with a pair of binoculars; he aimed the heavy barrels at Jaworski's pitted face and said, "Hey, you look about fifty times bigger, Jay. It's nasty, man. It's horrible." Jay made a grab for them, but Poppo said, "Nope. These are for beaver shots and I gotta be ready."

In a few minutes Dickie hulked in, nodded with a toothpick drifting in his mouth, and took a seat. Together they almost filled the "Cubs" alcove with their wide backs and shotputters' arms, big thickened hands throttling steins of beer. "This is a bitch," Jay complained. "Look at that broad over there. She's got a ass like Shirley."

Poppo held up a hand. "Wait, tell me something. What kind of chick is the best? With a fat ass or a thin ass?"

"A fat ass don't make it," Jay said. "It's gotta be thin."

Poppo gave him a look of pity. "Fat."

"I say thin. T-h-i-n."

"Bullshit! Nice and fat."

The darkness around them was walled with photographs, plastic leaves and clusters of plastic grapes. Pink light glazed their faces. "Fat," insisted Poppo.

George and Chip came in. With a grunt of pain George carried his injured leg under the table. Chip was Mr. Flash: black sunglasses and a white turtleneck sweater, a royal-blue sports coat slung over his shoulder. He crooked a finger at the waitress. "Bring on the martinis and the shrimp dip, wench."

"I'll have a Coke," George said.

"Chip," Poppo said, fixing the binoculars on him, "you're a big mover. What do you like better, a big ass or a small ass?"

"Decide for yourself, buddy. Do you like a nice tight little butt or a great big slobby thing that hangs down in *folds?*"

"Glaah!" Poppo let the binoculars flop on his chest and the others guffawed—except for Dickie, who sat there like a hill. Chip was feeling wild. He just barely stopped himself from saying, What are you doing out so late, Dickie boy? I thought they closed Flossmoor at 7:00 P.M. But his mother hadn't raised a fool. This was why he'd dragged George out; here was a chance to pull in one All-Pro linebacker and one tight end from Mangialardi's pack.

"Catching some night life, Dick?" he said.

"My old lady is pissed at me," Dickie said. "On account a that hassle." For a minute he stared at the pot of red light, crouched over the fire. Then he said, "Fuckin niggers. They don't love this country, they oughta go back to Africa."

"Right," Chip said briskly.

"Damn right," said Poppo.

"A nigger is a nigger," said Jaworski. "Unless he's on my team."

"And doin a job," Dickie said. "He's gotta be doin a job."

Then George spoke up, putting the words together slowly, with emotion. "That's the closest feeling there is almost . . . leaving out your family, I mean. . . . Say like a nigger makes a key tackle. Heck, I wanta kiss him."

"You got it mixed up again, George," Chip cracked. "You change your luck with a black *chick*."

Any reference to George's superstitions qualified as high wit. Jay picked up on it and said, "Hey, what about those great chicks, Poppo? Where're they at?"

"You're looking for pussy in *here?*" Chip gasped. "You're outa your tree. Gents, come with me. I have the key to the harem." He jumped up. When they hesitated he said sharply, "George, on your feet, buddy."

Obediently George pulled himself up and the others followed. "This way to the poon," Chip said. "Tonight is apple-blossom time."

Craftily he took them to a Polynesian restaurant on the Gold Coast. Bamboo and vinyl rain forest. Totem poles and glowering ritual masks by Mr. Dawn, Inc. The headwaiter made a fuss about suit coats, but Chip walked serenely to a table.

They shuffled after him, as big as billboards, stooping, intimidated. "Chip," George whispered, "they can keep their darn place if a man has to wear a suit to get in. Okay?"

"Not okay." When a waiter didn't come at once to take their order, Chip went down on the blaring red carpet and stretched himself out with his hands crossed on his chest. They whispered in horror, "Chip! Hey, Chip! Cut it out! Get up!"

A waiter came flapping toward them. "What's the trouble here, folks?"

Chip jumped to his feet and said, "We'll have five steaks, medium rare, baked potato and a salad. With Roquefort dressing."

"What?"

"And five orders of bacon. Make that double orders." The waiter shrank away toward the kitchen, and Chip seated himself with a grin. "Might as well drive up the price of pork bellies while I'm at it," he chirped.

"Man," they panted, "have you got balls! This kinda place, wow!" Every time they got out in public they froze into a great clump of distress, sweating and tampering with their hair, fidgeting awkwardly at their food. They went into paralysis at interviews and strangled out things like "In my opinion, uh, personally, I think we got more desire . . . They got desire, uh, but we got more desire."

To anybody not on the team—except celebrities and females—they were sullen and hostile. They scribbled their names grudgingly for fans and plunged back into the group, jumbling low half-words to each other, mostly about broads and games. "Like with Buffalo, huh? . . . You remember Gillie? Always wore a pink shirt? He could go, man, he could really go. . . . What kinda tits she got? Does she blow? . . . This guy, he's shootin in there, right? Really shootin the gap. So I pinch him in and ride him outa the play . . ."

Chip moved right in. He stroked down his scanty dark hair and said loudly, "You know, Poppo, I been thinking it over. What do I *really* like better? A nice big round soft ass or a thin bony ass with veins and tendons and pimples all over it?"

Poppo huddled over his steak, numb with embarrassment.

"Hey," Jay muttered, "there's no broads in here, Chip."

"Jay," Chip said reproachfully, "you don't want to screw on an empty stomach, do you? Finish your plate and we'll see."

He was Bobby Lane calling the shots now, all the shots, without George's help. They wanted to go back to Freyr's. He said, "Nope, we're making the Rush Street scene." They went along without a hassle, but he felt more and more restless, irritable, crazy. The date bars roared like electric hives. He picked up three secretaries in imitation fur coats and brand-new wigs. "Are you really with the Chicago Bears?" they asked, suspicious.

"Cross my heart," he said and introduced his teammates: "This here is Hawg Hollins, drinks nice and quiet, comes from Bean, Missouri. And this is Earthquake Jones, another living legend. Yonder is Bobo and that's Skeeter Tubbs, winner of seventeen awards for pass reception and good grooming." He swooped down in an elegant bow. "They're all married."

"You oughta be at the funny farm," he was told, and his teammates didn't exactly like it either. He smiled with his small icy teeth. "They were from the wrong harem," he said. "What we want is a nice cuddly type that screws like a mink and still believes in the Easter Bunny. Or the other way around, which is more likely."

He conducted a forced march from bar to bar, he

sold chances on a human-hair wig that an Indian friend had given him, he watered the plastic plants with their drinks. His frustration, his irritation kept snowballing and he pushed them harder and harder. "Fresh air is good for a rupture," he said fiercely. "Out!" A red neon horse galloped over his head in the freezing darkness. They tramped down stairs into a mob of voices and people sludging around in smoky light. Jay picked up a female all by himself, and Chip, turning the binoculars on her, said, "Poppo, what do you think of a nice big beautiful muscular ass?"

They took turns admiring size 96 boobs rolling out of a bra as big as a volleyball net.

Jay escorted her to the next booth and plied her with stingers, then went to work: "What about it?" he said. "Do you want to go to bed with me?"

"What? What kind of a girl do you think I am?"

"You're a drag, baby. A d-r-a-g," he growled. "Don't be a l-o-o-s-e-r."

Chuckling, Chip twisted around and whispered to her, "When he graduated from Pitt they retired his letter. D-plus. I think you two are gonna hit it off."

Taking the chuckle for approval, Jay tried to cut her up. "What d'ya know about hockey? Who's the goalie for the Montreal Canadiens? Who's the Blackhawks' leading scorer?"

"We don't have nothing in common," she said snootily. "I can't relate to you at all."

"You're nothing, baby. N-o-t-h-i-n-g." He came stamping back to the group.

"You lost the piece of ass," Chip said, "but you won the spelling bee."

That tore it. Jay's acne-riddled face went splotchy with rage and he said, "Watch it, I'll put you in the hospital, asshole."

"Yeah, sure." Chip bluffed him down. As he expected, Jay didn't even quit the party; he couldn't switch channels all by himself, and so he tagged along, sulking.

A fog of despair came down over everything. They were trooping toward the car. Somewhere ahead of him the guys were slap-boxing and bashing parking meters, one after another; the row of metal figures vibrated in the cold street. There was a snowstorm in his head.

Poppo was fooling around with the binoculars, holding the small end of the barrels right up to Chip's face. "Hey," he said. "I can't hardly see you, Chip."

"You and everybody else."

George asked him if he could go home because his leg was acting up, but Chip said, "You don't want to miss the sneak preview of my funeral, do you, buddy? Onward, goddamit, I want everybody to come back with at least six Easter eggs."

The next stop was Kayo's Stage Lounge. Electric guitars and voices splashing into each other. Bland doll faces reflecting in faces like mirrors. A fan swaggered up to their booth and said, "You Chip Hughes?"

The inevitable mustache and bubble eyes, pudge belly, atrophied arms.

"So?"

"I think you stink."

The other players told him to get lost, but Chip said, "No. Go ahead, get rid of your hangups. Live a little." The fan hesitated and Chip said, "Come here. A little closer." Suddenly he faked with his shoulder: the soft face burst open like a stone hitting a puddle and he was gone.

"Cocksucker," Chip was choking. "The nutless zombies. Yeah, I know, you hate their guts too, but not like me. The masturbators—they're shut-ins. They work on the old six-pack of beer while we do their fucking and killing for them."

Till now Dickie had sat drinking orange juice to help heal his forearms, which were like misshapen eggplants from the hammering on Sunday. "Fuckin fans," he said. "I don't play for no fans. I play for my pride. The other players, what they think a me." Probably it was the longest speech of his life. "That's my pride. That's why I'm a clean player, not like Lips. I don't ruin their knees or nothing like that unless I got to."

Chip said, "Fred, you're an inspiration to every living American."

"What I like is, I like to use my head when I nail somebody. Get 'em in the guts with the old helmet. That way they remember me good."

"Way to go," Chip said, and the others nodded.

"Look," Dickie said earnestly. "Chip, you wanta be on my radio show?"

"Sorry," Chip said. "I don't speak Polish."

Christ, he'd done it again. Oh well, he said to himself, might as well throw another interception. What the hell.

But this time he came close to getting the shit beat out of him. Dickie's hair seemed to bristle; his eyes crazed in his stump face. Chip could practically see the control centers in his brain short out. "It's in Polish, you fucker," he shouted. "I mean it's English."

George jumped in soothingly. "He didn't know. Cool it, come on. We can't afford any fights . . . no dissension. We can still put it together, guys. We scratch harder, that's all. Okay?"

Oh crap, Chip said to himself. Abruptly he got to his feet and walked away. George limped after him, asking what was wrong, why was he acting like this?

Chip whirled on him. "I heard this voice inside me, George, saying fuck it. And you got to listen to those voices, you know that."

"Aw, come on." His yellowish half-eye twitched sympathetically. "I know it's hard on you, Chip, but just hang in there. Put out harder and wait for your chance."

"Oh, horseshit! Don't give me that team-attitude jazz. You're programmed, for Christ's sake! You're a conditioned reflex! 'Coach says' and you twitch like a goddam muscle."

"Any psychological effects or traumas to report?"

"No, I don't think so," Chip said. He was lying on the couch with a glass of Scotch on his chest and a burnt-out cigar in his hand. "Well, I wet the bed, but I've always done that. Don't scorn me. Mickey Mantle wet the bed until he was sixteen and I'm only thirty."

He sort of grinned, but then he wouldn't talk to her for ten minutes; she simply couldn't get him unbugged. Finally he mumbled, "The green light is busted. It's all pfft!"

"Spell that," Dori said, yawning blearily. She draggled back and forth in a pale-orange nightie, picking up goop. Empty take-out chicken cartons, beer cans by the dozen and all the back copies of the *Sporting News*. And more work she'd brought home from the office. "You're wrong," she said. "It has three 'f's.' "

Her cubist print, "Nude in a Green Mirror," was on the floor. Blinking at the apple-green breasts and melon thighs, reflections, copulating images, she managed to hang it up again.

The last few days had been a marathon hassle. She had been up to her ass all week in ribbon copy and carbons for the Argo newspaper presentation. So who lands on her doorstep last night but Fuzzy, reeling across the threshold moaning his wife threw him out, but he was going to split a case of Schlitz with a friend who cared. If she was too busy to drink, well, he'd keep her company anyway, so he popped tops and ate chicken half the night to the beat of her frantic typing. By the time she packed him out of there, dawn was breaking and she was coming apart. Today had wiped her out, and if Chip hadn't sounded so absolutely suicidal on the phone, she would have told him she was out of town. God, she was whipped! And when she thought of finishing the Argo job, she wanted to upchuck and die.

She switched off the fireplace and the electric flames wavered, ducked out. "The weenie roast has been called off," she said, yawning. "Everybody on the bus."

Her guest belched morosely.

"Time to lay the body in the wheat, Chipper. Let's sack in. What do you say?"

"What kind of a farewell party is this?" he said. "I mean it. I'm hanging it up, Dori. Driving back to New Jersey tonight—if my goddam car can make it that far."

"Un-huh. And have you called Mrs. Hughes and told her?"

"Why the hell should I call her?" He gushed curses and pitched halfway up. "You ever hear the one about Omar the Camel Castrator?"

"Thirty-one times, Chip. In five different languages."

"Well, that's my wife. Socko! On the old grapes with two bricks. Good old Zsa Zsa." Smeary-eyed, he pawed clumsily at his wallet. "I ever show you her picture? Here. Here she is. She's the one on the right with the five-hundred-and-sixty-pound tarpon."

"You don't have to knock Martha to please me," she said. She tried to keep the impatience out of her voice. Wives meant no more to her than the other girls the players took out. Nothing. She dated X-number of players and former players and people connected with sports. She was fond of dozens (she had a *deep* bench) and she really let herself go with maybe three of them, but it was always there for Chip. She was honeycombed with little rooms of love, and for each one of them there was a neat little flag on the map in her mind. She was introduced and added a flag here, moved one there, quietly pulled another when a player was cut or took his pleasure elsewhere. The seasons changed and the players changed, and in March she took her vacation in Florida and hit the spring training camps, allowing one of her devotees to pick up the tab. Then it was July and the football camps opened and the long-distance phone calls from stir-crazy players began. And the seasons changed again in a whirl of phone calls and weekend trips, shop talk and gossip, expensive presents, trades, motel rooms and cab rides to motel rooms, and she never forgot anything, never blundered by dropping a word carelessly, and she never got carried away—well, almost never.

Dori jealous? Unh-unh, that was for the bodies, the

dum-dums. Corn-ee. "If you're not sleepy," she told him, "the booze is over there. Good night."

"Good night." He came trailing after her and spread himself on her bed. Wide and deep and plushy, it swelled out from the dark shelf of books in the headboard. She stepped up and walked across the bed to the closet and back to the pink fur bathroom. Her long legs flipped nimbly above his face, the joining up there a little strip of delicate fur, the puffs of sweet flesh glowing in the little tent of orange silk.

"Don't look up," she said, "or you'll go blind."

"You promise? I already got a fiddle and a tin cup," he said gloomily.

He tickled the hell out of her. She collected beautiful bodies, but Chip was much more—quick, smart, wacky. Tired as she was, she listened more compassionately, wrapping her hair with toilet tissue to save the set.

"It's a lost game," he was moaning. "I work my ass off to keep a hold of the team and so what? Grover breaks it all the way to win a couple games and the bodies'll go over to him anyway."

"Pooey! That won't do it, a clutch TD in the last thirty seconds wouldn't even do it. Look at Norm Van Brocklin when he came up. Dutchman had everything. He could throw with Waterfield, he was rough, he was a natural leader. And Bob was on the way down, too, but the Rams were his team."

"Yeah, yeah."

"No, listen. Ten guys must've told me about it, what happened. What Dutchman does is let a defensive end come in on him. He just pump fakes and holds the ball with three men wide open downfield. That goon comes in on him like a crop duster and Dutch just stands there.

Then boom, at the last second he straightens up hard and gives him a forearm in the mouth. There's blood squirting all over the field. I mean, he splattered him. The defense all come up off the bench, yelling and clapping. It was Dutch's team after that."

Her head by this time was a big white dome. She had pinned the tissue with clips and stretched a sheer nylon net over the whole structure; now she tied the strings under her chin. "Grover is dead, friend. He's no Van Brocklin."

"Maybe not, but he runs like a tank and he can throw a football through a stone wall."

"Pooey some more. He didn't show me that much against the Cardinals. And besides," she said, tapping her forehead, "Dragon Lady has been at work. At this very minute Jackie is screwing him out of his ever-loving mind. It'll take him fourteen years to learn a Power-Six."

But Chip was gray and silent. She coaxed him out of his clothes, but he lay beside her bitching about Gabe Simson. "Ever since Biggie coached the offensive line he's been trying to nail my balls to the wall in his rumpus room. I really ticked him off with my scrambling . . ."

"There's only one way to stop this," she said, switching on the night lamp. "Kiss me, my sex fiend." In the dim light his face was like a chunk of dirty snow, but she fluttered her tongue along his chest, along his belly.

"No sale," he told her. "Keep off the grass. Protect your pet, this lawn has been chemically treated."

She teased him anyway, petted, stroked his limp and fallen flesh, held it like a dark little mouse in her hand, crooning to it that she was a nice pussy cat, kissing it.

"Goddamit," he said, pushing her away. "I told you no. The act is dead."

She switched off the light with a shrug. "One kind of sleeping together's as good as another," she said.

But he was talking in the darkness, talking obsessively. "I've had it up to here. Tonight, take tonight. I'm impressing the guys into line, I'm dominating them, but besides, Dori, I really wanted to make them sweat. In that restaurant tonight it was sweet revenge. I've been sweating and bluffing it with them since I was twelve. My mother was this executive type, you know what I mean, divorced, ran this employment agency for women."

"It's okay, Chip."

"We got this pad in Far Rockaway, on the ocean—I never told you this stuff. Anyhow it was real Shangri-La, U.S.A., right on the flight pattern for Kennedy, Olympic-size swimming pool, a doorman that's a first-class prick. From the eighteenth-floor window I can see about a half a mile across to the playground by the projects. So I have to make it over there. It's off limits, and I mean strictly, but it's like a vision or something. I guess because inside I'm really chicken. I keep telling myself, 'Chip, are you gonna be a puppy all your life?' So one fine July afternoon I sort of creepie-creepie over there with my brand-new twenty-dollar Wilson basketball. Hot! Man, it's a hundred and ten, it's the inside of a furnace, and these cool-cat blacks and Puerto Ricans are playing B-ball. Real animal ball, you know? You go up for a rebound and they tear your arm off. . . .

"Right by the flagpole there's this like a plastic mat under the swings so the little kids won't fall off and get hurt. Well, every night they're balling the chicks on that mat and smoking pot and drinking wine and there's about ten radios blasting away at once. I don't recommend it for an initiation, I'll clue you. Anyhow, every day they rip off another new basketball from me and smear my ass all over that playground. But finally I hook up with this Jap kid—they called him the Orange Nip because he turned that color in the sun. He's got a brown belt in karate, and we have this deal. He'll flatten anybody for me for a nickel. It's beautiful! Now I can sleep at night, you know? So one day I forget and leave my money in my other pants, and Jesus, it turns out the Nip don't believe in credit. This big jagoff—his name was Fuck-Eye—he opens up and wears out the asphalt with me and the Nip just stands there laughing."

She tried to cheer him by saying, "Is that why you carry all that change in your pockets?"

"So anyhow, like I'm Mr. Super in all sports. Softball, track, and they respect that. I pitch on the baseball team. At ping-pong I'm so good they call me Slanty-eyes, like I'm Chinese. Hell, I won the state novice championship in tennis when I didn't even know how to keep score. I'm the best, Dori. No lie. I was team captain in three sports. I earned twelve varsity letters in high school and eight at Syracuse. But I don't know, there was always something missing."

"Maybe," she said, "it was something *not* missing. Like brains."

"I don't know, I don't think it's brains. Jerry Kramer wrote books and he was a jock. I been with jocks all my life and—I ain't one. I ever tell you how I went out for football? Well, I was just starting junior high and one rainy day the high-school varsity had to practice in our gym. Just running through the plays, easy, you know. They're all in pads and uniforms and helmets—all but the quarterback. Here's this good-looking kid in his tight white Levi's and tee shirt standing up straight and cool among all those big lunky guys. And he says a few numbers, real sharp, and the whole thing moves. I don't know, I guess it doesn't sound beautiful, but it was. And I said to myself, 'Chip, *that's* what you want to be.' "

"That's pretty! You never told me that."

"But did you ever see the agility drills for linemen? They teach them to get down on all fours and run like animals. But hell, everybody is an animal. I don't know. It's sure not skills, either, because there's guys that spend their whole life on the bench and they're jocks. I don't know.

"Look, I'm married to these guys and I love them, I gotta have 'em. They're like my arms and legs, and not just George, either. I feel like I'm married to Bird, but I'm damned if I know what goes on in his head. Or like my center, old Fifty-seven Flavors, he comes up to me and talks to me for a half an hour about motorcycles. He says stuff like 'All you really need is a two-sixty-five cc., and I say to myself 'What the fuck is this?' I mean, he's friendly, you know? His heart is on his sleeve.

"Anyhow, I'm the hotshot, you know, the lion tamer, but always it's been a bluff or like a fake. The edges never quite fit together. And don't think they can't smell it if I ain't careful. All the way back. The high-school team, they respected me because I was great, but they were kind of squeery too, because I got good grades. So I'd lay their fears to rest—fake 'em out. Like whenever I came first to a door marked 'push,' I'd pull like hell on it till somebody came up and helped me. Once I led 'em on to the wrong bus going home from a game, and it was two hours before somebody caught on. It kinda reassured them, you know? I wasn't really any smarter than they were. I was just the quarterback. I been faking in different ways ever since then. And I'll clue you, it gets real old."

"What doesn't?"

"Real old. Eighteen years of faking. . . . Well, fuck it all. I don't need this. I'm a big mover and knocker in the commodities market. How about loaning me forty-seven thousand dollars?"

She smoothed his high balding forehead. "Poor Humpty-Dumpty," she said and, tenderly, kissed the puckered line of the scar on his cheek.

"I told you, lay off."

"Well, my God, Chip! I wasn't being horny."

"Lucky for you," he said to the ceiling. "You heard the expression weak dick, weak arm? You heard of that one?"

"By Anonymous?" She smiled. But he was closed in on himself, ice-hard. "Hey, shake it off. You don't go with that sex-magic stuff. That's for the dum-dums, Chip. You gonna be like Babe? He had to make it with me the night before he pitched against the Sox or they'd knock him out of the box in the first inning. That whole virility mumbo-jumbo. Honestly. And the older a jock gets the worse it gets. They psych themselves till they drive me up the wall. I mean, they're *constantly* proving in bed they haven't lost that extra step, the old snap in the wrist—"

The sheet lay over him like snow. The phone rang, and impatiently she picked up the receiver and said, "Yes?"

It was Joe Mulvaney, who'd been a solid fullback with the Bears a few years ago.

"No," she told him. "I can't, no. Pretend it's Lent, Joe."

Well, then, maybe could they go to Cincinnati tomorrow?

"I can't. I have to go to work every day like a good girl for *years*. How far can a couple of rolls in the hay with the boss take me? Don't you want me to have a job like all the other girls?"

Yes, but Jackie was down there with Fuzz already and he thought they could make it a foursome.

Dori let the receiver sink to her waist, trickling Joe's voice. The bitch. The goddam silly, muddleheaded bitch.

All of a sudden her confidence about Chip's chances leaked away. Lying there in the dark, he looked like—what was it? She was tiptoeing upstairs in an empty farmhouse in Arkansas. There was a little wooden door in one of the bedrooms and behind was the dark old attic full of faded books and newspapers, mostly in some foreign language, jumbled together in the still air. A doll goggled at her from the sliding junk; she had a gimcrack crown pasted to her head and a skirt of feathers like dusty green leaves. Picking through the rubble of generations, she turned over a page and there was this real scary picture of a naked man tied to some stones. They were going to kill him because an old man in a long robe had a dagger held over him. She was a bloodthirsty little heller then, and she must've spent a hundred hours looking at the scary pictures of guys in armor fighting and hanged men and real neat spooky stuff like that. She got the biggest goose pimples in history; she even told her daddy about it while she drove the tractor to help him with the plowing. But this was Chip lying on the stones. Chip, her Chip. The poor dear bastard was so scared that he'd gone jock and psyched himself completely out. She could smell it in him: no hard-on, no TD passes. It was up to her. Now. If she couldn't break the spell, he was done for.

He really would cut out for home and Le Motte— Carsie might do any number of bitchy things—put him on waivers, anything.

"Good night, Joseph," she said and hung up. Goddam that Jackie! The entire counterattack had gone blooey. But before taking that on, she had to work big, big, big magic. The radiator hissed. She uncoiled the tissue from her hair and flipped the nightgown over her head. "Boo!" she cried. "Scare you?"

"You know what's the first thing in my life I can remember? I was standing in a crib and I had a load in my pants and—oh fuck it!"

"Ssh." Making herself cute and cuddly, she plumped down beside him with her legs crossed in front of the tuft of cornsilky hair. "That was Joe Mulvaney," she said. "Joe always gives me up for Lent, but he hasn't made it through the first week yet. I'm irresistible." She turned it on. She could feel her body shimmer into the darkness, a light delicious animal. "Pay attention," she said. "I'm irresistible."

He stared up at the slash, slash of traffic lights on the ceiling. However, they had had their best times in bed between jokes. The first time—it was the night after a Forty-Niner game. They'd been introduced at Freyr's, met again the next night, and after twenty-three minutes of moderate bliss she had stretched herself in the sheets and said, "Not bad, Mr. Hughes. That was all right." Without blinking an eye he'd said, "I wouldn't know myself. I'm a Baptist."

"A Baptist?" she said.

"A Bible salesman? A runaway bishop?" And they had been buddies for life.

Snuggling herself up to him, she began sort of tricking him into it. "Chip, when I was a little old hillbilly girl back in the seventh grade, another girl told me kissing was better than ice cream."

He wasn't tuned in. "At least this crap won't go on much longer," he said to himself. "I'll die on that bench in about three more weeks."

"Pooh! Let me see your hand, just for a second." She took his hand and gave it the old Gypsy tearoom squint. "Look at that life line. Eighteen-twelve to nineteen-sixty-five. That oughta be long enough for anybody."

He had to grin, and the icy darkness in him thawed a little. She kissed him on his tight, clipped mouth. "You're right," she said. "It's a profound spiritual experience, but it's not better 'n ice cream." He laughed. Throwing her hair out from her head, pink shadows blossoming over her face, she kissed the sad flesh, slipped her tongue around it, lifting it up, up in red throbs, erect, but before she could fit herself under him it leaned and wavered, shrank and went slack again, a gray little corpse. Cursing, he blundered away to get himself another Scotch. His desolation was beginning to reach her now.

He staggered back onto the bed. Threw his hand over his eyes. "Red Rover, Red Rover, let Chippie come over," she whispered. Her slippery little kisses became a dance, a speech of touches, strokes, slow wrappings and flicks of her quick tongue. It was a little pink snake twining on the pale sprout of flesh. With a sly sharp sideways look from her plump face, she took one of the ice cubes from his drink and plopped it into her mouth. They called this a cool cocktail, and it never failed. His frozen eyes warmed, warmed into sleepy pools, and he watched her roll the ice cube, bobble it around and around, juggle it in the spermy flows, juggle the weak flesh back to life.

It took her a whole week to get
the Grover Blitz back in motion. Then
she stayed home from work, curled
up in a bedful of magazines and books.
Yawning and stretching out her long
full legs, she turned over the pages of
Vogue and the *Bazaar*, lusciously
reflected in the Natur-elle Look, in
the models with the blank superb
faces of Siamese cats, furs, young
goddesses clothed in See-Mist, dreamy
lotions and her breasts peeping in
sweeps of pampered hair.

After a while the old girl from
across the hall came shambling in with
the mail. "Just put it down anywhere,"
Dori told her. "And get me some
chocolate milk, will you? And a sweet
roll."

"I declare, you just *won't*
cook for yourself," Florence
grumbled. "You live here like in a
hotel."

"What's the use cooking just for

yourself? It's all I can do to make myself pick up around here."

While Flo rattled dishes in the kitchen she muttered about Jackie's kids; they purely gave her fits, and wasn't the days getting shorter and why in heaven's sakes didn't Dori water the plant, it was dry as a bone.

"Take the damn thing back. My crop-raising days are over."

Florence was from the way-out country too, but today of all days Dori despised the feel of chickenshit between her toes that the old bag gave her. Damn and double damn.

Slapping the plate down beside the bed, Flo squinted at her through the fumes of the cigarette waggling in her hairy lips. "Took the day off, huh?"

"I should have taken off a week, what I owe myself for what I've been through." She snuggled deeper into the sheets and books. "Two weeks in Miami wouldn't do it."

Flo set her dyed curls in motion, rocking her head. "I declare you act like a martyr. I'd be in hog heaven steppin out with a nice boy like that Tommy Grover. Is he in love with you yet?"

Dori pulled down one side of her mouth. "You figure it. He gave me a bar of soap with 'Chicago Stags' on it."

"I wisht *I* had that bar a soap from him."

"Yeah? Personally, I'd rather not play fifty-three consecutive games of pinball. And I hate and despise cheeseburgers. You know what that hick did? Stole my panties! He *saves* them in a trunk like *scalps!* I had to come home with the wind blowing up my pussy."

"You poor thing," Flo hastened to say.

"God, I'm a wreck." She dragged herself out of the

bed and roamed around the room. "I'm dead stuck right back in the middle of it. Every single thing I tried to get away from. I don't want to be a Church of Christ country kid that had to take the school bus into Metropolis, Arkansas, with a greasy bag of sidemeat sandwiches. Stinky-stinky—don't you think I didn't hear them stuck-up town girls. They didn't have to even tell me, either. I knew it. Me and my Sears print dress. I didn't even try to get in their bunch. I was country and it wasn't no use."

"Now don't you go getting yourself all tore up."

"I'm so damn screwed up, the things I do for Chip, I swear. I sweat my butt off. That closet is full of Saks Fifth Avenue. I live in this slum so I can get my hair done by Mr. Edward and buy my shoes from some place besides Monkey Ward's. I'm into the best places. The Empire Room of the Palmer House and the Pump Room and Sage's East, that's my turf, that and Freyr's. And all the time I know better inside myself."

"Hush, now."

"And now Grover comes along and makes me feel like I'm that sixteen-year-old kid that lives eight miles from town. That couldn't even go out for cheerleader because I had to take the bus home right after school. Flo, I *wanted* that little gold megaphone hanging between my tits. You'll never know."

"I know, honey. And Jackie is so sorry she laid down on her part of the bargain. She come back from Cincinnati and the pore thing, I never saw such pain. She was cryin with ever breath she took."

"Mm. She wants me to give her Chip anyhow, huh? And if I do, what do *you* get? A pregnant pet? Her alligator purse with a dollar in it?"

"Why, hon," Flo said. And immediately tried to con her into helping Shirley, who was suffering the tortures of the damned because the Stags didn't respect her no more.

Naked except for black lace panties, Dori was examing herself critically in the mirror. She needed a shampoo and set, and she'd always known her nose was just a smidge too long and her mouth a teeny bit too small. But even without makeup she had that really *good* skin of a redhead. All over, like that Botticelli nude on the seashell. With this for a start she dressed herself ever so carefully, putting on only the most expensive things, a little wisp of a bra, her Givenchy necklace, and looked at herself again in the mirror, turning and posing, posing: Aphrodite in a Bergdorf Goodman dress, despondent.

"God, you're a perfect lady," Flo breathed hoarsely.

In silence Dori stripped herself back down to the skin and did it all over again in a cocktail dress, then abruptly shucked everything off and threw herself face down on the bed. "Forget it, Doris Nell. Just forget it. You're still wearing black cotton stockings and you've got pig shit on your shoes."

"Why, you don't any such thing, hon."

Naked, Dori sat with her face down and her hands in her lap. "And so what if I go shopping and pet myself all day? I got it to do again tonight. He doesn't know it yet, but he's got a date."

The old sow's eyes gleamed lewdly. "Jesus Christ, that Tommy Grover's pretty. He's a perfect Adonis." Her mouth smiled open on a few brown teeth. "I'd like to lose my panties to him myself. What a body. Jesus Christ. With a body like that he ought to be a good player in any sport. Personally I favor him over that Chip Hughes."

"You would, you old heathen," Dori said. "He's just your type. He picked up all his bedroom technique diddling the livestock."

Flo cackled through the roots of her teeth. "I like 'em like that. Green."

"Sometimes, Florence . . ." Dori checked herself and said, "I *wish* you'd stop knocking Chip. When I first saw him he was so . . . smooth and everything. The way he handled himself and talked. He was *born* in a Brooks Brothers suit. Not to mention his personal qualities, which I won't bore you with."

"That was my last word on the subject, it's a God's promise." She rustled away and in a few moments came back with a bottle of French perfume. "This looks like it's about gone," she said craftily.

"Take it," Dori said without looking. Chip was her guy and plowboys were blah, but it wasn't quite that simple. It was sort of too bad to chop down such an innocent.

"What are *you* doin here?" he said when she presented herself at his door.

"I want to see *Ben Hur* again, and play pinball, and watch you eat nineteen cheeseburgers."

"It's some kind of a movie all right," he conceded, tugging at the grassy fringes on his cutoffs. "Only, like I told you. I'm not foolin, Dori. I got to really hit the playbook tonight. Even Li-bary can't come over."

"Li-brary is a *man*. That's different."

"You ding-a-ling," he said, smiling. "You gotta stay

in the corner, though, and don't say a word. Just watch TV or somethin."

She slipped in. The middle of the floor was waist deep in strips of green carpet he was laying himself. Fan mail, advertisements and bills were messed all over a burly table. Barefoot, he stepped up on the sofa and flipped, came down whomp! on his back with the playbook resting, spectacularly open, on his chest. A flop of sun-colored hair lay in his eyes. Covering a page with his hand, he muttered to himself, "Four-thirty-two pass trap, drop back deeper . . ." Both the TV and the radio were on full blast and he attacked furiously, stretching his neck and swinging his caught head in a frenzy of effort. When he fouled up he raged at himself under his breath and jammed his ballpoint into his forearm.

She whistled. "I've seen studying, but this is giving me nosebleed."

He didn't hear her. All at once an alarm clock rang and he bounded up, his hair flagging on his wide forehead. For an instant, released into beautiful motion, he stood in the air, grinning boyishly at her. His Nebraska practice jersey bulged up there on his thunderous chest. "Wow!" He blew out his breath, landing softly. "Is it ever workin! Sweet!" Carefully he turned off the alarm and reset it. "Go ahead, guess what."

"It's time to get up?"

"Nah," he said. "Look here, it's a schedule, like. See, six-thirty to seven, study. Seven to seven-thirty, lift weights. Seven-thirty to eight, study. Eight to eight-thirty, watch 'The Outsiders' on TV, and so forth." The words came fluttering down in his breath, tumbling happily around her. "That way I always keep an edge on, like. You know, keep my concentration better. Li-bary deserves most of the credit, but I helped. Lay it on me," he said, holding out an enormous hand to be slapped.

With proper ceremony she slapped her hand down on it. "Way to go," she said.

"Thanks. Weight-lifting time," he announced. "You stay here. I'll be back in, uh, twenty-eight minutes."

"Can't I watch? I'll go with you and count."

"Uh . . . well, you see, uh . . ." Then he shrugged and let her follow him into the weight room. But he was embarrassed. The walls were all doodled and scribbled over, scratched up with plays and forgotten telephone numbers. A pair of tits was cut into the woodwork. This was maybe his worst bad habit. At the U of N he must have carved a thousand sets of knockers at least. But mostly he didn't want Dori to see Marsha's name spray-canned all over the place in great big branching red letters.

"I told you I was engaged," he said with a blush. "I call her every night long distance. Nine to nine-thirty."

"No big deal," she said. "I was engaged lots of times. I was even married. Great guy, too, except that he was a booze hound and kind of skirt-happy."

"Yeah?" Relieved, he took off his jersey and stooped over the barbell loaded with huge bronze-painted discs. "When I get married, I ain't gonna run around or anything." She said she knew. He came up with the barbell, swells and flexible strips of muscle surging, bunching up under his skin, and hoisted it up easily over his head. Sweet, it was sweet. His pores juiced open, sweet, releasing like sap coming out. He snorted with each heft of the iron. Between exercises he padded back and forth, panting and toweling himself off.

"Whyn't you do a few sit-ups yourself?" he suggested. "You're a little outa shape." She told him that was feminine fat and she needed it. Man, did he ever like to lift weights. He was really feeling happy; his whole body felt happy, like there was a fire in it. "Hey," he said. "Watch this one. Me and Li-bary call it the ball-buster."

"Do you think that's fair to Marsha? Or me?"

"Nah, don't worry. We just call it that 'cause it uses muscles we don't even have." Bent over with his monumental legs wide apart, his hands joined together on the bar, he brought the weight up to his chin twenty times. Then straightened up, laughing. "You know what I like?" he said. "I like to sweat. It gives me a good feeling."

The alarm clock rattled in the other room. His face darkened, but heroically denying himself a shower, he went back to the book, glaring at the pass paths that curled in and out, streaked and jagged in a wiry tangle. He plunged at it like a ram in a thicket. Beneath the diagram there was a bristle of description in code and at the bottom Coach's instructions for him. His fists bunched, concentrating. Again and again he drove the ballpoint into his bluey punctured forearm, as if he could print the code into his flesh. "Whip, stop in," he muttered.

"Whip, stop *out*," she corrected him.

"What? Hey, you oughtn't to be listening. I forgot! This is secret."

"I have," she informed him, "five of those playbooks at home."

"Five! Wow! Coach would sure be pissed if he— excuse my language. Do you really know the plays? Man, I wish I did. I'm pickin up on it pretty good, but Coach . . . well . . . My biggest hangup is the terminology, you know? I figure, including offense and defense, it's over twenty thousand things. It's like another language. Like you take 'Will,' " he sputtered intensely. "That means your weak-side I-man. And 'Stob'—uh—"

"Is the strong-side linebacker."

"Yeah! Hey, you're a smart chick! I mean for a chick with one year of night-school college, you're intelligent."

"Thank you," she said.

"Hey, what about if you quiz me on the short list? It'll put a new edge on it, okay?"

She took the playbook and fired questions at him while he paced around the green hill of carpeting—moving, always moving, exercising almost without being conscious of it. Prowling back and forth, he suddenly jumped up by the flickering TV, spouted straight up with his arms at his sides. "How close did I come?" he said. "To the ceiling? I'm tryin to touch it with my head." Standing in the doorway, he scowled at a hard one, almost cracking the wooden frame with the thrust of his arms. "Tucker!" he cried. "On a curl-in."

"Good. Now let's work on the sawhorse."

"That means a deep crossing pattern." He held out a fist for her to tap with her fist. "Way to go, Tom!" he chortled, lifting himself up and backward onto the radiator. "I like to sit on radiators," he told her happily. "It's my favorite spot to sit on." He was so pleased with himself that he took time off to tell her about the audible he'd learned today. "I was throwin the hell outa the ball, too."

"Bully for you," she said. "All right, on the thirty-three-zoom, how many counts do you wait?"

He wrestled mightily with that one. When he screwed up she helped him, going over and over the stuff. He was learning, but somehow it seemed like there was more of it; she kept adding lots more stuff he needed to know. He slid down off the radiator, frowning. He was losing it, just when he'd been getting on it, too, and more and more of the code kept coming in on him, star-in, flip, sponge-out, a dust storm of it, dry, parching his eyes, smothering him. He looked at the clock. When the alarm went off he mumbled, "We better keep goin. I got to hack it."

"If you say so. Okay, change of pace, Tommy. Let's take the first five tree routes."

"Unh!" A terrible grimace dragged at his face. "Maybe I better read it myself. Slower and everything."

He hunched down in the couch and blinked with gritty eyes at the shuffle of pages. The sweat drying on his skin felt bad. The numbers and letters didn't mean a thing any more. "Goddam you, Grover," he choked. "You stink!"

"Easy, boy."

"No, it's true. I cut it at Nebraska. I'd come in after practicin four hours and grub up and hit the books. And every time my head went down, my roommate would punch me on the arm."

"It's not fair, asking you to learn all this so fast. Plus timing and all your receivers' moves and all that. And under this pressure, o and six now! I mean it's unreal."

"Yeah . . . well . . ." He rubbed at his sandy eyes like a little boy. "I got it to do, that's all." He wouldn't blame the coaches for rushing him, or his teammates for making all those queer jokes. And in the life-and-death struggle with Chip Hughes, he didn't feel the slightest ill-will; he said Chip had it all over him for experience and football brains and everything. "But I should be doin better," he mumbled. "The thing is, I got this thing like. I always thought I could do the job if I worked on it. But I guess the competition, you know, wasn't . . . It's a lot rougher up here and . . . anyhow, thanks for tryin."

He asked her to excuse him and slumped away into the shower. At first he barely noticed the warm spray bursting over him, cuffing his head and face sweetly, drenching him, sluicing out the clogged muscle paths, but after a while he could feel the dry blind pain begin to soak through, melt and rinse away. His body drank greedily, lifted. He was joyously soaping himself when Dori came strolling in, naked!

"Hey!" He laughed. "You ding-a-ling, you!"

"I just wanted to try out this bar of Stag soap you gave me." Spray shattered on the plastic bag she had tied over her hair. Tickling and kissing in licks of water, she soaped his back for him: lathering the big muscles growing out of each other until they looked like part of a snowman and then dousing them off with sweet armfuls of water. "I'm kind of a water nut sometimes," she said to him. "I went to Bermuda once and I felt so good I walked into the ocean at sunrise. In all my best clothes! I damn near drowned, too."

"You're some kind of a ding-a-ling," he said admiringly. She was all shiny and foamy-slippery in his arms and her belly and legs sucked against his. He got a terrific hard-on. Laughing, she opened her mouth in the driving water and flooded it, then kissed the water into his mouth in giggling spurts. Blowing, gasping, he said, "I'm gonna initiate you," but she wriggled loose in bright kicks of spray before he could rip off her cap and duck her. "You're gonna get it now," he spluttered. Grabbing her and tipping her back in a hurricane of swept spray, he began to pull her knees apart.

"Oh no you don't," she said, and her steady look

stopped him, pushed him back. "Everybody out of the pool."

"What's the deal?" he said. "What's the deal?"

"That's no way to have an orgy," she said. She insisted that they dry off and go into the bedroom. He was all messed up. He had this big hard-on and he rammed his knees between her long elegant legs and came busting down. She slipped away from him again. "That's not the way either. It doesn't go wham, Tommy, and it doesn't go bam, and it doesn't go thank you, ma'am."

On his knees he gaped at her, hurt.

"It goes," she said, "like this." Taking him gently down to her, she moved skillfully underneath him, in and out and every which way, with some kind of crazy-ass rhythm he couldn't pick up, fishtailing herself before and after his banging great strokes, quick, quick, and then just as he was getting to it, slowing him down, reining him in. He was bewildered, struggling again, angry. "Hold 'er, Knute." She smiled. "These things take time."

"What for?" he blurted. "What's with you? Are you a nymphomaniac?"

"Well," she said, "that year of night school *was* the University of Chicago."

She seemed to think that was real funny. Sullenly he said, "I think screwing is just screwing and not all this stuff."

"Whatever screwing is," she replied, looping her arms around him, "it is not just screwing."

He was sore, but he needed a piece very bad, so he tried it her way. And pretty soon the pounding started again, the pressure inside him like a wind from the Rockies, like Current River piling up against Current River Dam, great big hills of water piling up and piling up. But he hung in there. Mostly out of pride and the old competitive instinct. Then, just for a second, it started going good and that worried him. He didn't like to do anything less than perfect and maybe, just maybe, that went for this too. She sure was something else for moves, he had to admit that. She was fantastic, out of sight. He went all out, but the pressure was beating and drumming inside him. And it wasn't only taking the pressure either, but using it, and that was one rough thing, rougher than the toughest coaching, when Coach Magus had hollered every time you fucked up and kicked you in the legs. He pushed himself harder and harder, but she wouldn't turn him loose, not yet, not yet; she wouldn't let herself moan and go under with him. He was exploding inside in fiery streams, rolling, plunging, heaping up like a mountain, and she put her hands on his wild hips and held them, checked them quietly, firmly. He was in agony. "See?" she murmured to him. "See how pretty?"

She'd got to him just in time. He'd been cracking it, but when she left at 2:30 in the morning his proud schedule was a shambles and his playbook somewhere in the carpeting. He made her take a solemn oath to stay away on Friday night. So at a quarter to seven she socked on his door and piped, "Trick or treat."

The door opened and she posed fetchingly in a mildewed Salvation Army gown and a witch's mask, warty and black, poking out a crooked icicle nose. "I'll take it in small unmarked bills," she said, holding out her treat bag.

"You ding-a-ling," he said, laughing. "Hey yeah! It's Halloween, ain't it!"

She didn't have to seduce him away from the playbook. Chuckling and pacing back and forth, he phoned Li-bary and told him to buzz on over, fast. Winking nearsightedly through thick glasses, the young reserve guard loomed near the hill of carpeting like a studious water buffalo. In a high squeaky voice he advised Tom to stay on it with the books, but Tom said he needed an hour off to clear his head.

Boisterously he whacked together some costumes. He unearthed a decrepit track suit, added a mini-skirt left behind by one of his fans and then strapped on shoulder pads, glossy overlapping bowls that rocked the upper air around his grinning face. For Li-bary he jerry-rigged a skirt out of a sheet and roped three sofa cushions to his belly to make him look pregnant.

"How's that?" he said to Dori, heaving out big laughs. "If we don't win Best Costume it's a rob."

"Right," she said but with less enthusiasm.

"What's the matter?"

Plenty was the matter. Dori Frazier, the idol of the American and National Leagues and points in between, was coming down with a bad case of clay feet. Her campaign to get Chip off the bench was still in progress, but goddamit, Tommy was so boyish and sweet.

"Nothing's the matter," she said to them. "Nothing at all."

"Okay then! Let's hit it!"

They bought plastic pumpkins to fill with candy, a horn and a cowbell, and roistered down the streets. Li-bary and Dori hung back while Tom lollopped along with the tiny maskers, a patchwork giant wading happily in the little scarecrows, spooks and skeletons, monsters with glistening nylon fur, red-white-and-blue spacemen and kindergarten princesses, pitching along in front of the meek little houses.

Dori watched him yawp on his plastic horn and devour everything he collected as soon as it was dropped into his pumpkin. How he enjoyed things, she thought. He drove a car like flexing a muscle, effortlessly but joyously, completely, taking his shoes off to get more feel. "Ain't this great?" he said, galloping up. He was mashing corn chips in his shining teeth. "Come on, Li-bary, let's hear that old cowbell."

Li-bary said that this kinda stuff turned him off. "It's a travesty," he said.

"Don't tell me, let me guess," Dori jeered. "The commercialization bugs you."

"That," he said, "is minor. What bugs me is nobody knows what it's all about. What it denotes."

Tommy burst in. "Listen to him, Dori. You're a smart chick, but he's smart too. He's hung up on reading. You know how many books he's got? He's got over two hundred paperbacks, no foolin."

Pompously the big lineman gave the exact count and delivered himself of a few esoteric facts about Halloween: about the jack-o'-lanterns glowing like small idiot suns in the windows, about black cats and leering witches riding the sky on their broomsticks. "Yeah," Tommy said, "it's all about ghosts. This is the night, you know, the dead come out of their graves and everything."

"That's nothing," Li-bary said grandly. "It's older 'n that. It goes back to a savage people called the Celtics."

"You mean the Boston Celtics?" Dori asked. It wasn't fair, but he was so hard to take.

Li-bary gave her a pitying look. He was referring to

a savage tribe, he said, and this was the dying of the year for them. "I read it in the *Trib*. Also, you take men wearing dresses like this." Unhappily he poked his inflated belly. "It was a very sacred deal with the people of long ago. It was religious with them. Now it's perverts. And I ask you, what's it doing in Halloween? How's that for a screw-up? In fact," he said expansively, "it's all a king-size royal screw-up. Nobody knows nothing, and what we got in the world today is bits of junk out of past times pasted together and a fresh new coat of paint on it. It's like new cars rollin off of the assembly line and they're junk already. Most of the steel is made out of old cars and scrap."

"What did I tell you?" Tom said proudly. "He's an expert on the Cold War too. And the Panama Canal."

He romped off to trick-or-treat some more. His shag head bobbing along, his shoulder pads flapping, he towered away in a glaring cartoon procession of kids. Li-bary kept talking. It was cold. Along the sidewalk came a girl slopping in her mother's faded dress. Her bawling little brother dangled on her hand wearing a bedraggled Mickey Mouse costume. Somehow he reminded her of Chip. His big round furry ears were smashed and half his tail was missing, and as he stubbed along he sobbed out yellow shreds of candy corn.

She couldn't shake it at all. She took off her mask. The dead leaves and scraps of paper swirled on the new sidewalk, around and around in a dark skipping dance. "Counterclockwise," Li-bary informed her. "That's how witches dance. Opposite to the stars."

"Li-bary," she said, "you're an asshole."

"You're not the first to say so." Profoundly hurt, he

took the cushions out of his skirt and walked off into the darkness, a great dismal snowman hulking away.

"You want a popcorn ball?" Tommy had come back and his face glowed down at her, smiling. "Li-bary head out?" he said. "Hey, don't look so depressed. He's always depressin people. Did he tell you the one about history was a garbage pile? He really depresses people—except me. Hold this," he said and handed her his horn. Holding the pumpkin like a football, he sprinted down the alley toward a pile of boxes that some kids had set on fire. It blazed in windy lashes, ugly, dangerous. With a whoop he jumped clean over it. Pleased with himself, he trotted back to her. "I jumped every bonfire we ever had when I was a kid. No lie. I never missed."

"Way to go," she said. "If you don't mind, I'd like to go home."

"Now? When we're just gettin started?" Very disappointed, he got the car and drove her to her apartment. She took off the decaying dress and put on something. Then she made herself a martini.

His sweet, heavy face was concerned. "What kinda hassle was it? Hey, you gotta cheer up. Hey, I got it! Come on to New York and watch me against the Giants. I'll get you a seat on the fifty-yard line." She sat there with the martini in her hand, and he said, "I'll play good. No lie, it'll be a romp."

"Fine," she said. "All right. Fine."

For a while he was stopped, but then his face lit up. "How about if we, like, bob for apples?" He laughed encouragingly. "You get the joke? They used to tease me about it when I was a kid. I mean, you know, that's my nickname, Apples."

Before she could say anything he slammed out. In a few minutes he came blasting back in, his arms full of brown paper bag. "Hey, you got a big pan or a bucket? I'll fill up the sink. Come on, I'll show you how."

She let him take her arm and pull her along with him. He filled the sink with apples bobbling in water and said, "Watch this," dunked his whole face in and came up with one in his teeth, laughing. "Now you," he said. "It's easy."

And, ah, what the hell, who could stay sad with him rollicking like this? Cautiously she dipped her face in, snapped at a sliding-away roundness and came up with her nose full of water, coughing and choking. "Good first try!" he said. "Watch again now. You got a small mouth, so what you do is you kinda nudge it over to the side so you can get a grip on it."

She couldn't help herself; he was so full of wonderful life. She finally came up triumphantly, dripping, holding an apple in her teeth, and he took a bite off the other side of it. "That's for good luck," he said. Her hair was ruined, her housecoat was a mess, but she was pulled back and back, all the way to when she was in the second grade.

"We used to make popcorn balls, too," she said. "And we sat around that big old oil stove telling ghost stories. There was a great one about an old witch that lived up on Crowley's Ridge and she'd come down with an old tow-sack on her back and carry away bad little kids in it. . . ."

He was a nice kid, but that didn't mean he was going to be the Stag quarterback. Not over Chip's dead body. At noon on Saturday she flew to New York. It was drizzling, and faded yellow leaves were plastered to the glistening cars. Lowry had the team socked in, marooned out at the Sea-View Motel where the major distractions consisted of mermaids and the Pan Am flight pattern. Thinking all the time, she checked into the Sea-View while everybody was upstairs watching the Arkansas–Texas game on television.

Then she rang up Apples. "I'll meet you in the Davy Jones Locker Room," she said. "I'll be right next to the sunken treasure."

"Dori? Is that you? Hey, I can't do it," he said. "I can't even eat dinner with you. It's not personal or, you know, like that. It's basically I'm a loner the day before a game. If I even talk too much, I lose my concentration and everything." He wouldn't even give her his room number, and he meant it when he said, "Wish me a good game for tomorrow, for luck. I can't see you till after."

And click, he'd hung up.

It was suddenly a long way to the eggs. She'd been here a couple of times with Chip, and she knew how tight the security was. One entire wing of the second floor was sealed off, with assistant coaches playing watchdog at each end of the corridor. After supper there would be card-playing and TV and for Apples a final coaching session. At ten o'clock the team would be locked up, at eleven the lights would go out, and some time after that Daisy or one of the coaches would run a bed check.

However, they were up against a redhead who had twisted both in and out of tighter spots. She dialed Chip, got Grover's room number from him and told him to slip the catch on the kid's door. And to relax; there was more than one way to skin a cat and she was using them all. There was just a touch of resentment in her voice as the apple-dunking laughter echoed in her memory.

Twenty minutes after lights out she glided up the stairs and past the room where Gabe Simson was snoring like the creature that guarded the treasure. Into Room 239. Two massive bodies overloaded the twin beds. Pink light from the neon sign in front rippled over and through the frail dike of the drapes. Shucking her nightgown and slippers, she crept into bed with Tommy, kissed the sleeping mouth and whispered, "Guess what I brought you for Valentine's Day?"

Tom opened his eyes, reared up. "Hey! You nut, you! What's goin on?"

"Rape," she said softly, blowing sweet air on his chest. "Cold-blooded, heartless rape."

"Anhnh!" The lamp went on, a barrel of light next to the TV set. "What's the deal?" Li-bary said. He groped for his glasses and blundered up clutching blankets and sheets to his large naked body. "You!" he gasped. "How'd you get in here?"

"Ssh! With my usual cunning," she said. She helped Tom off with his jockey shorts and paid homage to the erect and throbbing organ with a kiss. "Will you kindly look the other way?" she said to Li-bary. "This is gonna get intimate in a second."

"Miss Frazier," he said, "I must ask you to leave."

"Sorry, Li-bary, that's my line."

Trailing sheets and blankets like three or four togas behind him, he announced, "I'm telling Coach."

"Go ahead," Dori said, twining her feet under Tommy's ankles, stroking his back, "kill off your roomie. Lowry used to be a priest or something, and one time before you came up he caught Joey Hill with Maybelle and cut him from the squad."

"Blackmailer! Filthy dirty blackmailer! Don't leave her do it, Tom."

"Ah, relax. One piece won't hurt me. It'll help keep me loose."

"This way to the honey pot," she said.

Li-bary draggled into the connecting bath, but they could hear him agonizing: "Your vital energy will be exhausted, Tom, I warn you. It's a medical fact." He groaned as the waltz of the bedsprings grew louder.

"Why don't you sing along?" she said. "No? Okay, read a couple of dust jackets."

"She calls me an asshole," he moaned in the bathroom, "and then sneaks in here and throws me outa bed and gets her kicks with my best buddy. It's not fair."

She was smiling. The springs skreek-squawked like a barnyard full of chickens. Tommy panted, "Am I gettin better?"

"The next few hours will tell."

"Hours!" Li-bary squeaked. "You said one time!"

Tommy called to him that, in the best circles, it took a lotta time. Li-bary filled the bathroom with sorrowful noises. "I can't stand to hear," he said. "Through a door even. I got too much imagination. I got a hard-on and I hate your guts, Dori. I got too much imagination."

About midnight, bumping and thumping came toward them down the hall: bed check. Li-bary came in and threw himself on his bed. Nimbly snatching up her things, Dori popped into the closet and stayed there till it was safe. Then she zipped back into the bed. Li-bary said, "I can't permit it no more, Tom. Your vital energy is at stake!"

Grinning at him in the pink light, Tommy spread his

arms in a gesture eight feet wide. "Do I look worried? Okay, then. If I don't worry about it, why should you worry about it? I'm all set for tomorrow. No lie! I have very good morale for the game." Enthusiastically he re-mounted.

"Morale," his buddy said bitterly. "I got to do something. I oughta unload on you, Dori . . . something." All at once he plunged through the bath into the next bedroom.

He returned with Lips, in polka-dot shorts, ambling behind him. Tom stood up and the three men filled the whole room, huge hairy growths in the rippling pink light.

"You, huh?" he said to Dori, a big butcher boy scratching in the red hairs on his belly. "Get lost, Frazier. Kid, she's just changing brands from Hughes. You're gonna be the number-one quarterback and she wants you so she can stay queen of the Locker Room Annies."

Dori draped the sheet over her in elegant folds and said to him coolly, "That crotch rot seems to be spreading, John."

"Sh! Watch it!" Li-bary said as John started to bellow at her. "If Coach hears us he'll bench Tom."

Lips kept his voice down to a frothy snarl: "She's poison, Grover, I warn you."

She merely grinned. "Go back to your hole in the cheese, Mousie."

Lips almost fell down, but he kept trying. "Kid, think of your future. You're hurtin yourself and the team. You gotta stop thinking about your dick and think about the Giants."

Swiftly Dori said, "You better start worrying about your own dick, Lips. You're going up against Heraman tomorrow."

Hoisting a ponderous leg, Lips discharged a fart of contempt. "That's for Heraman."

"I wouldn't do that on the field tomorrow," she said. "He thinks that's a love call. You know what he's gonna do? He's gonna throw you on your back tomorrow and play with you. And when he's had enough, he's gonna hang your nuts on the goal posts."

"Bullshit!" he said, his ox eyes staring at her. "I'll destroy him."

"I'm trying to tell you he's queer, John."

"Bullshit!"

"No lie. He's a dick-shaker. Lance Rentzel is Mr. Straight compared to him. They caught Heraman exposing himself in a park to two little boys, but he got off with disorderly conduct. But last winter he put the make on a thirteen-year-old boy and the front office had one hell of a time covering it up. It cost twenty thousand dollars. Ask Fallon."

"No shit. Well, I'll be fucked. My kids are boys, you know? I'll bust the lousy queer in half tomorrow."

"Then you'll need your rest. Good night, John."

Big John went back through the bathroom, and Li-bary resigned himself to sleeping in the shower. Three complete orgasms later Tom said, "Hey, I can sleep and screw at the same time!"

"Not and get the game ball, you can't. Rise and shine both."

Just before seven o'clock rackets started up all around them, the swish of showers, voices, flopping steps. Li-bary wailed, "Tom, please! Team breakfast is in twenty minutes! Coach might come in!"

"Just one more," he mumbled into the pillow. "My way this time, Dori, 'cause I'm in a hurry."

Her lips were swollen and raw from kissing and she was sore between the legs, but she hung in there. Afterward she sneaked back down to her own room while the team was eating, leaving him lying face down in the crushed bed linen. Man oh man, she was used *all* up; she was as weak as a greased goose. But she had really done the chores. Apples wouldn't be able to throw the ball to the line of scrimmage.

The coaches were finishing breakfast at the big round table by the dining-room window. They were going over strategies in low tight voices while Gabe Simson, his flipper hands spread on his bulk, waited for another order of steak and eggs. When Ellis said the Giants were vulnerable to short flare passes, Gabe growled, "A game is a bitch in heat. You don't tickle her."

Gazing out the window at the blown gulls and the desolate beach, Jim Lowry let the brutal words drive into him. He was whipped. He didn't know or care when Le Motte would decide to sack him; he'd prepared a game plan according to Gabe's caveman tactics and he'd taught it patiently all week. And that was all.

The steak and eggs arrived, and he shut himself behind the *Examiner* and sipped at Al Whitman's daily cup of hemlock: "STAGS

VISIT GIANTS, READY FOR WORST. The losingest team in football joins battle with the Eastern Division leaders as the Great Blight goes on. Still hoping for a bolt of lightning, they are sticking to the powerful right arm of Tommy Grover . . ."

Jim couldn't help himself. With vengeful pleasure he handed the paper to Gabe.

"Asswipe," Gabe said through a mouthful of yolky meat. Jim flushed, but Gabe didn't notice. This was game day, and all the checked ferocity of the week came crackling and hissing out. Bashing the paper away, Gabe raged upstairs to roust the players out of their rooms. "Move out, move out," he said, kicking doors. His voice shocked like an electric cattle prod. "Let's bust ass today," he said, cursing the team onto the buses.

On the way to the stadium he stared blankly under the bill of his baseball cap. The brawling years in the pit kindled again, flamed up in his rolling flesh, and he sat in a fiery wind of pure fury, pure exaltation. "They ain't shit," he said over and over, hypnotically. "The Giants ain't shit."

Behind him the players were quiet, grim. Then a couple of the blacks started running their mouths. "What a man for moves and speed. With them great hands."

"Who you talkin about?"

"Me!"

Gabe breathed like a volcano at the hoo-haws. Then that little asshole they called Jellybean began speechifying: "Today, my brothers, we will achieve. There is victory and glory for all. Even Elijah here, he gonna knock down a pass today." More hoo-haws. "So look out, Giants. Also, if you play the numbers—"

Gabe's face came around, little eyes simmering. "Shut your ass."

The blacks slunk down in their seats, quelled and angry. Jellybean clawed at his glistening, coal-black skull. Elijah muttered, "He talkin like we got tails."

Raising himself in his seat, Daddy Wilson looked at Gabe steadily. When Gabe plunged back around, blazing obscenities, Daddy soothed them. "Be cool, brothers. You know what kind of bag he's into."

Every man, Daddy reflected, styled his own way, had his own formula to get up for a game. In pro ball you had to have all the skills *plus* that wildness or you were gone. So all around him blacks and whites were doing their own thing, psyching up, building a hate, hypnotizing themselves into that superhigh. It was easiest if you were natural mean and got your pleasure by putting a hurt on people. Or if you were Mark Youngblood. Now that honey-colored man always had that joy in combat. Irresistible. The divergence was, some of his brothers didn't sullen up; they got liberated into it by joking and so forth. Like the Green Wolf there, looking so fresh and fine in green everything, suede jacket, pants and shirt, two colors of green polka-dot tie *and* that green wool cap with a bob sprouting on the top—now that man was in outer space, but Whitey couldn't see that.

Himself, he didn't have to get up. He *was* up. All he had to do was think of Hosea, his sweet-stealer of a poorass little brother. And days back when, after they'd come up North from Louisiana. Every night the meat was locked up in the frigidaire and the bread and so forth in a tin box, but some scraps had to be left out on a piece of newspaper for the rats. Something like an offering.

Come lights out Hosea, he steal it and eat it up. Mama beat on him and beat on him, he do it anyway. She hit him upside the head and go to cryin, "Them rats is devils, Hosea! They bad and they hongry. They gonna bite my chillun you don leave 'em somethin. Hosea, I swear before Jesus, I hope you be the first piece of meat they gits." But he go on doin it, and now he was in police trouble and nefarious things of all kinds. Those days were all he had to think of to do the deed today and do it well. For himself he had his own Promised Land, money enough to keep his family and him out of that ghetto. For that he would kill.

The tension in the lead bus jammed tighter and tighter. George, in the seat across the aisle, was in sad shape. Last night he'd lost twenty-three consecutive games of solitaire in a vain effort to break the spell and get the Stags turned around. His cropped head sloped down into mournful little eyes looking out the window, looking feverishly for a lucky sign, trying to *will* one, *force* it out of the cold, empty Sunday-morning streets.

The buses shouldered into the parking lot. "Don't sweat it, roomie," Chip teased George. "I saw six pregnant women last night. Two of 'em nuns. It'll be a romp."

George stumped along, his hammered face plowing low in front of his chest. He felt like he was going to his execution, but he wasn't about to accept it. No way.

It was taboo for him to be taped by anybody but Daisy. Kneading the faded tattoo of a snake on his biceps, he waited for Mangialardi to get accommodated. Big John was usually one of the last to be taped. Today, though, he had a beautiful hate going. Instead of horsing around and giving the shaft to Daisy he sat quietly on the end of the table, coiling up inside, coiling tighter and tighter. Daisy wound each foot with gauze, then hooped it thickly with tape, breaking it off sharply—flick!—after each spiral. Then he built out the instep and bound it in firmly. A light tap ended the ritual. John continued to stare with inflamed pop eyes at his swollen, clubby feet. "Hey, John! Wake up!" Daisy had to say and nudge him. By this time the room was monumentally filled with lounging men in jock straps. Mangialardi trance-walked through them. Everything was Heraman, one burning intention. Back at his locker stall he slipped the hard plastic cup into his jock strap and fastened the metal snaps, making a small helmet for his genitals. Then he went to the coaches' dressing room and asked Coach for the first play.

"Gimme a thirty-four-crack-and-out, Coach. That fuckin Heraman is *mine*. I'll bust him in half."

His lion neck and his wingy ears were gorged red. A Babylonian astrologer's squint floated toward him: Jocko crossed his fingers and nodded up at him, hexing the Giants while he passed out face masks, chin straps and shoelaces from a trunk. For once Big John didn't mess him up. "I want a mouthpiece," he said absently. "Come on, get your ass in gear."

The only cheerful white player was Poppo. As he taped his socks tight on his lunking calves he was whistling "The Friendly Skies of United." But nobody on the team was more dangerous. In a pre-season scrimmage, when the adrenalin was streaming and fights were breaking out between teammates, when it was really bad in there, he would do these weird-ass things. He might do nothing but protect himself for half an hour, then suddenly, for no reason, he'd fire in from defensive end and cold-cock Toof, the offensive tackle, keep charging and sack the quarterback—Grover, Olson or his own buddy Chip—it made no difference. Then, chuffing back, he'd pick up Toof and ask amiably, "You ever go to Dyon's place?"

Groggily Toof said, "Yeah . . . couple times" and staggered back to the huddle. Poppo was scary, man. He was good-natured and wild at the same time.

"Hey," Poppo boomed at Short Stuff. "You're an expert. What do you like? You like a nice beautiful fat ass or a nasty little skinny ass?"

"I'm married," Short Stuff said without swiveling around. "I say Grover is shit," he snarled at Dude. "We're playin with ten men when he's in there. It's inconceivable, you know? Inconceivable."

"Don't piss and moan at me. Is it a bet or not?"

Fiercely Short Stuff locked thumbs with him. "Bet. If that shithead lasts the whole game again you shave me bald. If he ain't pulled I shave you."

Cheerfully Poppo asked Heinz which he preferred in the way of asses. The head of 57 Flavors hung like a ham, and he snuffled air futilely with his plugged nose, which would have to be rebroken and set at the end of the season. Heinz was praying hard: "Bless the Stags and everybody on the team. And bless You, God." The idea was to tell Him to take care of Himself, and then when He was in a good mood ask for himself: "And bless me, God. To eliminate my mistakes and not get injured. Also Chip. Leave him get back in." It was the only way to get it going. Staying with the kid was strictly a crud move. No matter how many times he told himself that the kid threw a real dart and ran like a buffalo, he couldn't, he just couldn't build up a love for him. And you had to have that love to be like one thing with him, centering the ball and working audibles. And especially pass-blocking for him, chopping down that wild-card rusher when he came shooting out of nowhere at the pocket.

The toilet kept flushing. And caught between mirrors, Chip went on puking. After each heave light and crowding reflections splintered into his eyes. Choking and bucking forward, he retched sour air into the white porcelain bowl. Goddamit, the pre-game runs all night, shitting his goddam brains out, and now right on schedule, the pukes. All that hyping up for nothing. The pats of sympathy, of loyalty, the bleak glance he got from the Bird, and now this, his other wide receiver Tucker, simply standing near him mournfully—real heart-warming, but what good was it? The Stags had to lose this one, and it couldn't be a squeaker, either. They had to get slaughtered and tighten the squeeze on Carsie and old Two-Ton. Not only that, Grover had to be Mr. Wrong out there, Mr. Nothing. The real way out of this box, of course, was a nice little compound fracture, but there was practically no chance of that. The kid was so big and strong it usually took two or three tacklers to level him and then he went down like a fucking pillar.

"Keep count, damn it," he said between retches. "Don't just stand there."

"One," Tuck said obediently, "two."

"No, you asshole, from the beginning."

Tucker blinked at him, hurt, and Chip hit him affectionately on the ass. "Only puttin you on, Tuck. You go on and dress out. I'm okay." Finally he got past it and dragged weakly back to his locker. The kid was lying on a bench like a great big tawny cat, asleep. He had seen Poppo read a porno mag while he was being taped, but this . . . It was fantastic! Dori had done the complete job on him last night, bless her. That chick was the best friend a quarterback ever had.

"Upsy daisy," he said, shoving at Grover with his foot. "Quarterback meeting, pussycat. Time to go over our new see-through game plan.".

The kid rose, yawning and stretching up his arms. "Hi," he said.

Chip had a ball at the meeting. The plays ran the gamut from "You run with it" to "Everybody go out for a pass." But Lowry read from his charts anyway, exactly as if he wasn't going to shuttle in all the plays again himself: "Remember, on third and short, they have a sixty-five percent tendency to pull in their free safety." Drab and fanatical, rattling it off like a missionary holding services in the Congo.

However, it was all Nome in November after that. Chip had to watch the team charge up, get in tight with it and with each other. When you played for the Stags you played hurt, and he watched the ghastly injuries washing away. Screwed-up ribs, a groin pull, a broken hand in a cast, a leg mummified with elastic wrappings from ankle to crotch—all of it sweeping away in waves of energy heaping up and up and up.

During the calisthenics the guys clapped and talked it up as if they were 6 and 0 instead of 0 and 6. And he was on the outside of it. Cold, iced in on himself, he watched them build that beautiful mystical drunkenness. Their emotion reverberated in him like a great sad gong.

After the warm-ups they went back into the choked locker room. The different parts of the team came together like parts of a super engine. George and the rest of the front four met with the linebackers and the defensive secondary to review signals. Simson blistered them with final instructions: "Remember, everything overhead in the first half is 'bingo.' And I want at least four sacks from you cocksuckers today."

Solemnly, fervently, George touched each of the men with him as he did before every game, Daddy, Poppo, Roger. It was a thing he did to mean a feeling like a blood bond. His forearms were bulging with pads and his hands were taped, turned into blundering stubs. He sat in front of his stall, sunk away from the turmoil of last-second taping and equipment changes, bug-sized trainers, gum-chewing coaches. He sat there like an expanding ball of flame. There was a red throbbing in his eyes. He stood up and began to hobble back and forth, back and forth, in the mob of players. Lifted by cleats and bulked out with pads, huge barred helmets in the crook of their arms, their faces slashed with blacking like ritual scars under the eyes, they were skyscraper men fusing backward, backward into something inconceivably old and magnificent.

Now the whole team assembled. George felt swollen and lighter, lighter. He didn't hear Coach Lowry's halting "If you want this game enough you can do it" or Coach Simson's "There ain't but one commandment in this religion and it's thou shalt win" or the little talks by the players. The words of the team prayer were a drum pounding inside him, the thudding ecstasy of god-drunk dancers. The swelling ball of energy exploded and he shouted, "Get it rolling!" And the other players shouted back in a chorus, "Stags, get it rolling!" He shouted it again and they chanted back, "Stags, get it rolling!" Daddy Wilson picked up on it and drummed with the sheafs of taped fingers on a chair. Then Youngblood came in with his talking hands beating a tom-tom of prayer.

With a yell they locked themselves together, they grew together, a green knot of men become one delirious emotion. The yells beat up Dickie's spine and came flapping out of his mouth, incoherent, a Holy Roller gibberish, and then they were pouring outside and up the ramp, flying. He and the right-side linebacker slapped at each other, and the beating frenzy went up into his eyes.

The teams stood at attention. The color guard strutted before the enormous shelves of fans and the band played the National Anthem. The Giants kicked off: a $50 official football (that had once been a soccer ball and seven hundred years ago had been the bladder of a hog filled with air and battled back and forth between villages to bring luck, good crops and babies, and sixty centuries before that had been the skull of a human sacrifice) whirled end over end through the freezing sky, hit in the end zone and flipped on through.

The ball was brought out to the 20-yard line, and in seven plays the Stags had scored. High up in the second deck over the 50-yard line, Dori watched haggardly. There was nothing fancy about the drive, just basic hand-offs into the line with straight-ahead zone blocking, a power sweep and two passes on third and long. She hated and despised this kind of ball, and it was coming in more and more. Simplified Vince Lombardi. Animal ball. Muscle and execution on offense and tons of brutal defense. Still, she had to admit it was awesome. The vast tiers of fans had gone silent in their downy scarves and blankets and mittens, all the soft life sucked out of them.

And that Grover! She shivered, feeling tired and somehow frightened. There he was down there in the jubilant, bouncing players on the sidelines, strong, untouched, stamping in his green cape. His windy hair flamed on his powerful male head. What he had learned he *knew*. All his faults were still there, but he was throwing hell out of the ball to a spot, and he had lost none of that brilliant body action.

She had pulled out all the stops, too. She had done everything she could, but Chip was going under. The worst part, though, was that somehow she felt she was losing at least as much as he was.

Dude kicked the P-A-T, and big John Mangialardi came off the field at a gallop, pumping his fists over his helmeted head. He was having some kind of an afternoon. On the first play he had blasted Heraman out of the action and for a bonus got in a beautiful lick after the whistle. Somebody was down. It was 57 Flavors. His bell must have really been rung, because one of his legs jack-knifed slowly and froze there. Instinctively, like all the other players, Lips turned his back and walked away: a man down was poison, was death, and some of it might rub off on him. Screw the instructions to stand over an injured player and act sympathetic until he was helped off to the sidelines. Anyhow, Heinz was Chip's soldier. The Rook came running on to sub for 57—one of *his* boys. Grinning with satisfaction, John swatted him on the ass and used his real name. "Let's play some ball, Pete."

Helmets clashed against golden helmets painted with antlers. John grunted, catching a knee in the neck from somebody in the pile-up. But every single play he put the shit on Heraman and the big goon took it, defending himself halfheartedly. How the stinking lousy queer had ever made All-Pro was a mystery. He was nothing but a hymen, a glorified hymen. The lousy queer. In a fury of virtuous punishment John moved him, handled him, worked him over, roughed him up good, real good. Blood came gurgling out over the heavy lump jaw.

At the same time Lips wasn't overlooking any opportunities. On a busted play Grover twisted loose and went into the line like a plow, jolting, wrenching forward in red-shirted tacklers for eleven yards. There was a red furrow of Giants behind him when he finally went down.

"Way to go, Tommy," Lips barked. Grover climbed back to his feet, his chest working hard. Mangialardi held out his fist for him to pound on. It was an important thing. The kid had never gotten even a friendly word from a starter, and he gave John a grateful look, banging fists with him almost shyly.

On the next play he'd buzzed one to Jay for thirteen yards and another first down. Lips clapped it up, and Jay and Pete came in with "Way to do it, Tom." The tackles, Toof and Harry the Hawk, added grunts. Lips could feel it, a deep hot swell in his rivering blood: the kid and the team were *his*.

"Beauty, a beauty," he'd puffed to the kid heading back to the huddle. "We're gonna have a little celebration tonight, and this time you'll feel like coming. They ain't nothin but a light blow job."

Man, it was Dream Street. Two plays later they broke it all the way from the Giant 40. Tucker sprang off the line of scrimmage and herky-jerked through the cornerback. Accelerating in smooth, moving-in-oil strides, he slanted down and across the secondary. A deep man picked him up and covered him like a TV ghost, step for step. Sprinting all out, Tuck laid a move on him that was out of sight—he twitched at him in midstride, just a light flick of his hip, the slightest altering of balances, and lost him completely. The ball came in a long, fierce, astonishing line, spinning like the bit of a high-speed drill. His hands did the rest. They streaked in the same direction as the ball to shut down the velocity, braked it gently, sweetly took it in and cradled it. He was leaping in the end zone, dancing in crazy-legged ecstasy as the official's arms stiffened straight up to signal a TD.

Chip? He'd forgotten Chip. His head was thudding and he was jabbering, shaking all over like a high-voltage line strumming in a March wind. Deliriously he slammed his hands down on palms held out to him like battered altars. He was smacked and hugged. Youngblood picked him up in his sweaty arms, crooning, "Now we doin it, little brother."

With 10:29 gone in the first quarter they led 14–0.

The kickoff unit hammered down the runback at the 17-yard line, and boiling out onto the field, the defense stopped the Giants cold again. The punt was short and feeble, dribbling out of bounds. Shouts of "Pour it on!" went off like charges along the Stag bench. "Beautiful, you cocksuckers are beautiful," Simson bawled. "We got 'em in the grasp of our hand."

Clutching his clipboard of charts, Lowry shuttled in the plays, standing in a madhouse of players streaming on and off and consultations with Gabe and Ellis, who was on the hot line to the spotters in the press box. Against his will he was excited. It was like blind man's buff compared with Hughes, yet the kid was moving the team.

On first down Short Stuff made six over tackle. Red pom-poms throbbed hopelessly in front of the glum acres of fans. Straggling out of the wreckage of the play, the Stags re-formed and dipped their heads into the huddle. Harris loped in with the next call, a quarterback draw—

Grover was to set up shallow, fake a pass and hit straight up the middle. The huddle broke open with a clap, like a monstrous seed pod. The receivers scattered out and set wide. Pete came up and squatted over the ball. Next to him Youngblood hunkered down in his three-point stance, his taped paw planted in the vicious artificial turf that flayed off skin and wrecked knees and ankles. He was working against a hard motherfucker today. On the last play he'd been whiplashed and everything seemed to be under water. "Got a message for you this time," he snuffled groggily.

All over the field there were matchups like this, private wars going on. A cornerback was chattering at Bird, "Come to me, shithands. Come to me. You gonna drop another one this time?" His blond hair spurting out of the back of his helmet, Tom coupled himself to Pete like a stallion mounting a mare. "Sally! Sally!" the Giant linebackers yelped, stunting in and out. "Burn! Right! Right!" On "hut" Pete snapped and the line came off the ball, springing into head-on collisions, grunting blocks. Cleats dug and ripped in the plastic grass. Lethal forearms battered, battered and crashed in front of Tommy dropping back. Growling like a Viking berserker, the middle linebacker came storming. Pete dived across to chop him down. There was a stunning bong in his helmet, and the white stripe of the 45-yard line spun around, whirled like the spoke of a great wheel . . .

Everywhere in the carnage there were accidents, wasted heroics, confusion. The blitzing linebacker overran the pocket, clearing the middle better than a perfect block by Pete could have. Tom raised up, pumped the ball, saw the ponderous heaving in front of him slide away and the gap open up for him as sweet as a pussy. He exploded into it, driving, thrusting. The right linebacker took a high shot at him from the side, out of nowhere. He staggered on, tripping and hauling the big weight on his shoulder.

All the time there was the close-up sound of the play. Under the dim waterfall noise of the crowd it was a horrible groaning and grunting. It was the sound of heavy bodies slamming, grappling and flailing. Taped hands mauled, tons of muscle surged and wallowed, yelling, squashing. Obscenities detonated in the ruck, grunts of tendon-straining effort, pain. Nailed again and again, Tom hurled himself forward in the struggling red mass of Giants. The dying play heaped up and up and toppled over, rolling him under, burying him in red tacklers. And still the terrible sound went on, a blubbering moan, a lamentation that seemed to be as old as history, as old as mankind, older. The whistle shrilled like a tiny trumpet. But deep in the heaving, kicking mound the groaning went on. The officials jumped in and yanked players off, peeling down to Tommy, curled up like a fetus on the factory-made grass. Miraculously intact, fresh, strong, he sprang up with the football.

It was an ordinary play, one in a long procession of plays back and forth. It gained nine yards and another first down—mostly because Heraman hadn't put on a pass rush or pursued on the play. But this time he hadn't stood there and let Mangialardi break it off in him. He catapulted into Big John like a blood-spattered boulder and laid him out. Then he landed on top of him and wrestled his helmet up so he could work on him better in the pile-up.

"My eyes!" John screamed. "Ref! He's goin for my eyes!"

Nobody heard him.

His chest was jerking painfully. Blood was coming from the furrows in his cheeks and forehead. He blundered over to the ref and said, "Look! He's tryin to blind me."

All he got was a nod and an "I'll watch for it."

John was shook. They fanned out along the line of scrimmage again. He was really snakebit. Crouching on his arm, he glowered unconvincingly at the lopsided face snuffling in its cage. At the snap, instead of destroying him again, Heraman humiliated him. He put two great inside moves on him, left him staggering and thundered by to the outside untouched. Down went Grover for a six-yard loss. On the next play Heraman put the crunch on Big John, hurdled clear over Short Stuff and clubbed Grover to the turf again. Tom's helmet popped off and wobbled away, his mane of yellow hair flopped out, and Heraman was standing over him, enormous.

"Hey, what gives?" The Stags on the field and on the bench were openmouthed. "Holy shit! Back-to-back sacks!" They called time out to regroup. "Wipe it out! Get tough, John," the offense puffed at him. From the sidelines the coaches were yammering, "Shut the door! Goddamit, John, does that man own you?"

It didn't help. Tom went back to pass on third and long, and Heraman simply threw John away, blew in on Tom and undressed him with a high lick. His legs went soft at the terrific clout in the face; his hands let go. Scooping the ball out of the air, Heraman churned into the end zone with it. A tremendous spout of cheering went up.

"Goddamit, mister!" Dewey shouted as John groped

toward the sideline, dizzily pulling at his chin strap. "Be alive out there! What happened?"

Bleeding down his face, John sank onto the bench, took in a mouthful of water and splatted it out. Numbly shook his head. Then Coach Simson came down on him, flogging the skin off. "You fuckin beer barrel, what're you tryin to do, protect your virginity? You gonna hold his fuckin hand?"

John didn't dare show him his ripped face. He knew Coach would say, "What's comin outa those cuts, spit or blood?"

Tiny eyes burning under the lid of his cap, Gabe waddled off, clapping his stubby hands and blowing, "Let's get hard, let's get hard." But though the Stags still led 14–7, the air had gone out of the ball. The first offensive play was stacked up. On the second John was swept aside and came crippling off on one leg, his gory face squirming and his hands clamped to his groin. Wincing down onto the bench, he ducked his head under a white towel.

Dewey gave poor Li-bary a push and said, "Get it done, boy." Right away Heraman got to him in a pile-up and all but squashed his guts out of his mouth. He was a bellowing maniac, a six-foot-seven terror, marauding, running amok in the Stag backfield. The dead crowd had come to life. The bland, cared-for faces were howling. Double-teaming him didn't work, cut blocking and traps didn't work. "Bad news, you know?" they panted on the sidelines. "Man, he ain't human." A dozen times he did it all. Pouring in on Grover, he leaped up to bash down passes. On a simple handoff he reached Shorty as the ball smacked into his hands and stomped him under, then sat down on him in showers of cheering, his jersey hanging out like a red skirt on his brutal, straddling legs. He came trotting off with his half-witted face turned up to the great splashes of delirious applause.

By now all the Giants, offense and defense, were pumped up, and it was one black hell of a bitch out there. Poppo fractured his wrist. Daddy Wilson was racked up; Daisy hit him with the needle and he hauled himself back and forth trying to shake off the pain chewing like a rat on his leg. Winded and foggy in the eyes, Jay collapsed beside 57 Flavors and croaked, "Did I ever take a shot! Man, I'm so fucked over I can't move." 57 Flavors was still on test pattern and muttering to himself.

Only Chip was having those *good* vibrations. In fact, he was lapping it up like the zealots in the seats. Man oh man, for most of the first quarter he'd thought the lid was on his coffin. What could have touched Heraman off? Anyhow, it was beautiful the way he'd put the hurt on Big John, just beautiful. He'd smeared his ass all over the field. And the kid—it was disaster incorporated for him. Four sacks, a fumble recovered for a TD and two interceptions already.

Ho, ho and ho. Carson Strangelove's instant Promised Land was still just a mirage.

Early in the third quarter, with the Giants ahead 21–14, Chip waved a clearing in the mob behind the bench and started warming up. A paunchy guy on the TV crew put a field camera on him, aiming the goggling lens of the black machine strapped on his shoulder. The small white sun was falling behind the stands, but under his jersey Chip had on a special rubber shirt to keep him from stiffening up while he waited for just this chance. A pocket passer like the kid was dead meat against that big rush. It took tricky, off-cadence signal calling to screw up the charge. It took play-action passes and scrambling. His game. Besides, the kid took a good whack, but he was being crucified out there. If only to keep him from losing his confidence they had to pull him.

Chip blew on his hands and flipped the ball, flipped the ball. The players wanted him in too. "Fuck this noise," somebody panted. Their brushy heads were hanging, their faces gaped in sweaty hair and scrapes of grime. "All we doin is build scar tissue for nothin," Elijah said. "Look at that, they blowin the kid away."

Lowry was on the hot line, half of his head cradled in a mouthpiece and earphone. He glanced at Chip, hesitated. Chip threw the ball harder. Lowry gave the phone back to Ellis, hesitated again and then walked toward Gabe, wallowing and cursing along the sideline. "Wipe it out! Get past it!" he barked as Shorty came off in agony, two dislocated fingers knobbing out on his right hand. A gold penalty flag went down on the field. "What for?" Gabe bawled at the officials. "Hey, shiteyes, what for?" Grover unloaded the ball as he was swamped and the interception was run back for a TD. Down 14 points now, Gabe raged like a warehouse in flames. "Fuckin cheap shot. All right, all right, let's take it to 'em."

"Gabe," Lowry said tentatively. "Maybe we better—"

"That Heraman," Gabe snorted. "He's twenty foot tall out there. When he gets caught on fire I tell you." And his red little eyes juiced with feeling, with something like reverence. "Whatever he had for breakfast I'd sure like some."

Chip let the ball drop from his hand. Scraps of paper shambled around him in the cold wind. They had him in the deep freeze. Biggie didn't see anything when he looked his way. Exit Earl Hughes, the one and only invisible glass man. Ice man. Abominable Snow Man.

By the fourth quarter the Stags were through. Even George had to admit it. Down in the trenches he spun off on all fours, shouldered two blockers up and over him and yanked down the ball carrier swinging through. "Valiant stand in defeat," Whitman tapped in the press-box. "The only Horatio at the Stags' bridge . . ."

But that wasn't the deal with George Schmidt at all —no way. He was playing ball. Hitting and hitting, drunk with hitting, in a trance of hitting, he'd forgotten his tortured back and leg, forgotten even the miserable figure of his roomie standing off by himself at the end of the bench.

It was a pass situation. Coach Simson signaled a three-blast-trigger: Dickie was to go headhunting. Hold on, the Giant quarterback was checking off as he chanted signals. Number 67 was leaning forward on his knuckles, which tipped off a run. Automatically, instinctively, he took in the flickering cues, and zip, like a reflex, there was the answer coming out of his terrific mindless concentration with the speed of a computer: sweep, this way. He shouted but Dickie missed it. The lines were jarring into each other, and Dickie was crashing the middle instead of slanting across to help. The blockers were coming out like tons of clay-red water flooding a spillway. He hand-fought to the outside and went underneath, smashed and galloped under, rammed with a knee, slugged and still plunging, rocked with stunning bursts of light and still submarining, grabbing as he took a blast like a depth charge going off. Blank light. Roars. He was being hoisted to his feet. All in a dazzle, he reached down to help up the ball carrier.

It was like that. You decked a man, really clobbered him, and then you picked him up. Heck, you loved him and everybody. His breath sobbed in and out. His pants were soaked with blood. He didn't know if it was his blood or somebody else's.

The plays came in red waves, shock after shock breaking over him, and with each bloody, terrible effort he went deeper and deeper—into something, some kind of beautiful feeling. It was what Daddy felt when the soul music was rising in him and he began singing to himself in the pit. What a warrior he was then! To an old-timer like himself it didn't come so often any more. Not this way. When this happened you did everything perfect; you took a hit and your whole body seemed to suck it up and burn all the brighter, like a great burning bush. And the feeling—it went beyond beating your man; it went beyond moves even, and they were holy to him, his own particular fakes and the routes branching off them. It was—it was a kind of glory and a music and a fire, and there was nothing else in the world, just playing ball.

The gun went off. Dragging his numb leg with him, he barely made it to the dressing room and out of his gear. Then he caved down against a wall like a heap of bloody stones. Stinks and wet sounds puddled around him. Weary voices. The rip of tape and bump of equipment into lockers. His bristly face was chewed with exhaustion and defeat. The pain was starting in on his back. There was a commotion and slowly he raised his grizzled snout. John Mangialardi must have tripped over 57 Flavors because he was skidding that slobby bulk around and grabbing air. "Wake up, asshole," he rasped at 57 and limped toward the shower.

George let himself down again. But this curious uneasy feeling—it was on his balls, it was scratching away at his spine. He had a responsibility as a twelve-year veteran, and he did what he could to break up fights and to help out with personal problems, like he'd take a first-year man aside and say "I'm not one to tell you what to do, son, but smoking pot ain't good for you and it hurts the team."

But if he was right, seldom was there anything as mean as this to handle.

If he was right. He couldn't go by a hunch, that was for sure, and he was so wore out he didn't trust himself to think straight. To the best of his recollection they'd lost by 20. Anyhow, the Giants had drove the ball down their throat. But Lord have mercy, it had sure looked like hay in the barn in the first quarter. The kid was performing adequate at quarterback and John Mangialardi was doing a job on Heraman—till he pulled that groin muscle. No, that happened after Heraman went on his rampage. Things were all melted together in his head. Still, he was pretty sure Heraman had turned into an outlaw; then John had come up injured, and shortly thereafter it was "turn out the lights, the party's over" for the Stags.

Which added up to . . . nothing.

Frowning with it, he stared at Mark Youngblood, who was already dressed and working on his hair, scratching with a sharp-tailed comb at the trenches and dents and flat places where his helmet had took hold. George sighed. He didn't have thing one to go on, just this curious itch. Meanwhile, there was 57 Flavors still in his spotless clean uniform, muttering "Bless you, Jesus" to himself. Concussion. George toiled to his feet, pain sweating his face, and took 57 into the training room to be doctored. By this time John had finished showering. Gimping forward with one leg pinched in close, he chucked some waterlogged towels at the hamper.

George was convinced he'd been wrong.

His long arms moved with a kind of fear, but they snapped Mangialardi off his feet. George was as surprised as John. Grunting and swiping with his arms, he went into a fatty-muscled reel, caught himself and flipped nimbly around to throw a punch.

"So I suspicioned," George said somberly. "You faked that injury, John."

"Fake? Your ass, fake! Look!" Roaring out of his thick mouth, he pointed at the bruise on his chest, a bluish mass of crushed blood and flesh trickling down into his belly hair. He pointed at the welts burning on his face. "The crazy bastard, he tried to blind me!"

"So I can see. You're hurting, to be sure."

"You better believe it."

"But everybody took a hammering. I say you faked the groin pull, John." He spoke in a tone of grave reprimand: "You laid down."

Already seven or eight players had collected, some of them wearing only a bleared tee shirt, some naked with a towel and toilet articles. All of them were very quiet in the hiss of the showers and the waspy vibrating of electric shavers. John snarled in fright, "Laid down, my ass! I called him a lousy queer—which he is. Dori Frazier said so. And he went berries on me! You seen him!"

George rubbed at the white-hot wire of pain running

from his back down his leg. He hated to call down a man in public—Lord how he did. But John Mangialardi could only be handled if you put his reputation at stake. "That's not my subject," he said, fitting the words together carefully, one by one, as if with his hands. "Sure, you were stupid to jack your man up and it cost us the game. Which tears my balls, I assure you. But that's not my subject. I'm saying you faked that injury."

Mangialardi jabbed a thumb at his genitals. "You're outa your tree."

"Do that again, son, and I'll hurt you."

Under his breath John muttered, "Get fucked." And letting out small coughs of pain, he hitched himself toward his stall.

George spun him back, his long grim arms dangling in pastes of dried blood.

Mangialardi yelped and gripped his crotch. But George said, "If you couldn't handle him is no excuse. My idea of a football player is, he'll go against any man alive. He might get his brains beat in but he'll go."

"I tell you I'm fucked up!" Mangialardi shouted. "Are you a doctor?"

"Are you a horse shitter maybe?" somebody growled at him. Because groin pulls were weird-ass things. They could lame you for only a couple of days or a week or they could put you off your feet for a month. Immobilize you. And no doctor could tell for sure.

So it was John's word against George's—strictly no contest. "You fuckin puppy!" "You pimped out, you son of a bitch!" The underwater air heaved with angry voices. Shoulders bumped. A solid gut plastered with wet hair surged forward. Poppo hurled down the icepack he'd been holding on his wrist and said, "I oughta piss all over you, Lips." And Mangialardi, swaying on one whiskery leg, screamed at George, "Are you? Are you a doctor?"

In a sorrowful, used voice George finished: "A man that's either a coward or puts his reputation before the team, he don't deserve to be a Stag."

Around six o'clock on Monday evening George came into Freyr's. Listing heavily to one side, he made it onto a stool and ordered a soft drink. He was still underneath from the game, half sunk in a watery dimness with the shapes of pain and worry looming in dark jags all around him.

Shorty came from the back, his shaved head swaying glumly. "That fuckin Dude," he said. "It's inconceivable, you know?"

Poppo was at a table with Jackie. "You look like Mr. Clean, Shorty," he guffawed. Part of his cheek was erased by tape and his wrist was a white lump of plaster.

"You know where it hangs," Shorty snarled.

"Where does it hang?"

"Right here, big man," Shorty said, jabbing his taped fingers at his crotch.

George sighed and put his bulk between them. "Let's go outside, big man," Shorty puffed, butting at George. Poppo, staggering jovially against him on the other side, swatted away with his good fist. The bartender squeaked.

Jackie chose this particular moment to ask where Chip was. "Don't pester me, woman," George said. After considerable talking he got Poppo and Shorty pacified. But every player that came in pecked on the little guy. They either rubbed his raw head or said he looked like a plucked chicken or something, until he was driven completely out of the place. George could feel the team pulling, ripping apart in the guts. o and 7. The loss to the Giants hurt, his back and leg hurt, Chip . . . It was a mercy when the Monday-night game came on and he could ease back under.

"Hey there! Buy a girl a drinkie?"

He raised up. Shirley was posing in a sparkly tunic and black tights and smiling nervously at him.

"I'll have a Snapdragon, Freddie," she told the bartender. "It's raisins and flaming brandy," she informed George. He didn't catch much of what she said after that, soaking himself in the game between the Eagles and the Dolphins. Glare licking off plastic helmets, crimson piping, incandescent green turf: he lost the moves, the work in the line, staring at the plays washing back and forth, commercials, plays, huge bright sweeps of motion and sound.

The game against the Giants melted into this one.

"Well, I'll blow it out myself then," she said in a bitter voice. Puff! She extinguished the bluish halo of fire on her drink, sipped at it—and forgave him. "Have a taste," she said with an anxious smile.

"I don't take alcohol during the season. Much obliged, though."

She clutched at his arm. "I saw you limping, George. It's just awful."

"A little heat lamp and I'll run it out. The older you get, you generally stay sore all week." He broke off. It was a jinx to even think about the disc problem. When he got popped a certain way his leg went out and he didn't know if he could hang on to the end of the season before he had to go on the operating table. It wasn't so easy this time to lull himself in the stream of pictures. She went into some kind of a rigmarole, using plenty of profanity. He didn't like profanity in a woman. He sure hoped she wasn't fishing for him.

"I have a right to be pissed," she said fiercely. "Don't you think so?"

"At me?" he said. But it turned out that her grievance was more general and included a certain somebody who had failed to meet her at the Sand Box. "I'm en ' l d to respect like anyone else. Could I help it if the other girls didn't show?" Her face was beginning to crumble around the eyes and mouth, he noticed, and her throat was sort of wilted. "Do *you* think I'm skanky?" she demanded. "Do you?"

He blushed with guilt. He was about to say that time takes its toll—on him, too. But she rattled right on. "Don't bother to lie. You dear friend Earl Hughes called me skanky and ever since—God, I mean it's unreal! Of course a lot *he* knows about women. I understand his conceited cunt of a girlfriend Dori is taking on other quarterbacks on the side."

"Don't say nothing bad about Dori to me," George warned her.

Her face went into ugly pouches, but her voice came out feverish, wheedling. "Could I buy you a drink? Just a teensie one, Georgie?"

"Much obliged, but—"

"All right, don't!" As far as he could tell she seemed to be in some kind of hysterical state. One minute she was cringing like a kicked dog and the next minute griping at the conditions certain people made, the things she had to do. She glared at him. "A person like that can kiss my a-double-ess."

He was lost. "Who?"

"Nobody's forcing you," she said.

"What's that?"

"Come on," she said, squeezing his arm. "I'll take good care of you." Her eyes glittered in cakes of blue shadow. "I'll do anything you want."

"No! That's all right." In a sweat of embarrassment he looked away, his sad little eyes blinking faster and faster. He wasn't much of a hand with women. Bluish-black tears were sliding down her cheeks.

He didn't know what to do. She was yowling like an old cat in heat. Oh well, he thought muddily, she was bound and determined to have her way. Also, he didn't get many chances, and he hit better if he slept with a woman. Maybe it was just his superstition, like Chip said, but it increased his football concentration. He went to her apartment.

She said she had just redecorated it. "Look! Isn't that cute?" He blinked at a glow-in-the-dark poster: blackness squirmed with orange boys and girls, a wheel of them doing it all different ways, with the girl on top and even worse, like a couple of dogs, and that was only openers compared to the next one. His eyes shied away.

"It's a Zodiac of screwing," she said. "What's your birth date?" He mumbled it. "Oh, wow," she said. "It's this one."

Highly indignant, he turned his back on it.

"And see here? It's a water bed, silly. It's fantastic! It makes all the moves *for* you. You don't have to do anything, just *lay* there." Twisting into anger again, she added, "It's practically unused."

He frowned. If it wasn't more perversion it was mighty close. Nor was that all. She had just bought herself a strobe light, and nothing would do but she had to demonstrate it for him. Lightning flashes swarmed around the goggling doll in the mirror and pelted his eyes.

"Hey! Stop that fool contraption," he said.

She cut the switch, but his head was still numb. She was taking off her clothes, unzipping her white elastic girdle. Flesh came gushing out, breasts and half-deflated belly. "Get with it," she said and danced her spongy dugs at him. "You like that? I'm told it's like I have a motor in them."

It was pitiful to see. When he didn't move she plunked down on the water bed. Her thighs slobbed out on the rocking chunk of water. She lay back smiling at him, and the bed pitched her sideways, rolled her up and took her down into its mixing cross-currents. "What's the matter?" she asked him, and her face was scared. "Don't you want to?"

"Oh," he said. "Sure." He turned his back, shyly, to undress. He was always embarrassed with a woman, and at first he was too flustered to notice a strange alertness, wariness, almost a sense of danger. It passed off in the general turmoil. Ruefully, he looked down at his peter. It was bulging and lifting, heaving itself up: the size of a bull's pizzle. Regardless of the woman or how beat down he was feeling, it would invariably come to attention. It sure was a hog for pussy.

Shamefaced, he let her see and began his spiel. "If you don't care to, I won't blame you atall. It's cost me many a predicament and many a joke . . . like it's bigger than any white man's."

She was in a panic to begin. But he plodded obstinately on. "Whores have even turned me down. In Billings, Montana, one . . . You can ask Jackie. She was sore for a week after, so . . ."

"Will you stop?" she almost screamed.

He stared down at the pole of blood-crammed flesh. It was throbbing and a milky gob of fluid came out of the blind, sideways eye in it. Even so he had to warn her, he had to tell her he was a divorced man but not in the market for another wife. At least he didn't need to tell her he still felt unfaithful to Vada, bad as she had turned out. "Also, if you get tired, just leave me know."

"Will you kindly shut up and fuck?" Moaning dirty words, she grappled to him and pulled him onto her wallowing body. Cautiously he stuck her. The bed slurped and gave deeply under them, sliding away. Her breath stunk. Her mouth sucked greedily. He sure wished he hadn't started this, he sure did. She reached behind her and switched on that darn strobe light. Dizzy throbs of light, like a dozen car lots rippling at once, like a hundred flash bulbs going off, stunned his eyes. Again and stronger that strange feeling came back—like he was on the other end of a deer rifle, dead in the sights of a hunter he couldn't see.

"Cut off that thing," he told her.

She whined, "It's more fun this way, George," and

after a time the suspicion dissolved in the hot splatters of light.

Tormented as he was, his peter had won out as usual. Won out though she groaned like a sick cow and suggested things that made his flesh crawl and though her crazy bed drifted off and slid back under till he thought he was going to be seasick before she got her fill. It was a wonder it didn't spring a leak and sink with all hands.

"Much obliged," he said politely as he left.

At least she wasn't having her period. It was sure calamity to do it then, and he'd broke his luck more than once because he lacked the guts to tell a woman so. When he got home he sank down in front of the TV and let a talk show gabble around him while he took off his duds. Now that Shirley and his peter had finished their business, all his senses felt pleasantly asleep. He took out his partial and massaged his gums.

Chip came in.

"Yo," George said with a gapped smile. "Where's your future ex? I thought she was staying till tomorrow."

"She just came to pick up my check and try to scare me. She's threatening to hire this big divorce lawyer—a real bomber. I wish she'd picked up my bills too."

He looked sour and tired. Hurriedly George grabbed his boots and hunting jacket and stuff, dumped them in his room and shut the door on the whole mess. Chip hated sloppy habits. His name for George's room was the Snake Pit. And it *was* pretty bad in there; somewhere in the ruck were about thirty traffic tickets he'd forgot to pay.

"How was she?" George asked.

"You want the true life story? Okay. I met her at the airport and we stand there for two fucking hours watching the baggage go round and round because she'd bought two new bags and forgot what color they were. I drive her to her hotel room and the first thing she does is get on the long-distance phone to the kids and go, 'Don't you cry, sweetie, Mummy had to go away and make Daddy be good.' I said, 'For Christ's sake, Martha, you just left the little bastards,' and for that I had to talk baby talk to them for half an hour. And you shoulda heard her yackety-yack with the bitch from next door that's baby-sitting 'em. Bad-mouthing me while I'm right there."

He said all of this very quiet like, leaning against the pool table. After seeing her, he generally always said bitter things, like she was a ball cutter or she had his balls at the jeweler's and was going to wear them in her ears, and like that. Now he said nothing. Nor did he pour himself a drink and sit down with the *Wall Street Journal* as usual.

Chip was sure in a bad way. George sat in his shorts in front of the TV, his heavy head pulled deep into his chest and shoulders. Martha wasn't but a little addition to the problem. He was very fatalistic himself. In pro ball you held your position against all comers until an injury or a better man killed you off. But Chip—this Grover thing was bleeding him to death by drops.

They were a funny assortment to be such buddies. Outside of football, he couldn't put his mind to anything; he was always late, he bought the wrong sizes, forgot the laundry and generally screwed up. With Chip it was just the opposite. Like this apartment. George lived here the year round now, but it was still Chip's place, a cool pad with a professional pool table, a leather bar and a Las Vegas poker table, all sitting on great big white and black squares of rug. "It makes me feel like a darn checker," he'd said once. And Chip had grinned. "Well? Move."

That was Chip. Who else would turn up to go hunting in a suit and say loftily, "I don't need any tips. You shoot it and then you eat it, right?" Who else would buy a telescope to watch the girls across the way and call his room the astronomy, or whatever it was, and when he was benched go in there saying, "I feel so bad I'm gonna watch the goddam stars."

Once he kept a daily serial going for months about the perilous adventures of Super Mouse. Super Mouse and the Pancake People. The Pancake People captured him and tied him up. Was he ever shook when they poured three gallons of syrup on him! He didn't know if they were initiating him or baptizing him or going to eat him. Or all three. "Which is it, Chip?" he'd asked. "How you gonna get him out of this one?" "Beats me," Chip teased him. "Looks like his ass has had it."

Naturally when Chip first came up, the team thought he was some kind of an oddball or nut, as well as a hot dog. But George had a kind of hunch about the rook, and sure enough he turned out to have a brilliant football mind and ability. So George backed him. And took to honkytonking with him in those Rush Street places where Chip was cock of the walk—keeping on the sidelines, of course, with a bottle of Coke. Somehow he felt restless without him, sort of lost and not himself any more. It wasn't long till he was telling Vada almost every night that he guessed he'd go see what Chip was doing. "Are you married to that guy?" she'd say. Neither she nor Martha could ever understand, but heck, Short Stuff and Dude ran together the exact same way. Himself, he counted Chip his friend above everybody. Chip was a great man, he sure was, and it was pitiful to see him miserable like this.

What he needed was a joke or two. Unfortunately he wasn't any hand at that himself; it would take Dori. He wished she was here, all fancy in her expensive duds, saying to Chip "You know, I feel like a little hopscotch and Polish cooking tonight." Which meant dinner at the Executive House. The three of them would go there, Dori and Chip as cool as you please, and while he stayed on the sidelines they would go at it. Like once he'd been bitching to her about never getting money for endorsements.

"You had that offer from Gillette, didn't you?" she said.

"Yeah. A hundred dollars to *grow* a beard." And they went to laughing like crazy and saying how it was a trap and Gillette was looking for a eunuch to demonstrate the perfect shave with. They were a sight, the two of them, laughing like it was kissing. "I do have one speaking engagement, though," Chip said. "At the Salvation Army Officer Training Corps. You think I can learn the trombone in two weeks, Dori?"

Poor Chip. He was standing over at the window. Seven stories below, the circle of bushes by the driveway was froze up and rusty, and the birdbath in the center was a stone cup full of leaves. Chip was just looking at it.

"Wasn't it funny about the Pancake People?" George tried.

Chip said it was a barrel of laughs, but in a mournful way. In a minute he started going through his mail on the pool table. "They're all after me, goddamit," he said.

"Thirty-four hundred bucks, that's what I dropped this week in the Pit. And Sweet-Ass Le Motte has turned off my valve. Shit! He won't trade me, and he's got me sewed up so I can't even play out my option. My ass is lunch, George."

This was no time to remind him to work on his charts for the Commodities Market. George couldn't understand it at all. If Chip would only put his mind to it he'd be a millionaire, easy, but he said it bored him and that was that.

George went to the bathroom to take a leak. Two seasons ago, in a game against the Packers, he'd gotten a shoe in the kidney and ever since then, whenever he was interviewed or had to speak in public or there was a bad problem, he always had to take a leak.

When he returned, Chip was playing pool. He was a master at the game, good enough to be a coast-to-coast hustler, and it usually gentled his nerves. George sure hoped it would tonight. He was banking shots of three, four and five rails, bent over in the hooded light, sighting down his cue. Stroking it, stroking it, absorbed in the action of the white cue ball on the flesh-red one spinning, caroming sharply as the English took it off the rail at amazing tangents. But his face was all whitish and drawn. Steadily, fiercely, he stroked the cue. The ball smacked into speed, whirling and zigzagging all over the table; the red ball cut six pure angles on the dark-green felt, angles linking with angles in a kind of invisible design, and suddenly streaked out of it—thunk!—into a pocket. "Way to go, Chip," George said. "Real perty." But all of a sudden Chip rolled his cue into the balls and staggered past him into the bathroom.

George could hear him throwing up in there. The poor guy—he took and took the pressure, but, Lord, how it told on him in private. George went in and slapped his back while he retched and retched, just pitiful. Pretty soon George had to go again himself, but out of sympathy he held it in, in spite of the swelling, bulging agony. Finally, though, he had to go in the sink because Chip had gone into the dry heaves.

Still kneeling over the bowl, Chip was talking between spasms. "Weak arm, weak stomach," he said. "Old habit of mine. The first time was in class in the fourth grade. I had to sing solo in music class next period and I got my first case of pre-game heaves. Christ, the janitor had to bring some kind of mint-smelling sawdust and all the kids were going 'Yuck!' and 'Blah!' at me. Just great. I was sweet on a little bitch named Janice and she went 'Pee-you!' too. Real sweetheart." He gagged again, feebly. "The teacher let the whole class go out for a toilet break until it was cleaned up . . . but I was a fucking leper for a week. It taught me to pick my spots, buddy. I guarantee you."

A lumpy bristly thing with poor nub wings plucked bare. A broad back loaded with muscle. A whiskery ass and feet sprawled out on both sides of it, kicking. Confused, his face going red, George stared at the glossy enlargement tacked to the bulletin board outside the training room. "George and Shirley" was inked at the bottom of it. "True love."

Six or seven of the Stags, some of them already in sweatsuits, jammed around him, snorting and hooting. "Man, that's something horrible."

"Talk about *raunchy!*" Jay said. "R-o-n-c-h-y."

"Hey, tell us about it, George. How much did she pay you?" Gooch asked.

"Her whole pension check!" Short Stuff hollered. "Haw, haw! She paid him her whole pension check."

Chip tore the picture off the board. "Grow up! You guys are sickening!"

"It's okay," George mumbled to him. He picked up his mail from the table by the cooler—and Lord, here was another one, writhing in the pile. "Lemme see" came the voices. "Hey, use that one for publicity, George." "Hey, George! You didn't use your *dick* to ball that stuff!"

It was some kind of razzing. He went to his locker, tipping painfully to one side on his bum leg. And there, a shining horror on top of the gnawed shoes, elastic bandages, corn chips and candy bars, rotting supporters and sweat clothes—there they were again, humping.

Chip blew his top. "What are you gonna do about it?" he demanded. "George? What the *fuck!*"

And worse was to come. Coach Ellis started the projector to go over the Sunday game. There was a wild dazzle, a hail and lightning storm and what looked like the Goodyear blimp or something, a big glowing whale plunging and thrashing the white water. "Go, baby, go," the guys shouted, clapping the beat. "Move it, George. Slop it around!"

Coach switched off the projector, laughing too.

The players booed. "More! More!" they chanted, and for the rest of the movie session they giggled, called George a skin-flick star and super-wad. Shorty, a wool cap hiding his naked head, was the loudest of all. Every time it quieted down he trumpeted through his hands and everybody came in with "Go!"

It was some kind of razzing, but George took it in

good part. They would rub his nose in it for a couple of days, that was all. This peaceable attitude of his didn't set with Chip, though. "It twists my mind," he said at lunch and again on the way home. "You just stood there with your thumb up your ass!"

George wheeled the Thunderbird onto Lake Shore Drive. The wind was roughing the branches, and white shreds of snow blew in from the lake.

"Well?" Chip said. "Why didn't you unload on him? Beat the hell out of him."

"Who?"

"Lips, damn it! That's what I was telling you! You came down on him for pulling a softie against the Giants, so he sucked you in with her. That's called revenge, George. He made Shirley set you up for him and his candid camera."

George wasn't especially listening. He was thinking of John Mangialardi rocking on his metal chair, rocking and laughing soundlessly, taking in big scoops of air and jouncing them around in his chest while Jay and Bebo and Gooch made jokes about the George Schmidt Fan Club. "Yeah," he said at last. "I guess he roped me in all right."

"So make him bleed for it! And I mean in front of the whole fucking team."

"Yeah . . . well . . ." He kicked at the rug by the elevator. "I only meant for him to put out or get out, you know? I didn't intend no . . . big deal."

Chip shoved one of the photos at him. "Keen, huh, buddy? You'll be a centerfold yet. Something for the masturbators."

The glistening squirm of bodies—all of a sudden it

dislodged something inside him. Another sorrow tore loose, heaved to the surface and turned over and over in a slow muddy stream of thoughts. He got to his room and took the smudged manila envelope from the dresser. Sweating into his clothes, he pulled out the photographs.

"No, not again," Chip groaned. "I'll buy you some new ones, George. What kind do you want, girls with girls? Boys with boys? How about girls with boy? And a cocker spaniel?"

"That's her with a naked man. His face don't show, but I'd recognize that shingle ass anywhere. If I ever run across it I'll kick it in." He grieved over the pictures the detective had taken, the mother of his kids screwing like a mink in a car, in a motel room. "I'm gonna show these to the boys when they grow up. So they can see what kind of a mother they got."

"Shrewd move." Chip glanced around queasily. Towels and putrefying socks gushed from the closet, cheesy dirt, defunct game balls in tangles of underwear, trophies, awards twinkling with gilt and glass. "Jesus Christ," Chip said, "how do you tell the dump from the shrine?" He attacked the chaos, picked up sport shirts and collapsed suits. Then he saw them in the sliding ruck, the unpaid traffic tickets.

"Okay," he said. "You win. I'm a prisoner in a Tarzan movie. Where's the goddam python I got to wrestle?"

"Porno pictures of my own wife. I'm gonna show them to the kids when they grow up."

"Old buddy, your belly button lights up when you think. Whyn't you show 'em the pictures of you and Shirley too? That'll really help their development."

"That's what busted my luck," he said dully. "Nothing has went right since the divorce. The ranch . . ."

Exasperated, Chip took the pictures away from him and prodded him out of the room. "Now listen to me, George. You can't let Lips sandbag you and just put your tail in your asshole."

"Yeah, well," George said vaguely, "it's human nature for him to hit back on me, I guess. There was no hard feelings on my part. I mean, I was just trying to light a fire under him to make him put out."

"I know, I know, you weren't pissed. But *he* was. He put the shit on you, George. He fucked you over."

"Yeah . . . and it's mortifying, I grant you . . . but—"

"But my ass!"

George snuffled in the shattered passages of his nose, sitting there in a heap. Chip was generally the backbone of his thinking. When they were in a hotel room and called room service, he left the ordering to Chip and just said, "Make it two, Chip." But this was football. "We need Mangialardi," he said doggedly. "He ain't the pass blocker Youngblood is, but he's quick and strong and he pulls good. The team needs him."

"The team, the team—why don't you play something else on your kazoo, just once? What's so holy about a bunch of guys that kick ass for money?"

George hated to hear talk like this—though it was true that too many people on the team were playing just for their paydays. Deliberating over it, he missed what Chip was saying. Something about how it *did* affect the team because it was Mangialardi's word against his about the injury, and the team went with the big man and what the big man said and did. "So if they're laughing at you—George, do you read me?"

George shifted uncomfortably. His back ached and he had to go to the can.

"That fake injury, George. What is it now? What are *you* now?"

"That don't matter . . . if he puts out. And I'll see to that personally. He better put out a hundred and twenty percent against the Lions."

"You just don't get it, do you?"

"We got to keep it together, Chip. And sacrifice more. We're o and seven as it is and bucking the worst jinx I ever seen."

Chip's face was a cramp of frustration. "All right, all right," he said. "If you want to lay there and take it, go ahead. But this affects me, too. *Me!*"

"You? How?"

"You know damn well how. Lips is pushing to be top dog. He's been bucking me all along, agitating for the kid. You know that. So you put him to the bottom of the class. For Christ's sake don't let him up! Cripple him! For me! Take his fucking head off!"

George crouched down, abject, defenseless—and unshakable. "I wish I could, Chip, I sure do. But he's entitled to his favoritism as long as he puts out. You might hate a person's guts, but if he's doing the job . . ." He trailed off, squirming. "Well, every team has some different personalities."

"Oh, go take a leak, will you?"

George did so, guiltily. Even now, even when it was a team thing, he reverenced Chip so much that he couldn't help feeling he'd let him down, betrayed him. Chip had poured himself a Scotch. He was pacing around the room from square to square, ferociously.

"Okay, don't do anything about Lips," Chip said.

"Listen. Quarterbacks are funny. Ryan's sort of like me—he hates to take that first whack and he runs hot and cold. If you get to him early he never gets untracked."

"I know. He can't start the sewing machine, seems like."

"So *don't* get to him early. Do me a favor once."

George looked at him, uncomprehending.

"Give it to me, George." His eyes were terrible. His voice squeezed into a harsh whisper. "I got to have it! I can't ride any more bench!"

It knocked the wind out of George. "Chip! You don't—you're not selfish. The team means something to you."

"Piss on the team! I want it, George! I tell you, I want it!"

George got to his feet, massive, hunk-shouldered. The words formed deep in his great horse body. "Just don't say no more, Chip."

"Now don't freak out on me. Jesus Christ, nobody's asking you to throw the game. Just let the Lions put a couple TDs on the board so Biggie and company will *have* to put me in. George?" he said desperately, begging now. "It ain't like you're throwing the game. I'll pull it out for us. You know I can do it."

George stared down at him, more and more solemn. His pride, his honor, all his beliefs . . . All of a sudden Chip was a stranger. He'd always sort of known that Chip wasn't the same as the team, but now he was a stranger. There was a darkness in him that he couldn't see into. Not only that. In the last minute or so he seemed to have shrunk, the way he was carrying on, pleading and arguing. "I don't want to hear no more," George told him.

"Well, fuck you!" In a huff Chip went to the phone and called a cab because his car was in the shop. Then he began taking hangers of suits out of his closet, sports coats, slacks. "I'm leaving, George."

A damned spoiled child, that's what he was acting. He put on his cashmere overcoat and picked up an armload of cardigan sweaters and a bag. Leaving George to carry the rest, he slammed out into the hall. Grave with anger, George loaded himself down and followed. "I'll send for the rest of it," Chip informed him in the elevator. They waited in the lobby. The revolving door swallowed and went still. The dark snowy afternoon turned back the glowing lamps at the windows. When the cab came, George followed him out into the grizzling snow. Chip tossed in the clothes he'd carried and stood with his back turned while George bundled in the rest. Chip's face was warped and shriveled in the hub cap of the cab.

"Where you gonna go?"

"Fuck you!" Chip said and got in beside the driver. The cab went off in the falling snow.

"And you too! A man that won't even fight fair for his spot!" George shouted after him. He felt a great sad rage, pressing, bulging in him and bursting out uncontrollably. In horror he looked down at himself. A wet stain was spreading down one of his legs. Warm loose gushes sopped his underwear and sluiced down into his sock. Spurts, drenches. And he couldn't stop it, the letting go, the horrible shameful surrender. He was pissing himself like a baby.

She was lying melted into soft
flows. Drifting, rocking with the bed
as Tommy bounced up, hollering,
"Hungry, hungry!" Dori made a
sound in her throat, soaking in
delicious fullness. Her body was still
releasing, gently releasing, petal-soft
folds juicing and letting go. Her blood
dozed sweetly. She slid deeper into
the squashed sheets, her mouth
opening into the deep mouth of sleep
... deeper and deeper. She was eight
years old and it was just coming on to
spring. The warm reedy streams were
thick with sunshine. The cardboard
boxes of baby chicks came in the mail,
filled with cheeping and little claws
scratching on the bottom and soft
yellow fuzz peeking through the holes.

   Whomp! She was tossed into the
air. He had set a jar down and dived,
rolling over her, onto the bed. "Umph,"
she mumbled. "What d'you think
this is? The deep end of the pool?"

"Sorry, I forgot. I just felt good." He reached the quart jar and lolled beside her slurping and chewing: hunks of banana and pear, maraschino cherries, syrupy peach slices tumbled into his mouth in sluices of milk. "It's a fruit milkshake," he told her. "I invented it myself."

"Give me some," she said and took big mouthfuls. There were splashes of milk on their naked bodies. "Hey," she said, "when you were a kid, did you ever go swimming naked?"

"Couple times. Mostly we wore trunks at the municipal pool."

"We used to do it all the time in the old stock pond." She was there, her lean body cuddled in the warm water flickering with bright minnows. There was a twitch in the brush across the pond. "The Jacobson boys always used to watch from the brush, but we didn't give a care, at least I didn't. I stood up and hollered at em, 'See somethin green? Dip your nose in kerosene.' So we all let 'em see, naked and splashin and slappin water at each other. It was great."

What was happening to her? Somehow, without her knowing, he had cut right through the achy, forlorn girl on the school bus and back to something naked and whole and clean.

Slurping, he said that once they'd dared him to walk the high trestle over the railroad tracks and he did it. With his eyes open and not scared at all, just walkin across between the rivets on the iron rail a hundred foot over the tracks.

"We use to steal watermelons," she said. "It was scary. There was a weighing station on the highway, for trucks, you know, all lit up bright as day. And the other kids were scared to carry the watermelons past it. But not me. I just stuck mine up under my blouse and sashayed right on by 'em. And then we all got the giggles and ate it right there, big old chunks of warm red, you know? With the seeds and juice running all over your chin?" She reached over and cuddled against him. "Oh, you make me feel so good. Not just in bed but feeling good, you know?" And he hugged her, grinning with his strong bright teeth.

"You think I'm better in bed, too?"

"I don't want to give you a swelled head, but man, you have really picked up on it. In no time you're gonna be up there with the great sack men."

"Thanks. You know, I believe this'll help my marriage. You know?"

He blinked at her—oh, the divine innocent—a beard of milk around his sweet loose mouth. Well, she had no intention of being jealous. That was rule one. And two and three. "Marsha," she said evenly, "should have a very interesting honeymoon."

Sitting behind her bare lovely legs, she helped him watch TV—just for five minutes. Propping up her hips, she boosted her legs over her head, glimmering there, the softest finest fuzz on them glimmering there in the radiance from the screen. She examined them critically. They were not, she decided, the teeniest tiny bit too heavy.

"That's the way," he said. "Now bike-pedal your feet."

"Throw me a banana first." She giggled. She felt cute and marshmallowy, six years old.

"You hungry? Me too," he said and sauntered away into the kitchen.

She pulled on one of his jerseys and pattered after

him, her hair a pretty red chaos around her face. The jersey was like another skin draping down to the middle of her thighs, slithery green. With a little shiver she stretched it tight over her breasts, feeling the nipples tingle, get hard and tip out like small green plants.

"Hey, neat!" he said when he saw her in the jersey.

"What's the matter?" she said, swinging a hip to one side. "Are you frigid or something? Tackle me!"

"You're some ding-a-ling," he said, laughing. He filled half the kitchen, sprouting great arms and legs at the table. He was eating what he called a cookie sandwich, five cookies stacked on top of each other and gulp!

"Not bad," she said. "But there's more than one kind of sandwich. You ever tried a double combination with lettuce, tomatoes, turkey, bacon and me?"

He stared.

"Take a drink of that Coke," she said. And slipped out of the jersey and walked toward him, raising her naked lovely arms. Smiling, she arched herself and plumped out her belly to his face.

"Oh hey," he said, going backward. "Hey, that gets me. I can't."

"Yes, you can. Go ahead, don't be shy." And softly she took the back of his head in both of her hands and drew it between her legs. "Please," she said. "Please kiss me there." Breathing in deep pulls, she pushed the front of her soft red-haired cleft into his mouth and felt the first, almost unbearable fluttering. With her lips pouting and her eyes half closed she looked down at him. Looked down at her own belly rolling out between her breasts, rolling back in with lovely tingles going up, trembles, crazy ripples of feeling spreading up from his mouth. Her breath shook. Smoothing and smoothing his head, dazed and moaning now, and the tender pink membranes inside her giving, giving into his boyish, eager mouth. "God, God," she was moaning. "You're beautiful." With a groan he turned away on his knees, embarrassed, dragging his forearm at his mouth.

"Don't," she said and pulled him up and kissed it like strawberries out of his mouth.

He said, "I still—I guess it's because I never done much—"

"Me either. Not like that." She could feel his strong rearing penis nudge and butt at her stomach. She wanted him inside her now, frantically. They were on the kitchen floor, and she forked out her legs to him, writhing and bucking on the chilly tiles.

But soon he was jumping at the ceiling, a flourish of muscle and flapping hair. Using the sink and the stove as parallel bars, he flexed himself up onto his arms and swung back and forth, his chest a great muscular arch, his sweaty legs glistening. He was so young and cute and sexy! His genitals loaded the pod of his jockey shorts.

He frowned, waggled his front teeth in and out. "Man, I took some blasts from that Heraman," he said. "I'll be okay, though."

"Sure you will." She hated to see the bruises that darkened the crests of muscle on his arms and legs. She remembered old Fuzzy coming to see her with his leg in a cast and fainting on her! Baseball players might be high-school dropouts, most of them, but at least they were intact.

The phone rang. It was Lowry, making sure Tom was on the stick. "Sure, Coach," he said and set the alarm, opened his playbook.

Oh God—she had promised Chip! And this was sure

no time to let up. After all, Norm Snead at Washington and Fran Tarkenton at Minnesota had made it in one year. Apples was *raw* material, but if Lips hadn't stirred up Heraman he would have beaten the Giants. But so far all the sportswriters were down on him, especially Al Whitman, who didn't know his sweet ass about the game. A couple more losses and Chip would be back.

But it was so hard. Reluctantly she looked over his shoulder at the game plan. "Dynamite," she sneered. "Old Lowry thinks that brain box is infallible, like the Catholic Church. That fool! How can you program the *talent* of a cornerback? Or injuries in a game? Or momentum? You only get out of a computer what you put into it."

"You do?" he said.

"A computer is a moron," she went on. "A very fast moron. Like Fred Dickie, hon. He's a human computer. You give him instructions, fill the memory spaces in that fabulous body and press a button. Zap! He goes storming and dumps the quarterback."

"What are you getting at?"

"I mean," she said, "Lowry called a bad game on Sunday."

"It was my fault," he said glumly. "Not Coach's. I started out good, but then I lost it."

Instead of following it up she dawdled away. She just couldn't make herself do it. While he worked gloomily at the playbook she went into the bedroom and counted the trophies in his footlocker. Twelve, counting hers, and he'd probably included a couple of fraternity gang-bangs and his sister. Jocks, jocks. The dear backward crude shy things. Joe Mulvaney hadn't had a date till he got to college. No wonder he'd taken his tool out in a bar by way of making a pass. Jocks. Most of them were horny monks, not swingers.

A pink trophy, a blue-lacy one. She tried them on, posing, smooth with light, in the mirror. "Ta-*ta!*" Beeping a fanfare for herself and spreading her arms, she paraded into the living room, all creamy nakedness with a pretty mess of rosebuds in transparent netting scattered on her pussy. "Wait," she giggled, covering her face. "Who does this remind you of?"

He glowered. His big worried fingers were tracing pass paths. Chip would have said, "Ah, school days! That first kiss behind the Ag barns." Sometimes she did miss the jokes, the intimate laughter, but right now . . . Lifting her tumbled hair behind her head, she smiled between her elbows at Tommy.

He scowled—while his beautiful penis came lifting up.

She dropped to her knees in front of him and peeled down his jockey shorts and took it in her hands, fondled the strong pulsing flesh. Just touched her lips to it.

"Hey," he protested. "We already done that lesson. And I got to study."

"Aw, c'mon, Tommy. You can study in a minute." She took it in her mouth, making small wanting sounds as she stroked, stroked with her tongue from the base all the way up. The first tiny flows came from the pretty little mouth at the tip of it, and sighing, she took it in, deeper, turning her head into hips and her mouth into a soft receiving place for him. He shuddered and she moved wildly with her eyes closed, wildly, violently, until he groaned and the beautiful thick bursts came, salty-thick, and she was holding his life in her mouth.

"Thank you," she said in a minute. "I'll be good and let you study now." She went into the other room . . . the taste of him in her mouth. She sighed. It was weird, really weird, that whole compulsive sex hustle. Sometimes, living around her job in a maze of phone calls and easy sex, players coming into town and players leaving, appointments at the hairdresser's, box seats at the game and nightclubs and more bedding down—oh, she enjoyed it mostly, but sometimes she went for weeks and months without any desire to get back into that scene.

But with Tommy . . . No question, she wasn't making love to keep him away from the playbook any longer. Worse yet: except for Chip, who sometimes needed encouraging in bed, a blow job was something you did just because the guy wanted it, and she had actually pleaded for one!

If she didn't cool it, and cool it right now, Chip was long gone.

She caught a break. The alarm clanged in the other room and Tom bounded to the phone. "Li-bary? B-ball in five. Get it on."

He was going to play basketball, of all things. Outdoors! In the dark and cold! "The snow's all blown off," he assured her. "No problem. Come on."

"You are out of your fucking tree! No! I'm not dressed. No!" She was still protesting as they went down the stairs. Mad Tom had a ball under his arm and seven pounds of shot strapped on each ankle, to even the sides. "That's right," she said as he pushed outside without holding the door for her. "That's right. Treat me nice, but don't spoil me."

It was ridiculous. Li-bary had brought along the zoo

people, Bebo and Gooch, so they played two-on-two in the freezing schoolyard while she watched, shivering by the baggy wire fence. "Slaughter sides," Tommy hollered. "Me and Li-bary against you guys." A goggling spotlight on the roof sent down pale glares into the icy breaths of wind. Thumps. Smoking shouts. Elbows. Boulder-jawed limping shadows slammed together as they drove, put the ball up and fought for the rebound. It was chaos out there. Eagerly she jumped at the chance to get her head back together.

"You see that one?" Apples shouted to her.

"Yea team," she said contemptuously. "R-rrrah, rah." Whatever it was they were expressing out there it wasn't basketball. They dribbled in pell-mell lunges, fouled savagely on every play and sent each other crashing onto the asphalt.

"Chalk it up!" Tom came loping toward her, snorting grins. And held out a big grimy hand for her to slap.

"Good *man*," she said. "All *right!*" Then she saw that his neck was bleeding. "Oh," she said in spite of herself, "you're hurt!"

"Nah. Gooch bit me on a layup. Didn't you, Gooch?" Gooch laughed and they all laughed, big and panting.

She sneered again. "Why don't you feed him before you play?"

"Relax. I fouled him too. We're just kidding, not playing ball. In cold weather you don't play hard outdoors—you'll bust a finger or something."

"Not hard, huh! I saw Li-bary get it in the head."

"Just light." Tommy grinned down at her, the edgeless words fluttering in his steamy breath. "Didn't you hear him? He said, 'You prick, you fouled me!' If he was hurt he wouldn't 've hollered—he'd a been out."

"Figures," she said.

He called for the ball and took it out to half-court, pounding it on the pavement. "No deuce this time," he yelled. "A squeaker is no good. You gotta win by a margin."

He dribbled in at Bebo, faked with his shoulder and jumped, stood in the black wind to shoot. The orange ball arced like a small sun and splashed into the net. Bloody and laughing, he pumped his fist coming by her.

It was ridiculous, it was childish—and it was great too.

The staid apartment buildings all around took up the racket, alive with echoing bumps and shouts. Tom leaped way up to take the ball off the rim, and suddenly Bebo tripped him. He was skidding, tearing clothes and flesh on the pavement. He came springing right back up, but she was frightened. "Hey, make it a friendly game," she said. "You could be injured."

"It's friendly. All I done was scrape some skin off my ass. Anyhow, in a game what's friendly? You gonna let 'em win?"

His whole life was always here and now. There was no important and unimportant, no "what if." He won again and came galloping at the five-foot cyclone fence— and cleared it with one yelling stride. "We're Number One," he panted jubilantly.

He crushed the breath out of her. Oh, she felt so uncertain now.

"I told you we'd put it on 'em," he said in the car. "It was a romp." Dirt-rubbed and oozing blood from a dozen scratches, he grinned at her. "We'll win on Sunday too. I'll bet you five hundred pushups we win."

He took just a quickie shower when they got back because he was an hour and twelve minutes behind on his schedule. Game films were next. Rambling through to the weight room, where he had the projector and screen, he said it again. "I'm not foolin. We're gonna win on Sunday. I'm not foolin."

Oh God, she said to herself. He wasn't just psyching himself up for Sunday's game. He *would* win if she didn't get her game plan back in action. He had that feel, that shine, that magic something players got once in a while when everything they put in the air was in the hoop, when every ball they hit was a line drive. Arnold Palmer used to have it, Mr. Balls himself as he charged from behind—power in him like a young god, whacking the ball a mile, nailing irons dead to the pin. Hell, even as he stroked a sidehill curling putt you *knew* it was already in the cup and the roar was already spouting up in the packed faces around the green.

Apples was getting that something. She could hear the projector crackling in there as he rolled film, and still she couldn't even make herself go in there and distract him.

Guiltily she thought of Chip stretched out on her couch when she came home from work. He'd conned the key out of Florence, of course, and he wasn't feeling any too sharp. Poor bastard. He had even accused her of copping out on her "Get Tommy" project. And he wasn't far off. Desperately she gave herself a pep talk. This was a *cause*, damn it. Chip's kind of quarterbacking *meant* something. Down with everybody who did it with just his arm or his 280 pounds or his six-foot-nine or his legs. Down with the high hard one and up with the knuckler, the breaking ball with fifteen different speeds. Down with Walter Johnson and Bob Feller and up with Whitey Ford and his jillion kinds of stuff, all of it brainy.

And there was still Chip himself. Even in some of her best moments with Tommy he haunted her. Chip was different—special. He tore her to pieces sometimes, but there was still that feeling between them—the way they always understood each other, the way he'd hear a racket upstairs and grin. "They're still teaching that dog to polka, huh?"

Off your butt, then, Dori. Poison the wells.

Tom was lolling in a chair and the projector was hosing a bright hot stream of plays onto the screen. "Hey, look at that," he said. "Look at him! He's a *ball* player." The screen flickered light over his smooth young face, watching raptly. "Look at that," he said again. "He's a champ!"

Flinching and slicking the jersey under her buttocks, she arranged herself on the cold, stiff mat. The screen boiled with another play: the weak-side safety cut in front of the receiver, picked off a Cleveland pass and came whirling up the sidelines. "Oh wow! Did Chuck burn him!" she said without thinking. "He's nothing but death against a deep swing."

"Yeah? Coach went over this with me, but I, you know, need more."

"All right," she said. "Roll it again. See, he overplays to the inside and switches at the last second." Poison the wells, hah! If she didn't watch it they'd be playing another quick game of pussy pussy *in* the well. The least she could do was not give him tips and inside stuff about the Detroit ball club.

The Cleveland quarterback stood in the collapsing pocket and pump-faked left, left again, and fired to the release man flying out to the right. "Perfect!" Tom said. "That was perfect! You know, if you do it perfect and everybody else does too, you get this—you know, feeling. Like it makes you feel bigger. You know?" He gazed at her earnestly. "I'm gonna be the greatest, Dori. No lie."

She laid her cheek against the giant locking bones of his knee.

"I mean," he said after a minute. "I thought I was gonna be. I never do it perfect, hardly."

She sat up and instantly, before she even knew it, she had seen the weakness and struck: "Don't get uptight about perfection," she said, "but there *are* a couple of things, Tommy. They'll be doubling up on Tucker, and if you don't start picking up those secondary receivers—"

"Yeah, I know."

"And you're still setting up too shallow. They'll run you out of the park with that big pass rush."

He clicked the switch. The river of plays froze in a black and white lump on the screen. "Goddam and fuck you, Grover," he said. "You're not shit."

Timing, breaking the pocket too soon—there were lots of errors, and the poor sweet kid blamed himself for all of them. "Easy. You've got to expect to make mistakes," she said, and now she didn't know how much she was killing him off and how much she was comforting him.

"Damn it, it tears me to make mistakes. And that's

all I ever do, is make mistakes and everything. I was a tail-back at NU, so I don't have a good college background. But I should be doin a whole lot better. A quarterback oughta be the most valuable player on the team, you know? And I ain't, by a long ways."

"Don't let it throw you," she said sadly. "You can still get it together."

"All I do is foul everything up. Coach oughta start Hughes over me. In my opinion, I think he's a better player."

His whole body sagged. "Don't talk like that," she said. "Please!" He turned off the projector and dragged on his pants, his shoes. "Where you going?" she cried, flinging on her clothes and going with him. Mute and heavy, he drove into the Loop.

His face was so dull, so burned out. He was just one of the bodies, she told herself; there was a fresh crop of him every year. But it was a damn shame. It took a terrible effort to get things back into focus. She was no 4-H kid blubbering goodbye to a pet bull she had raised herself. A cause was a cause and Chip was a super technician, an artist, a chess-master quarterback. Chip *mattered*; he was witty and smart and her dear buddy—and still she was sore at him for what she'd done to Tommy.

He parked the car on South State Street and got out. "Oh no," she groaned to herself. In both directions, skin-flick houses blazed dizzily. Tattoo parlors. A GOSPEL MISSION. Jackoff shops with signs in the blind windows "You must be 21." And good old FUNLAND, a shambling hulk of rotten bricks in an Uncle Sam suit of red-white-and-blue paint.

Every time they came here she felt like a hillbilly

again, fresh up from Metropolis, Arkansas, with a blue suitcase, a genuine simulated fur jacket from J. C. Penney and the phone number of the pitching coach for the Sox. Scornful again, impatient, she followed him into the gun-banging, popcorn-smelling glare. Toy thunder came down the aisle. The wounded hero was going to cure himself with four bacon-and-cheese sandwiches, two malts and thirty-six fast games of pinball.

A couple of undersized, goaty boys reeking with hair spray were bent over a pinball machine. Tom slumped to a stop beside them. The game was whizzing and flashing. The steel ball caromed from bumper to bumper, eyes of light blinked open, the ball skidded down but nubby wings batted it up again and again, fighting the long downward pull, the inevitable slope into the coffin slot at bottom.

"There's one open over here," she told him. He paid no attention to her. "Hey! Since when is this a spectator sport?" she said irritably. "Let's roll 'em."

His face swayed around and his mouth was slack; his eyes were all pain. Suddenly she realized that he was punishing himself! The way old Toby, after a poor season with the Packers, had put in five months at a bakery. And Kraus, he'd done six on the Galveston docks. "Tommy, Tommy," she said, and her remorse was a physical sensation, an ache in her body. "I'm sorry," she said, her eyes putting sad kisses on his face.

All that wonderful luster was gone, eclipsed. He moved outside, pulling himself along like a great sick cat. The sidewalk was the color of ashes. He stopped again. He seemed to be listening very hard or concentrating—not thinking, though, but waiting intensely for something to reveal itself to him. Then he was moving again, more quickly now, moving with the rapt, perfect intention of sleep.

"I'm gonna initiate myself," he said when she tugged at him.

Initiate himself! It didn't make sense and he wouldn't say any more. He kept plodding down the sidewalk with that sleep-locked purpose, and the lights of the signs swarmed around them, stinging the long row of parked cars. Three sailors came out of a "you must be 21" shop.

"What the hell?" she said. Tom had halted in front of a keyhole-shaped window with a neon sign stuttering and hissing in the cold: CLIFF MOSS, TATTOOS. He went trance-walking in and what could she do? The place was narrow and dirty. A couple of girls and a kid wearing a chrome-studded motorcycle jacket were watching in chairs. The heavy electric-powered needle burred in a wedge of light. Stooping and slit-eyed, Cliff Moss was stitching a pair of blue wings and a reddish star into a boy's forearm. He paused to swab off the wings with a bit of cotton soaked in alcohol, then dabbed the needle in a pot of blue dye. The boy locked his teeth, taking six hundred punctures a minute in the arm while his friends watched.

It was a cheapie manhood deal, for God's sake! Get laid, get tattooed, get bombed out of your mind on grass and ride around in your first car—that groove.

"Man," she said, "this is bush. Strict-ly bush. How is this going to do anything for you?"

Tom took off his jacket and stared at the board of designs on the mildewed wall. The needle rasped and flashed into the boy's skin. "She don't fool me for one minute." The words had trickled from a shrunken old thing who might have been Cliff's wife and might have been his mother. Propped like an antique doll on a soiled chair, she was smoking Luckies one after another, coughing and squabbling with Cliff.

Cliff finished and began soaping the red-and-blue wound. "You ain't sure, Sybil," he said.

"God will punish her," she said hoarsely. "In due course."

"Sybil, will you just shut up?"

He wrapped the arm in a paper towel, then taped it, warning the boy not to pick at the scabs or they'd get infected. And Sybil went on complaining: "I tell you it was her that poisoned Toby. Best cat I ever had, too. Three-quarters part Siamese. When I found him in the basement . . ."

She lapsed into senile muttering. Then all of a sudden she jerked her cobwebby face around and gave Dori a venomous look. As if she blamed *her!*

Dori was spooked. The foul breath of the old building, thickened with dye and burnt oil and the sweetish smell of blood. And the old man showing Tom the flowers and beasts and serpents coiling on his dried old arms.

Without actually hearing Tom say it she understood that he wanted a Stag's head put on. "Marvy," she said, frantically holding on to sarcasm. "If you get traded you can cross it out."

"Cheaters," Sybil said grimly. "He was a nice cat." Tom was sitting in the worn chair with his great arm prone in the light, and all of a sudden Dori wasn't so sure of herself any more. Maybe he *knew*. There was a solemn, eager, almost hopeful expression on his face. What could he be after? He was feeling toward something, groping toward it in a kind of trance like a blind man turning, instinctively, toward light.

The filthy room whirred like the inside of a hive. The metal stinger pierced in the outline of a Stag's head with branching antlers. He wasn't punishing himself any more, or at least not *just* that. He was doing something, incoherently but gravely, maybe dedicating himself. It was no cheapie way to prove he had balls. He was straining desperately for something.

The needle drove in, stabbed into smearing dye and blood, and the vibration of the motor echoed inside her, drummed inside her. He was driving the antlered Stag into his flesh.

She shivered. She could feel the terrible stabs all the way down between her legs. The needle was a metal prod covered with blood and dye. She was breathless; her head was flying away. But already she could tell that he wasn't making it; he wasn't getting there, wherever it was. He was staring miserably at the gaudy oozing beast on his arm. "I'm sorry, Tommy," she whispered. "I'm sorry."

The defense was groaning on the bench.

"Man, that prick is killin us," they snarled. "Get the motherfucker outa there."

"Look at that!" Daddy Wilson said. "That cat don't see *nothin* downfield."

The broken play staggered toward the sidelines, tumbled over and stopped in the rain. The players unpiled. When Grover made it to his feet, soggy and panting, the defense spewed curses from the bench. "Damn! Too bad!" "Hey!" they shouted to the Lions, "bust his legs, somebody." On the next play, dropping back to pass on third and long, the kid tripped over his own feet and sat down with a splat. The ball skidded away. More boos came out of the half-empty seats.

"He left the fuckin game in bed," a linebacker snarled

as the defense dragged out onto the field to do it again.

"Never had no game to leave," Daddy said.

Stadium horns mooed wetly. The field was an icy bog. The teams tugged and hauled, butted, slugged, floundered on the acetate turf and went down in crashes of spray.

The Lions splashed to another score. Sodden bed sheets flapped "Goodbye, Lowry" and "The Stags Stink." The fans behind the Stag bench were really giving it to Jim Lowry. "Hey Charts!" they called, "Charts! Fuck you, Charts!" Naturally he was the scapegoat, he thought, and so be it. The fans had a perfect right to call for his blood. The team had failed them, the coaching staff had failed them, himself most of all. If he had been harder-nosed about playing Hughes . . . But so be it. Le Motte had his undated resignation on the desk, and the sooner he filled in the date the better. Gray, remote, he accepted the debacle on the field, the catcalls, the beery voices singing, "Goodbye, Lowry, we hate to leave you now."

And yes, he accepted that too, the most painful thing of all. Gabe Simson. He could look without anger at the 310-pound ex-lineman whipping the team. Belly rumbles shook his ponderous front as he chewed out Tucker, their talented black flanker. "Run out those patterns, you little cocksucker," he was steaming. Tucker dangled his sullen face. When Gabe moved away Tucker muttered, "Bustin my tail for nothin. That honky ain't no quarterback."

"Get it up," Gabe was hollering. "You're all dead-ass." His quarterback couldn't move the sticks, the overworked defense had finally come apart, and the Lions were destroying people out there. The grinning Stag-mobile zipped away with the hospital cases. Short Stuff, his head shrouded in a white towel, hobbled back and forth behind the bench. Li-bary was retching between his knees. Jellybean took a hit of oxygen and sagged back, his burnt-out face staring into the sharp rain. Another play unpiled to a Stag sprawled like a body thrown into a sacrifice pit. Gabe smacked his short hands together, flickering grains of water on his green blazer. "Get it up!" he shouted. "Get it up!"

On a post-and-out pattern Tucker ran a beautiful route: He spun the safety completely around with a stutter of his running feet and turned for the ball, waited. The kid was looking downfield for the primary receiver, Bird, who had slipped at the line of scrimmage—he was looking and still looking, helpless, impotent. Finally he cut loose like a malfunctioning robot and gunned the ball ten yards over everything.

The players were laughing on the Stag bench.

A field camera that happened to be covering them swung away hastily.

"Beauty," they guffawed. "A beauty, kid."

"They oughta pay the fucker by the hour."

"Yeah, by the hour."

"They hired him from DayLabor."

Hunched by himself at the end of the bench, Chip bit on his gum in agony. Those were his jokes they were passing around, damn it; the guys wanted him in there, and what good was it? Rain slopped heavily into his parka. Rain slivered down on the helmet beside his feet. A few calls of "We want Chipper" lifted soggily from the stands and scattered away, beaten down with the rain.

God*dam!* It was the Giant game all over again, only this time without the suspense. He was going to ride this bench till his ass froze to it. 28–0, 35–0, and the kid was strictly sand-lot out there; the silent majority was throwing beer cans and programs, and Gabe did not give a shit. It bent his mind! He didn't ask for any breaks, just a fair shot at it, him and the kid head on, either splitting the time or starting alternate games, and if he didn't have what it took, okay, *then* bury him. But not before they had it out.

A hoarse cough exploded in his chest and plays he would never get to call twitched and scurried in his head.

"Fuck him over, Rog," Gabe was bawling on the sidelines. "Good lick, good lick!" Chip couldn't take his eyes off him. Now he was roaring like a blast furnace at a roughing call that didn't mean a thing in a wipeout like this. The fool, he used his ass to think with. Chip coughed again. Hate pressed down on his brain, searing, blistering, and there was nothing else in the world, nothing but him and that 310-pound pile of meat with a head like a paunchy dwarf in a green cap squatting on top of it. The prick, the goddam prick! Now he was talking with Lowry, his breath smoking around his jowls; now he was squashing away in the rain.

Lowry was motioning him to go in!

"Me?" Foolishly Chip pointed at his own chest, like a third-stringer in high school. He had jumped up and raced out onto the field before he unflipped and the gong stopped vibrating in his helmet. There was only 3:47 left on the clock, for Christ's sake, and the Stags were down 35–0. This wasn't another pop at it, a chance to win back his starting spot. It was a fucking insult. He was being thrown into the sausage grinder like a rook, like a noggin-crasher on the special units. His eyes scorched and he almost stopped halfway to the huddle and the ball lying under a white towel.

The lights had been turned on. The wet turf glared up at him, neon green.

Then the drenched and exhausted players saw him coming and began to clap, and back on the sidelines in the sleeting rain the rest of the team was standing and cheering. In a gasping rage he overthrew Bird on the first play. And Bird, taking off downfield, braking, then hurling over the swamped green carpet, went up like an Indian rope climber—the crazy hillbilly left his feet and shinnied up nothing at all (reaching out and still reaching, seeming to hang there in the flickering rain, light, suspended at the very top of his jump, caught there in instant replay) and came belly-flopping down with the ball.

He sprinted back to the huddle, his beak face glittering in rain and tears. Sheafs of fingers were bumping together, fists went up, mouths were yelling through the face masks: "Pullin it outa your ass, Bird!" "Some kinda catch, baby!" and "New game! New game!"

Well hell, with a miracle like that to start him—Chip loosened up, recovered some of that old cool. He faked a sweep to the right and countered against the grain, against the flow of the play, and back into the zero hole. Bad wheel and all, Short Stuff got eleven. Chip was inside himself now, bent over the dark chessmen in his head. Swiftly, easily, almost without effort, contemptuously, he put six moves together.

Six plays. And outside in the other darkness lights blinked TOUCHDOWN and a man of light seventy-five feet tall caught a 20,000-watt sun and trotted past a flashing goal post.

Running to the sidelines in a shower of cuffs and loving grunts, Chip had a moment of solitary triumph.

That was not just a 65-yard drive for a TD; it was brains and skill in action. A fucking work of art. A short demonstration by Bobby Fischer.

He'd proved himself *without* a chance.

The gun popped. The band farted damply, "This is my country." Mixed in with the muddy boos and the yells of the vigilantes working Lowry over were a few wet cheers for him. "Ah," he said. "Hughie's Horde. The God-is-dead quarterback's loyal adherents. Bless you, folks, both of you."

The glass moment burst in his head, splintering. He'd proved himself all right; he'd really put it on. And while he was pulling Easter bunnies out of a hat with one hand and squaring the circle with the other, who was looking? The ticket holders were out in the parking lot; TV sets all over the country were going *click!* or switching to "Wide World of Sports," Le Motte was crying in the powder room and the owners were trying to move their bowels.

Great, just great. Man, it blasted his mind. Super Mouse had climbed out of his plot in Sunset Acres and nobody was watching!

The team clattered slowly down the runway to the dressing room. Stained and soaked, lame, ripping filthy tape from their wrists and hands, they towered around him and swatted him on the ass. "Playing *ball*, Chip!" "That's gettin it, baby."

The guys were his now, they were with him, really with him.

And he was more alone than ever, inflamed, more frustrated than ever. What was the use if Biggie had discontinued him? He was burning with it. Mark Youngblood, bleeding between the eyes from his face mask, took him into his big meaty arms and beamed at him. "You doin your thing again, baby."

Chip said formally, "Thank you."

A lumpy sweating face, a mouth with empty spaces between the teeth smiling anxiously down at him. "Beautiful, Chip."

It was George, trying to patch it up.

Maddened, Chip walked away without a word. The locker room was off limits to the press, so he went into the anteroom where Lowry was performing the autopsy. "Everything was bad today," he was saying. "The tackling. The blocking. The whole team was dead. We deserved to lose."

"Just one little second," Chip cut in. "I won my five minutes of the game."

He freaked out the interview and it just left him tighter than before, wilder. Five minutes, hell! The Invisible Shrinking Man had returned for exactly 3:47. Man, he was in shock. Coughing in hard jerks, he peeled down and shaved, rubbing irritably at the trickly mist on the mirror. He scowled as Poppo mussed his hair fondly. Christ, he was even sore at the poor busted guys for congratulating him.

There was a drumming of voices and echoes in the hall outside: Dewey and Gabe coming through.

Hate pressed inside him, bulged, stretched tighter and tighter—and he was out in the doorway snarling, "How'd you like those apples, Gabe?"

Dewey stopped and Gabe stopped, the old bull of the herd snorting at a challenge: "What apples? That TD? My kid sister could get on the board in a spot like that."

"Yeah? Sixty-five yards in six plays?" he raged with

a dry mouth. "Four for four in the air? That's some kid sister you got."

"They were giving you the short stuff, Hughes. They had their subs in there. You didn't show me nothing to get religion with."

The showers were blasting and Dewey was chomping a bit of neon-green gum, his oversize jaw working impassively, and Gabe was turning indifferently away. "You don't know talent when you see it," Chip yelled at him.

"Talent, my dick," Gabe said. "In your head you may be the greatest of all time, but that don't do it. You don't have it downstairs, Hughes."

"Bullshit!"

"You got a spaghetti arm, Hughes, and you can't make the big play. You're a choke, a loser."

He might have been butting a sub out of his way in a game fifteen years ago. He was still steamed up from the game, and he was seeing red about their eighth straight loss. And that was it. There wasn't any feud between them, not on his side. He wasn't that interested. Scalded, Chip threw himself at the arms locked around him, lunged and ranted, clawed at the powerful gentle hands—feeling smaller all the time, smaller, frail, lifted off his feet and kicking like a little kid, a baby. He was just making an asshole of himself and he couldn't stop it. He was bleating out of control.

And the stupid sunface looked at him, that goddam stupid jock look that said, "You're nothing, asshole." Chip's consciousness boiled away, his eyes crazed and he twisted out of the hugging arms. "You big bag of shit," he gasped.

Insanely he went for Gabe.

The swollen folds of Gabe's mouth were smiling. "Why, you little fucker," he said with something close to respect. And he seemed to get lighter and lighter, to float there in his rain-glistening blazer and cap, murderously.

But before he could unload, put it to Hughes and ice him, Chip had been caught again, a little doll man gibbering and straining helplessly in thick coils of muscle, and Roger Garrett, moving in behind Gabe, had caught him in his big brown arms, beseeching him, "Easy, Coach."

"Hands off, nigger," Gabe rumbled.

It was like a boiler bursting in the locker room. Torsos blundered in the steamy air, eyes, the crumpled nose of a linebacker: steam and a wreckage of players toppling and then standing there in panting clumps.

Gabe shrugged himself free. "Lay a hand on me," he said to Roger, "and I'll plant my foot up your ass."

He moved off toward the coaches' dressing room with Dewey. Mouths stared. The showers hissed steam. Daddy Wilson removed the beach towel from his head and threw it down.

"Well, *fuck* you, man," he said in a deep voice.

"Yeah, fuck you," Chip yelled. "These brothers are earning your salary. They're doing a job and what are they to you? Niggers! What d'you think you are, a plantation owner?"

But he was unzonking fast, not just yelling. Old Fats had really screwed up and with this to build on . . . His head was back together now and he could see the possibilities opening up everywhere, beautiful possibilities.

A black kid in a tattered sweatsuit jogged around and around the indoor track, all by himself in the darkening gym. Roger Garrett hadn't thought about him, except in his dreams, for six or seven years, and he fidgeted anxiously with the faucets, getting the temperature of the water super-right. (After every home game he spent a couple-three hours in his king-size tub soaking out the aches and pains; then he got himself around some steak while Wandella read the first newspaper accounts to him.)

He had a shoulder hurt to soak away and a stomach hurt also. And Wandella's baby brother visiting for a month. And 'specially what 68 had did to him today. Man oh man, that cat had smelt out the bad shoulder immediately. And he say, "I hears they call you Mr. Hit." Then he start laughin. A brother, too. The whole rest of the game he just come poppin at that shoulder and workin on it in the pile-up also. "How you like that, Mr. Hit?" That's what he kept saying.

Daisy had put cortisone shots in it and still the hurt was breaking out in sharp fires that he couldn't douse out in the tub.

Little Billy peeked in and asked, "How'd it go, Daddy?"

Roger smiled. "Just fine, Bill." He didn't feel like talking though, and when the baby came crawling in too, he called to Wandella, "Keep her out, woman! I can't watch her."

Ordinarily she would have fussed over him, lit a cigar for him maybe and scrubbed his back, and he would have told her, "My shoulder is treatin me bad, honey." Today he watched her carry out the squalling bundle and knew she was rushing to get back to her dear darling brother. Those two was an inflammatory situation every time Tyrone came on a visit. Which made it all the harder on him. Slopping waves over the edge of the tub, he hauled his streaming big knees from the water. Of all the hurts that he wasn't soaking away this was the one that scared him.

Coach. What he said.

All his thinking was twisted up in tangles. He had such a feeling for Gabe. A reverence and a love. He would run through a brick wall for him. Gabe wasn't no racist. Couldn't be one. That word must have slipped out, accidental.

But even so . . . He couldn't decipher it. Or get past it, even, and be cool inside himself again. Nigger. His mind swayed with the bright sleepy water, rocked back and forth—hands off, nigger—and the polished green tiles spun around him, and the black kid was plodding more and more tiredly around that track; his mouth was a dry hole and his small sheared head was loose on his shoulders, and down below in the empty gym Coach went on reading the papers in his office.

In a couple of minutes came a knock and Jellybean walked in. And oh, Lord, he was *bad* hot! Instead of his cool velvet pants, bird-of-paradise vest and the rest of it, he was wearing an African tribal shirt. With no welcome in his voice Roger said, "Thought you'd be out doin c-couple changes."

"Tidings, brother. Now you hear *these* tidings. That fat honky got made head coach."

"Th-that all the tidings you got?" Rog stuttered. "He been c-c-callin the . . . sshots anyway."

"Ketch up, baby. That honky motherfucker, he insult a black man and they promotes him. That make the insult more so!"

He was spouting half-melted words, things about they were all in trouble with that cat running it. It didn't help to shut out what he said; just the tone of Jellybean's voice, the hot splatter of it, was catching his own blood afire. And Rog didn't want that. Nearly ten years ago that white coach had run his little cousin to death for smarting off. Little Gregory, ranked the finest basketball prospect in Cleveland history, and he run him till he drop down. Died in his sleep that night. And nobody ever done nothin about it. Nobody.

"Take yourself outa . . ." Roger said, the words breaking down. "Not gettin crazy hot like you. . . . G-git!"

When Jellybean didn't move fast enough Roger levered himself up, painfully, with one arm, shouldering bath water all over the floor; and Tucker got. Roger settled back down in the tub and adjusted the temperature with a great deal of care. The warm water wrapped around him like sleep, and he lowered himself deeper into it, floating his brown legs, until only his head stuck out, his neatly trimmed head with the dead boy running around and around in it.

Oh God, here it was noon and she hadn't picked up or anything. Dirty-footed, wearing jeans and a "Smile" tee shirt that stretched a loony grin from breast to breast, Jackie lit into the rooms jammed with antiques and animals. Furry little things walking and stretching up to the sofa, barking, wheezing, giving suck under the coffee table. Around and around and around, the caramel-colored kitten was chasing its tail in the middle of the kitchen floor, in the spills of Cheeri-Pops, grease and broken egg shells. Catching her up in a great big hug, she fired anxious questions at the kids: "When did he get up? Is he in his study? What did he have for breakfast?"

The two shaggy heads in front of the TV mumbled inconclusively. Kurt said it was *his* shirt. She put down Antygoney and said, "Whose turn is it to throw out the garbage? Okay, both a you assholes do it." Kurt and

Casey scrunched farther down with their peanut-butter sandwiches, their eyes fixed on the screen getting rounder and wider as the Headless Horseman of Sleepy Hollow galloped up with a message for homeowners. Then the adventures of Slinky Slim resumed. Slinky Slim was this retarded crocodile detective that used words a foot long, kept losing his magnifying glass, missed every single clue, but still always got his man by pure dumb luck. It was a funny enough cartoon but not exactly the thing for these two dummies to watch. "Why didn't you go to school?" she demanded. "You don't have to be brilliant like Shelley on 'I Married a Genius,' but you could at least pass."

Kurt and Casey both said they thought Shelley stunk. She retorted that it was the very best program on TV, and what about last week? What about Shelley (who wasn't exactly popular, due to his brilliant IQ and his horn-rim glasses) coming through when the fire hydrant busted by building a moat to keep the football field from flooding so the big game could go on and now he was the most popular kid in school as well as the smartest. What about that? Huh? What about that?

They said they still thought Shelley stunk.

"You would, you dumb shits," she said. "Mr. Hughes's kids think different. *They* get all A's on their report cards. And they don't get sent home by their teacher, neither."

They were still bickering when the bell rang downstairs. She flew down to the shop and sold the goat-feet table, circa 1923, and the simulated stained-glass lamp. Parsonage furniture of the Twenties was really in now, she said to herself, dancing back up the steps with $170.

She could feel it in her bones. It was all coming true, the thing she wanted the very very most in the whole entire world. Blissfully she filled and refilled the Olde Englishe copper pot with the long curving spout and watered her plants, dreamily wetting the ferns and philodendrons, the vine groping up the sour window toward the ceiling like Jack and the Beanstalk. Damn, she'd forgotten to water for three days and the pumpkin seedlings were dead.

And just look! One of the cats had eaten the baby shoots off the bamboo again. "Was it you?" she said to Leda. "You bad, bad girl."

Pale tan and whipped cream and fudge brown, her rosebud nipples tipping out of her belly fur, Leda continued her snooze on the radiator.

Oh well, the bamboo would put out more shoots. Anyhow, she was too excited, too thrilled, to stay mad. She had wanted this for so terribly terribly long. In her scatterbrain days she had forgotten heavy dates and mixed up days of the week, players, and even the cities where she was flying to meet them. But this was different.

But when he did finally move in with her, was he ever grouchy! Half the time he couldn't see her for dust, and he kept doing these absolutely weird things, like he pasted paper all over the TV screen and left a hole in the middle so *they* could watch *him!* Or snarling at the ferns, "Hustle! That's what I like to see in a fern—hustle!" Genius was sure close allied to madness.

But then, out of the clear blue, last night he came out of his icy shell. He hadn't showed at Freyr's after the game, but along about 4:00 A.M. he came weaving in, absolutely pie-eyed, and instead of hassling her about the animals in the bed with her he shooed them out with a good-humored joke and slept with her for the third time!

Just thinking about it was like pink bubbles rising

and bursting tickles into her throat. Everything was coming together like a charm. She was charting her temperature every day, and in his astrological forecast column Ozymandias had said Moon children were especially dynamic and fiery. And to accent expression and take the initiative to broaden horizons. As far as she was concerned Florence could go on babysitting for her, but that was the extent of their relationship. Florence was *too* gross. Telling her she was crazy choosing Chip when she had her free pick of all those gorgeous young men that just made her snatch hungry to think about them. Now that was *gross*.

She didn't need just another baby; it had to be a smart one. Like Dori if it was a girl, but she wanted a boy. The crisis was she had to keep Chip for at least two more weeks. "Hey guys," she said, "how's he feeling?"

"He sent us out for the papers and some cigars."

"But is he crabby?"

"He's layin around in there and makin phone calls."

"And readin the papers."

"He is not, dummy," she said. "He's thinkin up plans. He told me last night he had some real cool ones going. And shut up!"

She sent them out to the laundromat, then mopped the kitchen and dumped the slop water off the back porch into the alley. She would call him Shelley Earl. Oh! It was snowing! Big fluffs were dancing out of the luminous gray sky. Skipping around the garbage cans and leaning way, way out over the railing, she chased the flakes with her mouth and ate a whole great big bunch of them, melting them into her rosy tongue. Her eyes were shining.

Now that the place was halfway decent she decided to throw caution to the winds and take the initiative like

Ozymandias said. She shrugged into her hostess gown, all dreamy fluffs of satin and flowers (if you didn't notice some blotches of coffee and butter on one sleeve), and for good measure dabbled on some musk perfume—Cleopatra and practically all the famous women of history had used musk to cast their spell. She knocked. "Excuse me for embarging on you," she said, "but is there anything you'd like?"

"Yeah. A bowl of ice cubes and a paintbrush."

A paintbrush? Puzzled but ever so happy to serve him, she ran to get the things and brought them in: goddess born in midsummer, beautiful.

His back was turned and he was examining her jungle wallpaper. Lions and tigers stood in the stylized foliage, magnificent among the arty palms, bamboo, elephant grass. He plunked two of the ice cubes into his Scotch. He sipped. He took the brush from her, plunged it to the bottom of a slobbery half-gallon can and blithely painted one of the lions into a cage with six dark slashes of his brush.

"Chip!" she wailed. Oh, Jesus God, he was in his crazy jester mood. Gloating like a mad scientist, he stepped back to admire a tiger he'd framed with paint. Then in cold blood he swabbed a bar right down the center of its blank noble face.

She broke into sniffles.

He said, "This room is supposed to be a study, right? And I'm thinking up plans in here?"

"Right," she sniffled.

"Okay, did you ever hear of a study where you had to wear a pith helmet and carry a rifle?"

He was grinning at her, but it was a scary grin, and his cold sleepless eyes, closed in by dark sunglasses, were flaring at her. The kookier he was, the touchier he was, wow! And he had to be indulged in all of his moods. Like those old lawbooks he was reading to get himself in a foxy mood.

She swallowed her snot and asked if she could stay and watch.

Too late. He stopped and moved to the window. The brush dangled from his hand like a broken wing. She watched him, stricken, yearning. That dry balding dome of a head, she longed to hold it between her breasts; she ached to have what was in that head inside her, growing inside her.

But he got to thinking again, sort of talking out loud about his strategy. He was teed off at some newspaperman who'd said that four for four when the Stags were out of it was something less than miraculous. And for some reason it was important to "make" Fred Dickie. And then there was Whitman of the *Times-Examiner*. With a smile like a crack in a mirror (but it *was* a smile) he told her to read Whit's column.

"Huh?" She was about ready to pass out.

"Well?" he said. "What d'you think?"

"Me?"

"Tut," he said. "You and me, chick. We're gonna take the Stags apart and take *those* pieces and turn 'em into chopped sirloin. Now here's how I read Whitman. All along he's been bad-mouthing the Stags. Way back before the season. I figure he's got himself a problem. I don't know what it is, but I believe him and me can hit it off together."

She was radiant. "You mean it, Chip? You're not mad at me any more?"

He coughed again, looking out the window at the

hunched shops and asphalt-shingled houses, the abandoned church with the long-silent bell tower. The warped old roofs were white planes of snow with clean hard edges.

"What I want you to do," he said, "is call Dori and get a list of the places Whit hangs out. We're sorta pfft!"

"Sure! Oh, this is neat! You and me are partners, really and truly?"

"And don't take Jack's car back to him yet."

"Gosh, Chip, I know yours is busted, but he needs it too. I mean, I'm his mistress, but we only sleep together about once a month." But before Chip could frown she gave in. "I'll tell him I busted a fender. Providing," she added craftily, "if you'll let me chauffeur you around."

"Deal."

Humbly, timidly, she added one more condition: "And if on the way we can stop off at the Wishing Well . . . because I have a secret wish, okay?"

Kneading his bum leg, George crouched in front of his locker, his mind going around and around in its familiar grooves. He had worked his thinking around to where he took it back that Chip had asked him to betray the team and told him, "If Coach would 've put you in early we would 've bagged it." But Chip had only rubbed that little scar like a crust of ice on his cheek and said, "I thought Ryan played a fine game."

He was bad off, but the whole team was a crisis. Forgotten grudges were coming to the surface. He had personally heard Jay accuse Poppo of trying to cripple him, back when he was with the Colts. "I got some debts that are overdue" was said, and even practical jokes could be dangerous. A man would slap a buddy's ass with a towel and get a "Sonofabitch, I told you. Don't ever do that again." Without turning to say it, either, really itching to lay him out.

It was sure Lord discouraging. Vicious mean words buzzing and stinging like cattle flies. But nothing to compare to this race thing. It was like a terrible wound had opened up in the soul of the team. He could feel it bleeding inside of him, and he couldn't tell that hurt from the one about Chip.

Trying to balance on one leg, he floundered into his sweatsuit. When the offense and defense separated for the films, Poppo hesitated, then, instead of sitting in the empty chair beside Daddy Wilson, circled around to the other side of George.

Daddy didn't change expression, but the temperature in the room raised to the maximum. Poppo tried to cover it over with his time-honored joke. "Daddy," he said, "you're an objective man. What's your judgment—a fat ass or a thin ass best?"

In the silence Poppo started out on what a supergreat night he'd had last night, and George cut him off somberly. "I don't want to hear nothing or think nothing but football."

It was a crisis for sure. He sure wished that Coach had said something to settle the blacks down. This was not a trouble that was going to wash away by itself. Much as he hated making speeches, it was up to him to call a team unity meeting.

He told Coach. Before afternoon practice he went to the can a couple of times, then took up his position in front of the blackboard snowy with erased diagrams.

"Our goal is to win," he said in a blind fluster, "and we got to find out what's wrong. Whatever it is. Get it out in the open so's it don't fester. In other words, make our grievances come out and be settled. We've all been through a lot together and so—"

At last he was able to take in what his eyes were seeing: helmets and pads, brushy faces, gum-chewing mouths, and the blacks, ominously, all sitting and standing together.

And no Chip!

It stopped him completely. For a minute he stood there powerless, propped against the blackboard like a huge disconnected puppet.

At last he stumbled back into his spiel: "As far as the Lion game, we got our butts dominated and that's all there is to it. It was a dying flame from the start. So . . . So they beat the hell out of us and that's that. So let's look ahead instead. For Green Bay ahead of us. So let's clean it out inside."

Fred Dickie's bowlegged power filled the doorway. "If I was on offense I wouldn't be able to hold up my head."

"I mean something—you know, constructive-like, Fred."

Fred said if that wasn't constructive, what the fuck was?

George quieted him down, but then an argument broke out between the two tackles. It ended up with Harry the Hawk stabbing his taped hand at Toof and saying, "Outside, man! I'll see you outside."

About all people could agree on was that they couldn't win with Grover. While the poor kid went red as a beet and hung his head, the players called him a fucking plumber to his face.

"Hold on now," George said firmly. It was a terrible

hard thing for him because he wanted Chip in there more than any of them, more than anything. But he said, "I'll tell Coach how we feel, but it's up to his decision on that, not ours. It's up to us to put out a hundred and fifty percent no matter what our preference is."

After the meeting he at least had the satisfaction of telling Coach how the team felt about Chip against Grover.

"Tough tiddy," Coach said. "How's the leg?"

"It'll be okay for Sunday, Coach."

As one of the walking wounded he stood on the sidelines while the team cracked helmets, and it was sure terrible. Coach should never have called for a full-hit scrimmage with the situation already so serious. It got more and more vicious with every play, holding and hooking and every kind of dirty stuff.

Coach Ellis called a play to his offense in one huddle, and opposite to him Coach Simson called the type of defense. The lines set, haunches tight and rumps up, and George could hear the angry words, back and forth, from the sidelines. "Hut-hut!" The lines banged together and the play stacked up in a heap of slugging and kicking players. Coach Gabe roared, "That's enough, you bunch a cocksuckers," and plowed into the scramble, yanking people off right and left.

All at once he was down, like as if he was pole-axed. He'd taken a shoe in the head, accidental. A dozen people helped carry him to the sidelines, dead to this world, and the trainers all went to work on him. George hovered nearby. "That fucker is . . . somethin else," Gabe was muttering, lost in some game fifteen years ago.

With him laid out, it was stupid to keep on with the full go, but the other coaches knew the chewing out they'd get if they didn't follow the instruction sheet. "All right, all right," Coach Ellis snapped. "Back to work! And cool it, all of you!"

He might just as well have saved his breath. Without Coach Gabe in charge, the savageness built like fire in a canyon. Players were snarling, "Jig motherfucker" and "Honky asshole," and on every play they were clipping and face-masking, twisting at knees and generally hitting to hurt their man.

"That's enough rough stuff," the coaches barked. To no avail. Every matchup between a black and a white was a shoot-out. It was the worst shame George ever saw; it wasn't even football. Fred Dickie was playing with a shoe full of blood. Jay was put on his butt five times in a row and came off shaken up bad, his face bar tore completely off his helmet.

"Get the black sonofabitch," three or four of the white players said.

"Yeah?" he puffed. "You go in the pit and get him, not me."

George went limping over to quiet things down. "Nobody's getting anybody," he said, "till he gets me first."

They moved away from him sullenly. A reserve linebacker had to be helped off the field. A pitch-out stumbled into a wreckage of helmets, pads, torn jerseys, fists and murderous shoes. The players unpiled, leaving two giants struggling on the ground. "Kiss my ass, mothafucka," growled a huge black lineman lying atop a white linebacker and belting him. He was peeled off and hauled away to the sidelines to cool off. "That'll cost you both two hundred dollars!" Coach Dewey bawled.

"Wuth it!" Mark Youngblood panted, pulling off his

helmet. "Wuth it every dime." George tried to talk peaceable to him, but he said, "Sist on that noise. Nex time he try to cripple me he won't be roun no mo."

Daddy wasn't doing much better on his side. "Keep it cool, brothers," he kept urging, and they either looked surly or scuffed away grumbling, "That honky, I know his scene. He gonna be flat of his back."

George wished he could go over and ask the coaches to call a halt, only it wasn't his place to do so. On a deep pass pattern Bird Jones and Jellybean, the strong side safety, collided in mid-air—an awful crash, both of them hanging there stunned for what seemed like seconds, then falling backward from each other. Jellybean wobbled to his hands and knees, yammering something crazy. Bird made it to his feet groggily and started toward him and keeled over, gagging like a rope was pulled tight around his neck.

It wasn't anything but pitiful out there now. The worried coaches hollered and slapped fines in every direction. Dripping blood and panting meannesses at each other—"Whup me if you kin!" and "You black crud, I'm gonna lay you out"—the offense and defense battered themselves half to pieces. And Coach Gabe was still on the ground.

Only for Poppo was it business as usual. He came barrelling in on one play and really racked Shorty up—knocked him into a dazed bundle rolling over and over. Shorty staggered to his feet hollering "Fuck up a nigger, you asshole! Not me!" Poppo looked down at him kind of surprised. "You're wearin a number, ain't you?" he said.

Otherwise it was *mean* bad, an alley fight instead of a practice. George decided he *had* to say something. In the offensive huddle Coach Dewey called for a screen-left to Shorty and instructed Grover not to pedal back and burn it to Shorty but wait till the pass rush was right on top of him and then just lob it over to Short Stuff. George said, "Coach?" The team was straggling up to the line of scrimmage. Before Grover could even say "Hut," the two lines were hammering away at each other, and this time Daddy Wilson took a lick from behind that left him out of it, on his back.

George went limping over to him at top speed, scared half to death. "Are you all right, Daddy?" he said. "Daddy?"

"Don't bug me, man," Daddy said, not moving.

The coaches called it off without George asking them, but serious damage had been done. In the parking lot afterward, when he saw Daddy's silver Cadillac come gliding toward him, he waved it to a stop. Roger was with him in the front seat.

Daddy skinned down the window and asked him what was up.

"Well, look here, Daddy. The practice was discouraging. And it sure looks bad all around. But I figure we have to make the best of a bad situation. What I mean is . . . if you and me . . . we've played alongside of each other for five years."

"And that's a mighty bond."

Greatly encouraged, George said, "Right! And if you and me—well, this race thing, if we could work on it together . . ."

Very gently Daddy stuck out his long arm and roughed George's orange wool cap. "George baby, there's some things got to be done by yourself."

He put the car into motion. Only then did George

see him, lounging at his ease in the back seat with a cigar in his mouth. Chip.

A terrible awful feeling went through him, a shock and a premonition like. It was cold. The sky blew around like ashes. Hunched around the terrible feeling, he hobbled toward his car.

Daddy Wilson stood by his stereo, not showing the worry he felt. The big double room was a smoky roar. "Shit, couldn't *git* worse. Them ofays never have dealt us a straight hand. All we askin is respect for the black man."

Green Wolf said, "I'll make my own demands, boy. All I wants to."

Jellybean was jumping up and down and screaming, "Don't you go 'boyin' me. Firs you walks on me a little bit and then you 'boys' me. I'm a man."

"Shut you ass!" Wolf flared back. "You don't stop I have to bust you."

Before it came to something physical Daddy said, "Both you sit down. You brothers are too little to fight." His dark wise face smiled down at them from under the ceiling. Then, shaping his goatee with his long fingers, he said to the others, "Goes for all you cats. No more racket and gut-shovin. We are conductin this caucus orderly, each man saying his say-so in turn."

Man, taking charge over this chaos was some kind of hard. Every brother on the team was here, even them on crutches or in casts. Sweat-flaring brown faces charcoaled with whiskers and sideburns. Ballooning Afros. Beads. Sun-spoke medallions. Many black wrist bands. Angry voices buzzing everywhere: "Our brains gotta ketch up with our brawn. . . . Rap on, brother. It ain't gonna change nothin. . . . What *you* been smokin?" You could hardly see the honeycomb light of the lamps in all the fumes and clogging bodies.

If they were going to get anything done he had to keep it together, and that meant combining some very diverse elements. Brothers that couldn't think past "I got seven mouths to feed." Brothers that were colored white inside and brothers that were all the way into the Muslim life. Such ranges. Now add to all this Tucker: hot to start with because of Chip and crazy out of his mind now. Plus Elijah, after ten fine years at cornerback, had lost that quick step and was due to be cut anyhow. And so had nothing to lose.

"If we all sticks together and signs it . . ." Elijah was on his feet, blinking and baring his shattered mouth. His face twitched and his voice kept shrilling up and up.

"Well, I don't know," Youngblood said. "It's a bad somethin, all right. But the way I figure, I figure Gabe is the same hard on black and white alike."

Jellybean wasn't having any. "You outa yo mind? He the mos racis coach in the whole league."

"W-worst of it bein," Roger said, "it all s-seem like bitter ways. I c-can't believe in him no more."

Without waiting for his turn Tucker bawled, "Fuck all this jive! I am resignin as of now."

Daddy leaned back on the sofa and stroked himself around his mouth and down the narrowing cone of whiskers. "That's beautiful," he chuckled. "I think you lyin, but that's beautiful." After he'd pacified Tuck he said to the whole assembly, "One thing about this motion before us. There are discrepancies amongst us. But what we decide here tonight, if only by one vote, we all do it."

The Green Wolf shook his head, his floppy green hat sparking its golden discs. "Minus me, you will," he half challenged Daddy. "I'm All-Pro. I do what I wants to do when I wants."

Green Wolf had a mean mouth when he was coming down after smoking a couple of joints. That was all.

Daddy gave him a look and let Elijah have him: "You selfish, man. You one selfish cat. The black athlete has got to use his success for the benefit of the whole race." He was wearing a white cotton robe, and a white turban spiraled up from his black face and sooty whiskers. Used to be he was called Sun Child because he was always either tanning himself on a bench or lying under a sun lamp to get himself browner, more black. From being that much of a hothead he was now a human flame-thrower of bitterness. "This is the predicament of the black athlete," he gobbled and panted. "We are the tools of the white establishment. They underpay us, they use us up and then throw us away."

"Yeah! Workin for a salary of grits money," Jelly-bean said. "A five-hundred-dollar raise after the year I had—"

"We beatin ourself stupid for their pleasure! Knockin heads for their entertainment!" Elijah was flopping his white arms like a gun-shot bird, screaming crazed spit and pain: "Bein called nigger, that is just a symbol of our whole predicament. Where the black coaches and athletic directors in the colleges? It goes all the way from top to bottom—"

This was as much as Daddy could take. Man oh man, any more of this and *his* brain would by frying. "Hold it, Elijah," he said, raising himself stiffly to his feet. "In a minute you gonna have us jumpin off these walls. Just to be frank, I don't like Mr. Simson myself. And plenty else going on in this country. Howsoever, we have got to keep ourself cool and more cool. We can't just take the insult laying down, but we don't want to tear everything up neither. That way will just hurt us more."

Facing them from in front of the dark window, his back stooping with weariness in his velvet robe, he was still the Watusi man, the chieftain responsible for all his people.

"So," he said then. "On to you, Mr. Youngblood. Do we or don't we all sign a paper demanding to Coach Simson he apologize to Roger in public?"

"To all of us too!"

"We all of us insulted!"

"Yeah!"

"No way." For the first time Chip spoke up, sending out the words in puffs of cigar smoke. "Gabe ain't apologizing to Rog or no*body*. You know what he's gonna do? He's gonna wipe his big fat ass with that paper and then serve it up to us for lunch."

Fists. Mad garbling. Arms beating and blabbers, squawks of rage.

Lord, Daddy groaned to himself, look at them all rise up. Chip was the only white player he'd invited—not even George, not even George—because not only was Chip a brother inside but also he had that good brain power. But first he had brought along that Jackie chick, who had had to be put with the women in the kitchen, and now he was coming on hotter than Elijah.

As if he didn't have enough burdens already holding these fire-breathers down and staying cool enough himself to think. This was a very complex situation and he had to keep his concentration. Had to. Though he was still beat up from the game and hurting bad with a personal sorrow, not one of Hosea's ruckuses but something eating at him all the time. Here he'd come up all the way from a shack and a patch of sugar cane to that ghetto slum with those rats to the top of his profession. And now it was all going up in smoke because of Gwynn. His wife had turned religious maniac on him, beating a tambourine in Bishop Dallas' church five nights a week. Damnedest part of all was what she was doing to little Eddie, turning the boy into a sissy. Cutting his balls off. He'd told her, "That's enough, woman. Don't give me no more Jesus." So what did she do? Run straight to the boy and say to him, "Your Daddy is a wicked man." Now the two of them was praying for him. God*dam*, how could he think?

Meanwhile everybody was burning to a crisp in the wildfire Chip had fanned up: "You a turkey, Roger." Rog choked and Mark Youngblood came to his defense. "And you ugly. Ain't he ugly, Rog?" Wolf snarled back, "Gonna cut the perty off you in a little second."

Sighing with fatigue, Daddy angled out his long arm and for once spoke sharply. It was quiet. "Next one says something mean better have a stick," he said. "Mr. Hughes, I'd like to thank you for your shrewd opinion. Maybe you could have said it a little nicer, but even so." Wearily, wearily, rolling his face like a heavy stone to include everybody, he said, "We have all spoke our piece and now it comes to, do we sign that paper or not sign it? Somebody get a pad of paper. Each man puts his vote down in secret."

While the balloting went on he turned away from the smoky jumble and glare, brooding through the oil slick of reflections on the window, brooding. There was no doubt which way they would vote.

And he agreed with Chip. There was no way a petition would do it. As a matter of fact he'd only let this scene come about because it was the slowest and most reasonable he could keep things. And it was no good at all. Gabe was one bad motherfucker, and once you made a move on him you better be ready to keep digging at him. Harder. Or otherwise it would only mean more humiliation, more injury to Black Pride. This was just the preliminaries, feeling each other out and establishing turf. When Gabe tore up their petition, then what? What could he and his brothers do?

His tall shoulders sinking, he gazed out at Martin Luther King, Jr. Drive. The November darkness seemed to press all the light into endless pure lines, geometrical blocks, diagrams, words. Which even as he blinked dissolved into splatters, into red and green waves and the flash-flash-flicker of a gas station. He was so damned tired. And mad.

Behind him in the swarming noise he heard a cough, then Chip saying, "Not me. I'm not voting to get my ass kicked."

"Fine," Daddy said without bothering to turn around. "Nobody has to vote. Just abide by the outcome."

He had never felt so dog-tired, so alone. The murderous weight of all this made him want to cry out—he didn't know what, something speechless with grief and exhaustion. He wanted to get away, sink into those pretty splashes of color out there and be quit of planning and making peace and everything else. Wanted to be that little bitty boy back in Louisiana. Living in that board-and-tin shack by the levee. Every year, all along the top of the old grassy embankment, them Frenchies made trees out of wood. They nailed poles into a framework twenty, thirty feet high, a great spire filled with brush and pine logs tapering up like a church steeple. And then on Christmas Eve night they lit them on fire. Granny say if they blazes good it make the winter easier and so her rheumatism less. But talk about *some pretty*. All in a row, blazing in the darkness for miles. Fire trees.

He'd slaved his fanny off to get everything just exactly perfect. Instead of calling Gabe on the carpet at the club headquarters he'd made it a social occasion, a little dinner for two at his apartment. His young friends were under strict orders *not* to show their faces. And he said *not one word* about his art collection. The welded rhythms of his "Football Player," the Jackson Pollock original splattering its brilliant colors all over one wall, the Lichtenstein blow-up of a comic-strip red mouth— he'd just pretended they weren't there all around them, and Gabe's heavy-lidded eyes brushed them away.

But it was the menu that had required the most *grueling* self-control. Any chef cooking, any exquisite sauces and vintage wines were an absolute no-no. Just three-inch-thick steaks and a turkey which he was careful *not* to stuff with his fantastic oyster stuffing. Everything, every single detail had been planned and executed to perfection and still Gabe had said, "Fuck no."

"I don't see we have any option, Gabe," Carson said firmly. "You simply *must* or the whole pot of beans boils over. Damn, damn, damn! Why do *I* have to get all the poop? Why didn't the blacks ask *you* for an apology?"

"They knew better."

"And look, just cast your eyes on all these other grievances they tacked on for good measure. A black assistant coach, my God! What am I going to do with these?"

"Piss on 'em."

"I'm extremely sorry, but I'm afraid I can't do that. Oh damn! O and eight for the season and now this! I tell you, we're on the verge, Gabe."

Hands clasped sternly behind him, the GM paced back and forth on his miniature feet. Gabe squashed down one end of the sofa. His heavy head spread downward and spilled out in a paunchy face hung with necks and jowls. The face did not follow Carson's anguished movements.

"Gabe—oh, I just hate this! Why did you have to call him a nigger? I'm not 'Jay accusing' anybody, but it was very ill advised, Gabe. Very ill advised."

The round man finally looked at him. "Nobody lays a hand on me, Mr. Le Motte. Black or white. Any player touches me I'll put him on the floor."

"Yes, yes, I know. Team discipline. But, Gabe, this is not just another little case of the owsies and I'm not just overreacting as usual. Remember St. Louis? We have a very hot potato here. What if the papers get this? Our image," he dithered, "the franchise . . . the other owners . . ."

The dammed-up mass of flesh on the couch waited for him to get through. Sometimes Gabe was really *too* exasperating. The man was a monolith. And now, oh dear, he could hear a very distinct giggle from the master bedroom. Why, why, *why* had he made Bobbie that present of a trip to California to cure his state of depression? He'd come back with this beautiful blond *degenerate*. Who was on drugs! Why couldn't Bobbie have left him out there with his surfboard looking for the perfect wave? Now it was pure hellish torture. Bobbie dispensed his favors *alternately!* The bitch slept one night with him and the next with Billie! It was draining him, absolutely and totally ripping him to shreds.

Wavering toward hysteria, he said, "Gabe, it will do absolutely no good for me to take care of these other grievances if you don't apologize. You're blind, and I mean that. You simply can't treat everybody in the world in the same way. Just for example, you hurt *my* feelings sometimes. And very badly, but I can take it. But these Negroes are children. They're still basically savages, Gabe. Children of nature. You hurt their feelings and they take it to heart more than we do. It's a matter of emotional makeup. I've read about savages that just sat down and died out of heartbreak when something went wrong." He thought of the two of them in there, balling each other in his bedroom, and almost sobbed. "Sometimes I wish I could do it myself. Just sit down and never move again. But blacks will brood, Gabe, and not give it their all. And we need everybody putting out a hundred percent, not brooding."

"Brooding, my ass. They'll put out or get out. Anybody lays down and they're gone. Any color, black, white, or any color. If a nigger wants to brood, he can do it shining shoes and I'll get somebody that wants to play ball."

"Gabe, Gabe, Gabe," Carson wailed. This was so heartbreaking. "You're on a very hot seat, Gabe. Of your own creation."

"Shit. I told you. I wish you would've kept Lowry. Working in the line is my meat and drink. I only took the fuckin job because another head coach would go with Hughes."

"I couldn't keep Lowry. It was thumbs-down time for him, but *you*," he said eagerly, "I don't want to lose you. I *know* you can get us up there leading the parade—though I must say that Grover, your baby, looked just stinko against the Lions."

But Gabe was true to the vision in his guts. "I think he's got the credentials, but like I said, you never know. You just got to pay your sacrifice and find out. He needs a lot more games inside him, and till then we're gonna be bringing plenty of happiness around the league."

"You mean we're going to just go on losing and losing? The season is already—"

"Plow the fuckin season under."

"You can't be serious! My God! Oh well, it's ready for the embalmers anyway, I guess." He sat down limply and shut his perspiring white face in his hands. What an ordeal! He heard another giggle. Damn them! He had a sudden terrible vision of them, naked in each other's arms, doing things and watching themselves at the same time in the wall mirrors, kissing and floating up in the mirror-ceiling like depraved angels. Boy bodies. The ravishing, almost feminine litheness. The tender strength of loins and sweet testicles. The baby-soft shoot of Bobbie's penis swelling, filling and throbbing up, thrusting toward him. And now he and Billie—it was maddening. They were jazzing and sucking and laughing at him! In his own bedroom, in his own personal Versailles, smirking and laughing at him.

And it was *his day!*

Perfectly furious, he said to Gabe, "A believer I might be, but I kid you not about the racial thing. You have exactly one week to play it your way. You settle it by then or you're off the payroll—unless it all blows up before that. Which I firmly believe it will."

"That's the way I want it," Gabe said. "If I can't hack it, fire my ass."

He was busy and had to go now. It was infuriating! "You blind stupid moron," he screamed inside himself, in his cold stomach, as he walked his head coach to the elevator. "Go ahead," he screamed soundlessly, and the scream was like blood bursting inside him, "Go ahead and just ramrod it. That's all you know. Go ahead and see what happens! Screw it all up, you bullheaded—I'd love to give you the ax. It will be a pleasure."

"INTERNAL PROBLEMS HIT STAGS." Even before the elevator closed on Gabe, the first editions of Al Whitman's morning column were hitting the fan. "It's been no secret for some time," he lobbed one in there, warming up, "that the Stags are not a contented bunch. A team with eight bloody noses in eight trips to the well is bound to have problems. Earl Hughes, the gutsy little tactician, has made it clear that he would like to take his talents elsewhere. And he isn't alone. The list of disgruntled players is beginning to look like the Stag roster.

"However"—and now he whipped the cow plat into the blades—"the problems go deeper than that. In the wake of the disemboweling by the Lions, it develops that at least one of the coaches is in disfavor with the blacks. In fact, the black members of the team are disenchanted about a number of things. They have submitted a list of grievances and demands to the man at the top, Carson Le Motte.

"Are we going to have another St. Louis racial tragedy here? Pro football still quivers and shakes at the mention of that one!

"It looks like a long cold winter for Stag fans. If it weren't for the Bears (presently 6 and 2, bless them), it's possible that the sun wouldn't turn back at all on December 21."

"Black demands!" All through the brutal drills the phrase rumbled and seethed among the white players. As they tromped out of the stadium in twos and threes, it went splattering like hot grease all over the parking lot. "They got demands, huh? Well, ain't that just tough shit."

"Spoiled crybabies, pissing and moaning all the time. If I was Le Motte I'd tell 'em to get fucked," Jay said.

Bird nodded. "Hit's the same old thing. Ever team I been on, them goddam turds was bitchin about somethin."

"Man," Bebo said on the way to Freyr's, "there comes a point, you know?" He made a few jungle noises, ee-ah, oo-oo, waiting for the light to change.

Gooch said that he might be riding a lot of bench, but at least he was white.

Harry the Hawk's view was that the black players didn't stay in shape. "So where do they come off with that grievance crap? There's only two jigs on the team in shape."

"You fuckin right," Gooch said. "They're not doin a job. What I always said, if a jig is doin a job for us he can screw my sister. But the way them crap-mouths are playin they couldn't hold her hand."

Out in Oak Grove Short Stuff worked himself painfully out of Dude's car. It had been a bummer of a trip. For twenty-five slowing and stopping miles Dude had done nothing but run his mouth: "Black demands! That's real funny. Why don't nobody ever come up with white demands?"

Man, it was aggravating. To personally agree with every word Dude said and be unable to even say, "Yeah." It was lamentable, it really was. But ever since the head-shaving there was this, like a communications gap between them, that every damn single little thing seemed to make it wider. Like Dude's wife had a baby and he kept bragging, "Eight pounds four ounces at birth! Top that!" It got to be old, real old. "For chrissake, I'm ahead four kids to two," he'd finally snapped. "So what's the big deal about weight?" In the old days it would have been part of a good-natured competition; now it was just sad. Lugubrious. Everything was.

Dude rolled down the garage door. Half lifting his sprained hand in goodbye, Shorty cut across toward his own house. He was too lugubrious to pick up the toys scattered all over the frozen brown grass, a broken sled, one ski. Behind him on the driveway Dude was still rabble-rousing: "And I'll tell you something else. They're gonna get their demands, too. Every team in sports is shit scared of racial trouble. All they do is catter to the niggers."

Shorty found himself trembling, propelling himself awkwardly around, the sadness lurching up into his throat. "I hope they get every goddam one," he shouted, icy with shock at himself. "I like niggers!"

"The chickenshit jig-lover," Lips said, and all around him in the alcove at Freyr's angry players nodded and gruffed. This wasn't any formal deal. The guys had just sort of gravitated here, kept coming in until two tables had to be shoved together. Even Fred Dickie was here. The small grove of vinyl leaves and grapes hummed and swarmed, and the man with the stinger out and stinging was Lips: "Who else could have wrote out their demands? They couldn't do it by themself."

"Chip's the only white man they'll talk to, all right."

"Yeah, he's romancin the jigs."

Super, man, it was super. He could feel the tide coming back his way. Except for his beautiful game against the Cardinals things had gone piss-poor all season. First off he'd put his money on Grover. That dumb prick. Then George Schmidt had accused him of faking that groin pull and pushed him all the way to hind tit with the guys. But here it was at last, his golden chance to get back in solid and, for a bonus, to really stick it to Hughes. Man, did he want that guy's ass! So bad he could taste it. Nights he still waked up with that white mouse squirming in his sweat pants, biting with its sharp teeth at his nuts while he screamed and screamed in the darkness.

And now Hughes was just where he wanted him: with the blacks.

The guys were all torched up about it, too, with one all-important exception—Dickie. Every once in a while the great linebacker felt the weedy lengths of hair over his mouth which he devoutly believed was a Viking mustache; the rest of the time he just stared at the one bottle of beer his wife allowed him before he hit the road for home. "It's some kinda horseshit," Lips said to him. "We get screwed and the shines get what they want."

Dickie's neck muscles thickened and his little eyes flamed up. "Motherfuckers," he said. "They get everything. They took over the old neighborhood. They're all on relief and aid to dependent mothers. They're a menace to the United States of America."

Lips was jubilant. "And the team, man. They're tearing it *all* up."

"You goddam know it," Jay said. "Them pissers gotta be kept in line, that's all."

"Well, Gabe's the man that can do it. The only time the jigs got away with any shit in practice was when Gabe was out cold," Lips roared.

"Yeah, Gabe's my man," Hawk said, "but hey, man, that Grover is goddam fuckin nowhere."

Lips agreed loudly. "But what I'm sayin," he added, "is we got enough of a problem without the jigs makin demands. That *Hughes* thinks up for 'em."

Bull-shouldered, he brought his forearm down on the table. Glasses, bottles and silverware clanged in the jumping red light.

But out of nowhere Dickie said, "I'm against jigs but not Chip. He's okay."

Vacant mouths. Even the flame in the lamp seemed to droop.

"Chip thinks I oughta get more money," Dickie said, looking ugly about it. "He says I oughta renegotiate my contract. He's a better lawyer than that dumb Polack I got. Sonofabitch says I gotta wait till contract time."

Somehow Lips kept it inside. Somehow he didn't yell, "Wake up, asshole! Hughes is playin it both ways. Tryin to keep in tight with us while he plays soul brother with the jigs." He was not about to goof up with Dickie. No way. He was going to ride this bandwagon and ride it with the reins in his hands while Dickie pulled. "We all know you deserve more bread," he said. "Hey, you know what Daddy Wilson makes? Fifty-two five! No shit. And a bonus deal besides."

"He what?" Dickie came to his feet, snuffling. "That black motherfucker! He's the one that brung all this Black Power shit to a head. I'm for White Power!"

The other players picked it up, squeezed together in the leafy hollow, growling it, pounding it, blasting it out: "White Power! White Power!" The pale sexless bartender implored them to keep it down and fled. The chant swelled in the smoky blood light, "White Power! White Power!" Bebo came in with his ooh-ahs and monkey jabbers, yawps, bird screams; and Lips, his mouth curling off his yellow teeth, delivered a fart of magnificent, of superhuman, proportions.

"I'll tell you this," he purred. "Gabe don't have to do it alone. I catch any nigger not playin ball, he's gonna pay."

But Lips had it all wrong. In the contact session the following morning he worked Roger over and got in a couple of cute ones. Unstacking after a play, he worked an elbow into the bundles of muscle in Rog's neck and levered himself up.

Rog's jaws strangled open. "Quit that," he gasped. "I gonna bust you you don't stop."

"Yeah? Try me out, motherfucker."

While the coaches were busy chewing out Grover they exchanged threats and taunts: "Next play, I'm gonna

put the shit on you." "Quit jivin round an come *to* me."
Lips half turned as if to line up and jumped him. They
were flopping over and over on the harsh turf, slugging,
kicking savagely. A thrashing weight was sucked away
and he was on his back with a red face floating above him,
grim and bright in the cold sky. Looking down at him,
Coach deliberately kicked him again, swinging the full
heft of his haunch and leg into it, driving his shoe deep
into Lips's terrified rump. Yelping, he scrambled out of
range on his hands and knees.

"You started it," Gabe snarled at him. "You beer-
bellied piss-licker."

And while he was still gaping and pawing at the
numbness, George came down on him: "I'm watching
you, John. You don't just only put out. You cause one
more widge of trouble—now hear me—I'll put you away
myself. Personally."

He wasn't in pads and his gorilla face came jutting
out from the red cross on his chest. He was trembling all
over with the effort of holding back.

Jesus.

"All right, all right now," Gabe said, smacking his
hands, and they went back to sweating ass. Black and
white, he had them all *stretching*. What Frank Leahy used
to say when he was head coach at Notre Dame—that a
practice was no good until there was blood on the grass
—this was where Gabe started. Let up at all and it *cost*
you. It was bust a gut, baby, on every play, and if you
messed up an assignment he took the hide off, whatever
color it was. "What's the matter with you?" he said to
Jay. "You run that zig-in right or just keep goin out that
gate."

Without raising his voice.

He worked 57 Flavors, coming back from his head injury, as hard as he worked the rookie Pete. The wounded listened and watched from the sidelines; only Chip was out of it. In solitary. The agitator, the clubhouse lawyer shivered on the bench, then moved over to a salamander. The chubby orange tank expelled gushes of heat from a winding canvas colon. Weary players came blowing and stamping into its comfort and went back out there. Coughing, his arms cramped on his chest, Chip stood in the warm, gas-fouled wind. He wasn't sure, but somehow he didn't like what he saw. All morning long the grim round man flogged the stumbling team. Acres of empty seats swept away and away under the dying sun. 57 Flavors was down again.

By lunch break the players were dragging their tails and there was another full-contact scrimmage set for the afternoon. Gabe waddled into his office to eat. He'd stayed in his old cubicle when he became head coach, and there was the same bag of straggling golf clubs, the same screen and projector squatting on his desk, the same filing cabinet with the same comic statue on top: from the front it was an exotic dancer smirking out of an Egyptian wig; turn her around and she was a dick with a hard-on. When he was in a good mood he showed it to somebody he favored, laughing out his thick red tongue.

But not to this little candy-ass. Waiting for him with Dan Fallon was the sonofabitch who had been bad-mouthing him every day in his column. Whitman. "No press," he growled. "Didn't you see the sign on the door?"

Fallon wallowed around in his loose brown suit, apologized, explained that Mr. Le Motte had given it the okay and ducked out of there.

"Just a couple of quickies," Whitman said, pad and ballpoint at the ready.

Gabe gave his attention to the thermos of coffee and the spicy-warm cartons that Jocko had brought in. It was all there, three orders of barbecued ribs and a family-size pizza with everything on it.

Whitman hemmed and said, "Le Motte told me, quote, 'We do have a few conflicts.' Could you be more specific on this?"

He got a belly grunt for an answer. Turning his back on him, Gabe pulled himself up to the desk and began to feed out of the cartons.

Whit was not to be brushed off. He disliked Gabe Simson, hated him, but it went a lot deeper than that. He hated everything from the summer training camp to the Pro Bowl in January. It bored him, week after week the same endless tug of war up and down the field. The game belonged to ten-year-olds in a vacant lot, along with ring-around-the-rosie, Red Rover and all the other scraps of lost and dead ritual. *Not* to the purveyors of bloody entertainment, to big, BIG business, TV business. Maybe most of all he hated scratching columns out of nearly inarticulate players and coaches who grumbled the same stale answers, year after year, to his worn-out questions.

Once upon a lovely time, before the Stags opened shop in Chicago, he had been the outdoors writer on the staff. Hunting breakfasts in highway cafés before dawn. Fishing camps in the dark-green steeples of Minnesota pine woods. Good talk. Whiskey. But that wasn't it; not even the comradeship was quite it. What he really craved was to be out of it all, to be alone.

Then suddenly this season the defeats had piled up and there was his goal in sight. All he had to do was run the franchise out of town and he would be back at the old stand. This was where Chip Hughes came in—he was at least a canny SOB. The thing was to slash and stab with copy like "Chicago fans deserve more from the Stag orgnization. Wouldn't it be better all around if they took the plague to some other fair city?" And the civic crusade was picking up steam; the other sports-writers were demanding wins. Now! Pots of tar were bubbling; the search was on for pillows with real chicken feathers.

Attacking, attacking, he put questions to the thunderbolt man of the Stags.

"Why isn't Hughes getting more playing time? Is he in your plans at all?"

"Do you intend to go for a quarterback in the draft?"

"Or trade for an established quarterback? Somebody you *will* use while Grover learns his trade?"

Gabe stripped the ribs down to the oily bones. Hot coarse smells filled the office. Every so often, like a pit bull throwing a dog off his shoulder, he would shrug.

Whit came clawing back at him. "How much of the team dissension would you say is racial and how much is due to the quarterback problem?"

Blank chewing silence.

"Well, tell me this. Are the blacks going to get an apology?"

Now the torpid face came around, the mouth still contracting in a halo of grease. Gabe Simson was on his feet and moving at him with bristly red eyes. "No more questions."

Whitman was blown right out of the office. The little candy-ass. As the door slapped shut behind him Gabe grabbed his dong contemptuously and started on his pizza.

Then back to driving the team. He put in no new plays for Green Bay. He planted himself with his coaches, his face grim under the snaking bright S on the front of his cap, and worked hell out of everybody who could walk. They were reeling. Their muscles were sloppy with exhaustion. Their breath sobbed into frozen vapor. Eyes glazed in leaking faces, they hauled themselves into position and pushed, falling like sacks of grain, into each other. The sky froze into dusk between the scraps of temple on top of the stands and still he drove them. "Hit! Can't you do the job, Wilson? Do it, or make room for somebody that can."

Ass-kicker mean, cracking that whip. They were all dying and vomiting and shit like that, and still he kept it on. Talk about *hairy!* The whites were just trying to last it out. The blacks were too whipped down to have any feeling at all. Coach, he was one hard dude. He was *bad*. It got to you, all day long this "Die, motherfucker. Die or go home."

Fire the team up for the Packers? Crap. He laid it on and laid it on, he all but destroyed them, and on Sunday they won it 7–6. To be sure, it was not exactly an artistic triumph. Grover was only 5 for 16, and the winning TD was scored by Fred Dickie on a 27-yard run with a recovered fumble. Still, it was a win, and after eight straight losses it was a biggie. It broke the ice. As time ran out and the players came puffing off the field, a smile furrowed Gabe's broad face. Down in the locker room he hugged people, croaked joyous obscenities and swatted white asses and black. "You're beautiful," he burbled to Dickie and splotched a kiss on his streaky face. "Dynamite," he said to Daddy Wilson. "You played a dynamite game."

Fallon called him to the phone in the coaches' dressing room. Carson Le Motte was on long distance to congratulate him. "I knew you could do it!" the teeny voice trilled. "We're off the ground at last!"

Gabe was naked, stuffed with game fury and satisfaction. "It's a way to go yet," he said impatiently.

"No, no! Listen! I'm doing what you said about the black demands, Gabe. I'm stalling like you said. Listen, I'll pick them apart, issue by issue. If I give a point it'll be a minor one, fret you not. It's blowing over already. Especially with this win. I just want to say you're fabulous, a veritable steamroller . . . you and me, what a team!"

The tiny electronic voice babbled on, fawned, licked at him, apologized and prostrated before him. Gabe shifted restlessly, scratched under one of his hairy breasts and listened to the voices booming in the shower room. Ellis and Dewey pumped his hand and he forgot Le Motte entirely. The phone finally clicked and he padded back to the shower, humming like a hollow oak filled with bees. Gabe Simson was singing his alma mater, "On Wisconsin."

"There are," Chip observed to Jackie on Monday night, "three things for a person to remember when they fuck with me. Don't. Don't. And don't *never* do it."

He was mysteriously jubilant. Lying next to her in bed, he was releasing mouthfuls of cigar smoke, clouding over the naked bulb that glared down at them.

"Boy, are you ever spacy tonight. But I like you," she said and snuggled against him.

"What else? In your place I'd be wild to get my

hands on me. Ready? Here's another thought for today. It's always brightest just before it gets dark."

"You mean it's always darkest just before dawn, silly."

"I admit lately it's been a trifle on the 'Goodness! Whatever happened to Atlanta?' side. But no more. Gabe's ass has had it. We are coming to the end of the short, short reign of Fatso the First."

"BLACK IS HORSESHIT." Didn't care who wrote it on all the blackboards and everywhere, walls, floors, the mirrors in the shower room even. It landed on him and his brothers like exploding napalm. Instead of going home after practice Daddy went to the Club Mecca, deep in the South Side ghetto, to be with some of his people on the team. They had a king-size Naugahyde booth in the celebrity section, roped off with a twisted golden rope from adoring fans and customers. Serving them was a sleek young fox wearing a neon-glow cocktail skirt. The bandstand was in shadows, but the jukebox was pushing some *sounds:* streaming organ moans and drum thuds, voices wailing. Tucker and Elijah and the others were carrying on and proclaiming and just plain cursing: "Tuk all that kinda stuff I'm gonna ofay mothafucka gonna bust both his knees tomorrow White is horseshit. . . ." And he sat in silence, blazing. They were hot? He was hotter. Anything they said to him he replied, "Ain't sayin nothin yet. Too hot to talk yet."

A thick fur of Louisiana and South Side had grown over his speech.

More patrons. Rounds of drinks sent to them in homage. Menus to autograph. Messages. "He's tactician," said Roger, but he wasn't thinkin nothin. Every idea he got seemed to melt in the swollen bowl of candlelight. "Get the big nigger," the white cats were sayin while they crouched into their stance; that was him and they was specializin on him, and meanwhiles across the field his stands yelled, "Pok chop, pok chop, greezy greezy. Gonna whup Lakeview, eezy eezy." Easy it was not. Got his bad leg twisted after the play till it was twisted 'bout off. They paid for it, but easy it was not. Hunh, hadn't thought a that in yea number of years, Lord God, the Crane Tech high-school game versus that white school in the city playoffs. Some kinda riot after, unh. *P*olice couldn't do nothin packs a kids' buses tipped over gangs roamin the streets blue lights flashin and whirlin an Miss Evans his math teacher layin like a broke umbrella in a puddle of busted glass . . .

Unh, he wasn't nothin but hot. It was time to activate and they was all waitin on him and he wasn't nothin but hot. So he made a phone call and told his brothers he had to be gone for a little bit.

Thirty-five minutes later he was at Chip and Jackie's. To "Hey, what's happening, baby?" he responded, "Nothin much." Accepted a hug from Jackie but refused a drink. Took a seat on the antique couch. Formal. Dignified. Silent.

Jackie could hardly believe her good fortune! Wow! Her face was shining in the black frame of her new Cleopatra wig. She'd been calling all Chip's hangouts, just about crazy, *praying* he wouldn't stay out all night tonight or come home so bombed he couldn't lift a finger, much less something else. But suddenly he'd come tearing in like a madman, asking if Daddy was here yet. This was *it,* Chick, what he'd been waiting for. Clean up the pad, damn it, and as soon as they got into strategy go milk the cats or something. She'd just had time to pick up the *surface,* stick Aphrodite in the bedroom with the kids because she was in heat, zip into her green brocade, wind her hair up under her wig. She was still fastening her bracelet of tiny planets swinging on thready silver chains when Daddy came glowering in.

In her best hostess manner she said, "Daddy, this is Antygoney," introducing him to a fluff of cream and cinnamon with ice-blue eyes. Daddy was up there with Chip for smart, so she bragged on Antygoney's intelligence. "She can even open a door by herself! Isn't that *unreal?*"

Daddy barely nodded, pulling air in and out of his deep nostrils. Quickly Chip said, "Ter-rific. Can she close it behind her on the way out?"

He signaled to her to keep it up. Rattle, rattle, she hardly knew what she was saying. In a breathy, schoolgirl-reciting rush she told about Osiris, who was missing an ear and several square inches of fur, and from there launched into the epic amours of her Oriental queen, Aphrodite, who had been turned down cold by Tony's white Angora but what could you expect from *that* spoiled thing, but she had made it with Zulu and Mickey and Cesare and that gorgeous stripy *monster* from next door, so who could foretell the outcome; personally she hoped it was Zulu—was she talking too much, Chip?

"What?" he said. "Oh, excuse me. I was meditating."

"Hey, really?" she cried before she caught on. He was putting her on about the meditation she was into now with Shirley. What you did was empty your mind and groove on Alpha waves, the ones you put out when you were sleeping. If Chip only *knew!* She was so excited at the *thought* of Shelley Earl that she couldn't even meditate!

"You got enough animal history?" Chip asked Daddy.

He was really uptight, waiting for Daddy to do it, let it out for Christ's sake. And Daddy couldn't or wouldn't. "Proceed, little fox," he said to her. Gentle. Even though his face was a stiff black mask with terrible eyes looking through it. He sort of went for her, always talked to her and introduced her to the colored players and their wives and girlfriends.

"Go ahead," Chip groaned. "Tell him how you put catnip in my Scotch."

"I do *not*," she said, kicking her foot at him. "But you oughta see Christopher when I give him some. He goes round and round in these *orbits!* I mean he goes wild!" She felt so lightheaded, so sort of floating away. Whenever she fell in love there was this kind of summery brightness, but this time, oh, there was the wonderful dark secret too, inside of everything, that was almost too precious. She wanted so bad to tell Chip. He would only say she was kooky though. She wouldn't say one single word, and just as soon as him and Daddy finished their plans . . . "Do you like my new wig?" she asked. "Maybelle and Shirley both say it expands my personality."

Chip laughed and sent her to get more ice cubes. That was to give Daddy a chance to conspiracy with him, but when she came back they were setting up the chess pieces. Her gorgeous decorator set!

"Isn't it gorgeous?" she said to Daddy. "Chip says he couldn't beat the firehouse cat with it. He can't tell what the pieces *are*, but I think it's gorgeous." Daddy took her part and she sniffed, "So there, Earl Hughes."

She backed off to a respectful distance, expecting a super battle of minds. Chip did a lot of relighting his cigar and fiddling with the scar on his cheek, only he had his mind on Daddy and not on the game. While Daddy stared at the board. It was like one of those Westerns where the chiefs gather for a powwow on whether to make war on the settlers, only first they had to sit around the fire and pass the peace pipe.

Her kids snuck in, barefoot, shaggy, their mouths painted with Goofy Grape drink, and flopped down with her and her fat diddledums, Leo. Casey wanted to play too.

"Well, you can't!" she whispered. "It's a game for grownups, not kids."

"Like fuckin, Ma?"

She slapped him across the mouth, then held her hand over it to stop his blubbering. "Shut up! Didn't I tell you not to say that word? Now be quiet and watch."

Rats! She was too jumpy to sit still herself. The program on TV was really *too* glucky and dumb. The only good thing was this divine commercial about old man winter freezing a darling little house practically to death until it got a thermostatic gas furnace with twelve or thirteen months to pay, plus a lifetime guarantee, then it smiled all warm and snuggly and safe just like a baby bird in its nest, while the roly-poly furnace glowed away like anything in the basement.

"Hey, turn it down, will you?" Chip said. Wow, he was about to *faint*, he was sweating Daddy so hard. Well, he didn't want Daddy to shit or get off the pot any more than she did. She had the picture all sketched out and colored to the last detail in her head. Shelley Earl getting all A's and representing his high school on "It's Academic" on Channel—whichever one it was.

"See what's burning," Chip said. "And take the kids with you."

She ordered them back into their bedroom and no fightin, lay down and go to sleep. She sort of danced into the kitchen to get a Pepsi, wishing, wishing, rocking with her green belly. In a litter of coagulated grease, dishes, petrifying pork chops, gobs of dog food drying on newspaper and segments of a stained-glass window. Chanting ever so softly,

"Shake it, shake it, shake it,
Shake it if you can,
Shake it like a milkshake
And shake it once again."

Pretending she was in the fourth grade back on Noble Street. The other girls were walking around her in a circle, real solemn, with their hands locked together, singsonging about some guy going to a fair, she forgot who. Anyhow, they all stopped and done the chorus—shake it, shake it, shake it—while she belted her stomach in and out and switched her skinny hips like mad. Then another girl got to be chosen and they swirled around her in the sunshine and the leaf shadows with the sweet oil and gasoline smell of Miska's Body Shop floating to them from across the street.

"He's had enough time to eyeball it."

She could tell by Chip's voice that whatever he was after he was getting it, which would put him in a really supergood mood—for afterward. She couldn't wait another minute. She was standing with the refrigerator open, breathing in its cold stale breath and wishing, wishing with all her heart. Holding her feather-soft hope inside her, pressing her arms over herself. " 'Course I'm hot or I wouldn't be here . . . play it super cool . . . fear not, his left sweetbread don't know what his right one is doing . . ." It took forever before they got finished and Daddy was towering by the front door in his beret and coat.

"I'll be at the Club Mecca till midnight," he rumbled to Chip. He was a whole lot calmer now that he had come to a decision, only in a hurry to get started. "Bye now, little fox," he said to her.

"Hey, what are you gonna do? Can you tell me?"

Daddy flipped a tall shoulder at Chip. Chip was an icy glitter, his eyes, his teeth, as he said, "Chick, there's gonna be a strike. Daddy is gonna send the ultimatum to Le Motte—stop the stalling, and that includes the apology by Gabe. Everything, the whole package. Or we don't suit up for the Vikings on Sunday."

Her breath stopped. He was putting on his red-ochre jacket!

"You're *not* going *out?*" she wailed. "When will you be back? But you got to know when. You *got* to. Can I come with you, then?" She was trembling. She made her hands into a cup, into a shaking little nest. "Please, oh, please, Chip. Today's the *day!*"

"That it is," Chip said. "Give me a lift to some low dive, Daddy-O. Something *bad.* I'm gonna unwind for a couple days."

"Hey man," Daddy said, asking him to let her come along.

"Can't do it," he said, and her hands broke apart and fell at her sides and the long black fibers of her wig closed over her face, eclipsing it. She didn't really hear him say, "Take care of the livestock, now. Tell you what, you stuff a turkey and I'll be home for Thanksgiving."

It must have been hours and she couldn't stop crying. Casey and Kurt bawled with her and fell asleep and she went on crying, huddled naked among little animal bodies. "Oh stop that," she said to Leo, who was licking her titties, and pushed him away. Today, *today*, the temperature line on her chart had shot up, which meant they could begin Shelley Earl, and Ozymandias had said the day was an extremely productive one for Moon Children, and she hadn't made a single mistake, not one. Chip just didn't like her very much; he really liked Dori, in spite of they'd broken up. He was too far above her; she was just a dumb piece, a phone call and a fuck. She shivered. There were tears pushing up into her throat and eyes. Desperate, she called up Dori, but she was out with Tommy or somebody. She called Shirley. She called the Club Mecca and, swallowing at the cold slippery tears, asked to speak to Mr. Wilson.

"It's the next exit," Lips said, and the orange Starfire 360 swerved out of the traffic, stuffed to the windows with big confused bodies, blurts of anger and helpless profanity, sweat and beery inspirations.

"How do you know they're gonna strike?" they kept asking him.

"I told you," Lips said savagely. "Shirley said so."

"Well, screw them. We'll win by ourself," Hawk said.

"Get your head outa your ass," Lips snarled. "There's no way we're gonna take the Vikings without the niggers." It tore his nuts off: Chip and his niggers had it made. Chip had pulled it off, the little pisser had pulled it off.

On the radio the Led Zeppelin thumped and twanged. "I hope they do strike and get their ass fired," said Jay.

Furiously Lips informed him, "They ain't gonna get fired, stupid."

"Who's stupid?"

"You're stupid, s-t-u-p-i-d."

Narrow highways angled off at wicked tangents into the darkness. The fields were prickly with dried cornstalks. "Hey, Lips!" they grumbled more and more fiercely. "Where the fuck are we? This is your fat idea."

"Just hold your fucking water," Lips said. "Turn right up there and keep going till you hit a pizza factory." The shopping centers were closing; darkness swallowed the dim glows of the tract houses. He was so pissed off he must have blew a turn. When Shirley broke the news about the strike the guys had asked him, Now what? And there wasn't one goddam thing in the world to do. Great! Finally he was running it, and the only thing he could come up with was Let's go out to Flossmoor and check with Dickie. That cockroach-watcher. But at least it would take some of the weight off of him—if he could find Fred's house.

"Hey, man," said Bebo, "this don't cut it."

"We better ask a gas station or something," Lips said, but the next two gas stations were closed. God*dam* that Chip. The guys were about ready to kick his ass off. The road jolted between decapitated lines of boxcars.

"Piss on this noise," Gooch snarled.

A headlight splashed over the windshield, dissolving

the road sign, and the car raced on, heading at sixty miles an hour up shit crick.

"Hey, will you *kindly* tell me what you're celebrating?"

"Sure thing. I'm celebrating the little mouse that nibble-nibbled off all the roots of the whole fucking apple tree. Not ordinary apples, you understand. Golden apples."

Maybelle's wide sweet face crinkled with effort. "Like on TV?"

"Exactly." Bending like a demented priest over the eight glasses of vodka, Chip tuned them into a ladder of notes, taking scrupulous sips to adjust the pitch and then tapping the rims of the glasses with a steak skewer. "We'll start the game as soon as we get this right," he said, "and not before. Okay, places everybody. Put your hand over your heart, my love." Humming and clanking, his streaky bald head darting this way and that, he performed "The Star-Spangled Beaner."

"You mean *banner*, Chip Hughes. Are you ever sick in the head!"

He quaffed off the fullest glass, coughed and applied a handkerchief to his eyes. "Plays hell with the melody, doesn't it? Maybe we better just finish these off and do it solo."

She cringed under the waiter's frown. "Why," she quavered, "why are you acting like this?"

"More patriotic this way. Can't start a game without the national anthem." Attending to the nuances of harmony and phrasing, he regaled the patrons of the Four Seasons with his rendition of "The Star-Spangled Boner." Maybelle departed. Shunned, that's what he was, shunned.

By a warm-up girl for the Stags at that. As he took his leave the headwaiter, in his autumn-colored tux, asked him for the steak skewer. In reply Chip handed him another with which to defend himself. "Swine," he said and advanced to run him through, pointing to the scar on his cheek. "Heidelberg," he said significantly.

His ochre jacket slung over one shoulder, he made his way toward Old Town. Broken darkness. Glints, watery shines and fogs blooming around the billboards and neon signs. An old hag passing out religious tracts hissed venomously when he said, "I'll take forty. No, make it forty-five. The coaches have strayed from righteousness too."

"There's a light drizzle, fans," he said briskly. "Temperature up in the sixties, amazing for this time of year. T. S., you snowman builders." Slipping between parked cars, he placed his skewer on a fender where it would be handy for the kills. Shaking out his jacket and stamping his foot in the grand manner, he shouted "*Toro! Toro!*" And took the hurtling Oldsmobile past him with a superb red flourish, his back arched, his jacket slapping the flank of the car as it yawed away with its horn bawling. "I'll never be as cute as Belmonte," he said to nobody at all, "but maybe I can win your heart with my technique."

He worked closer and closer to the cars in slashes of wet light and wind, pivoting, swirling his bruised jacket around his hips in classic veronicas. "Come on," he yelled at the dark windows. "Let's hear it! *Olé*, you assholes." Hands clasped over his drenched head, he paraded the empty street. "Louder!" he said, scooping his arms. "More phone numbers, more frilly underthings!"

Then he took up his cape once more. For this one, he swore, he would be awarded both fenders and the muffler. A sporty little Vega came buzzing toward him behind its headlights. Chip, leaning out with his draggled cape, caught a glimpse of the pale, deflated face behind the wheel filling up with excitement, with hot sweet passion. He threw himself back from the thing veering, charging right at him. "Tut, tut, tut," he said to the midget skidding and then racing away. "You have to buy a ticket before you get to do that."

But he'd had enough bullfighting, not that he was all that shook up or even so teed off at the slob trying to turn him into an ornament on his radiator. He was cold and wet. In small collapses he let himself down onto the curb, too disgusted to put on his smashed jacket. "The bitch," he said out loud, "the stupid bitch." That beautiful campaign, that masterpiece of double and triple dealing, angles linking with angles inside of angles, playing the blacks and the whites, playing Whitman and Dickie and Le Motte and Daddy and Two-Ton . . . A real beauty, damn it, completely out of sight, aiming all the time at a strike, and beyond that at Biggie, and beyond that . . .

Nothing simple like Fran Tarkenton at Minnesota lining up players till he got his coach out of there, Norm Van Brocklin, the great Dutchman himself. This was really *wily*, and, man, he'd completely had it *knocked*; he'd had Biggie in the crunch. Biggie would never have apologized, never; he'd have played the taxi squad first, and that would have been all she wrote for Two Ton. And beyond that was *it*. The ultimate. His starting position, his team back again.

And Jackie had mucked it all up with her pussy. Brought it all down by jumping in the sack with Daddy. The stupid horny broad. But why, *why* would that make Daddy back out and kill the strike? How could one dumb white piece do that? Maybe Mr. Soul felt he'd betrayed the black cause or something. Who could tell? Anyhow, at practice today it was clear right away that school was out: Simson was kicking butt and the blacks were working on that plantation. And Daddy, the fire-breather of a day ago, wouldn't even look at him.

Crop forecast: a surplus of golden apples next year. A goddam fucking glut. Enough to bring down the international price of gold and save the dollar.

But what really frosted him was the way that pile of meat and shit had lucked out, won it with a break like that. And his fair-haired boy, the cluck in the fairy story that stood around with his mouth hanging open and his thumb up his ass had won the princess and the kingdom like always.

And so the celebration (the vodka solo and the great-new-model-loaded-with-extra-features-so-luxurious-you-forgot-how-rugged-it-was-power-steering bullfight) was actually a wake. A wake for a rodent that didn't get it done. Super Mouse was back in Sunset Acres.

Was Fred Dickie steaming! He
sweated ass all day at practice, then
spent three hours doin a one-minute
commercial. Three hours jumpin in a
pool and climbin out and sayin, "Next
to sacking a quarterback, exercising at
the Chicago Health Salons turns me
on most." Three fuckin hours of that.
His head was full of water and his
elbow was screwed up worse.
Goddamit, he'd took two years of
speech and diction courses and still
it was "No, no, no, Mr. Dickie." That
time it lacked pizzaz, that time he was
too wooden or he left out a word.
Finally he lost it all. Come up blowin
and drippin, his elbow hurtin like hell.
And nothin. He opened his mouth in
the streamin water and nothin come
out.

Then the faggots say, "I guess
we'll just have to dub." Why the fuck
didn't they say that in the first place
and save all the grievance? Fuckin

faggots. They turned his guts. Their idea of a joke was "My *dear*, Harvey is so *changed!* He got into a fanny-reducer backwards and now he's in *love!*" Fuckin faggots.

On top of that, tryin to make it home and into the sack by midnight, he put a $150 scratch on the Caddy. Some hippie was dancin around in the middle of the street and wavin a red coat at him. So like a dumb asshole he cut the wheel to miss him and sideswiped a Chevy. Should of gone back and left him for somebody to scrape off a wall.

Pissed? He wasn't nothin but. Lousy season. Team wasn't shit. Fucked-up elbow wasn't healin good. On top of that it was him that won the Packer game. Single-handed. It was the perfect time to renegotiate, but that jagoff lawyer still said wait till the season was over. The niggers got what they wanted. But was that good enough for them? No, they were gonna strike.

That's what really blew his stack. Bullshit the strike had been called off; that was bullshit. Those coons were puttin up a smoke screen. Tomorrow they were gonna fly with the rest of the team to Minneapolis as ordinary as you please. Then just before "The Star-Spangled Banner" and the entire nation glued to their TV, whammo! They pull a sit-down strike. It was all bullshit they had pulled in their horns.

In front of him a mammoth truck farted up the ramp to the expressway. It was foggy. Off to the side and way above, the haze had a kind of a misty radiance and it started to come to him. Like an inspiration, the answer. Like a vision or something. Growing in the sky coming around in the windshield as he turned with the ramp and he could feel the answer inside of him, stronger and stronger, collecting in the ripples and blinks PHILLIPS 66, growing bigger and bigger.

He fuckin *knew* how to stop the strike and save the team!

At the first exit he got back off and tore ass north toward Freyr's. Up until now he hadn't been enough of a leader. That was his big defect. His way was, he didn't say much and let his actions do the talking. But you had to take charge too. Coach even called most of the defensive signals from the sidelines. And that hurt. He was proud of his rep as a one-man gang. He was All-Pro, for God's sake, in a class with greats of the past like Bill George and Ray Nitschke and Dick Butkus.

Well, he was gonna be a leader. Startin now. He was gonna put the plug in by himself and stop the strike. Nip it in the bud by nippin the ringleader of it in his big black bud—hey, that was a good one. He was gonna cold-cock that big jig Wilson—no, he didn't want to put him out of action. Only rattle his dishes for him and say that was only a sample; he'd tear his goddam arm off and beat him to death with it if there was a strike.

Coach didn't allow fightin on or off the field. But this was private. Between two individuals. He would put the fear of God in all those coons, and the beautiful part was, Daddy lived on the South Side somewheres and he could take care of the whole situation in ten minutes. Drop in, kick ass and keep goin because the expressway to Flossmoor cut right through Cannibaltown.

All he needed was Daddy's address, and somebody at Freyr's was sure to have it. The bartender sent out Christmas cards to all the Stags, the shines included, so he would know.

He stopped for a shot of Early Times and said, "What do you see after every fuckin play? Jigs on opposite teams pickin each other up and pattin ass. That ain't football."

A guy wanted to talk about the Viking game, but he didn't. That wasn't where his head was at now. Pretty sloshed and goin on automatic pilot, he made it to Freyr's.

So of course the crud had the night off. And nobody else knew where Daddy lived at. Damn, he was all jacked up to get a piece of Daddy too. There was a hassle about jigs, but everybody was on the same side. On top of that, he was hungry and tired besides. So he ordered from the kitchen and added, "Bring me a pitcher a orange juice first." Margie could wait another half hour; he was pissed at her too.

Spilling her guts to that magazine writer. "The Many Silences of Fred Dickie." The ones like his psyching up for a game silence, okay. But "Fred don't mingle easy," that was somethin else. Including how they met in high school, for Chrissake. And how his buddy's girlfriend fixed him up and he never said a word for weeks, just rode her around on the hog.

All right, he was shy. Fuck, why tell the whole world? Now it didn't matter about the tailor-made suits and all the lessons. His image was back to something they threw raw meat to. A cave man or the missing link. Something on all fours, and it really hurt.

A female—what a terrible piece a livestock she was, at least forty years old—came over to his table while he was grubbing up. He told her to get lost.

"Hey, Fred!" Now it was Poppo. And he was really sloshed, bombed out of his mind. Staggering around with this withered-up old flower-seller on his shoulders, a gypsy or something, handing one flower to everybody in the place. "Fred a whole bunch," he slurped, his face all red and laughing. "Free . . . my saint's day . . . celebratin St. George."

Up there straddling his wide neck, the old hag picked around in these bunches of wilted flowers she must of got off of a grave or something.

Fred said, "Thanks." He didn't like to be disturbed while he was eating. But Poppo was on the team, and when he felt like playin ball he could do it somethin special. Only he didn't always feel like it.

Plop! Mangy roses came down all over his fried oysters, his roast-beef sandwich, his pizza, his plate of ham slices.

"What the fuck!" Dickie got to his feet, brow ridges bunching and muscle ropes moving the big plates of bone in his back.

The old witch laid these brown, four-tooth smiles on him. Like it was a favor to screw up a guy's meal, for Christ's sake. "Some more, *moja mila majaka*," Poppo said. By now Dickie was sieving air through his teeth. Her tiny seed-eyes shining at him and her tiny feet kicking, she dumped messes of roses and different kind of flowers all over everything, into his pitcher of beer and over everything.

"Poppo," Fred panted, "that is *all*."

Poppo beamed. "Saint's day. St. George . . . and the dragon."

The nut. He was some kind of nut when he got sloshed. Pitching boozily around, Poppo lugged the old witch away to another table. In a minute he was asleep in one of the leafy alcoves. But the old witch, she was like a handful of rags, she kept giving him these mud-pie smiles and flapping a tiny branch of a hand at him. Even after he said savagely, "Get fucked, will you?"

His hands moved in the greasy leftovers, acting out what he'd like to do to her. On the field his temper was one of his biggest pluses, but off of it it was his worst. He wasn't about to waste ten bucks on another meal, so he ate what he could of the garbage, then went to the can and took a five-pound crap. And he was still burning. Sucking at the food in his teeth, he read all the stuff on the walls, squinting in the tan light and the stink of piss and chemicals. Names, initials, phone numbers, "Cubs 8 Cards 6 May 1st," "Shirley sucks," with a drawing of it, "White Power," fuckin jigs anyhow. His slow stumbling thoughts wandering among grievances, he did the legends and art work all the way back to last year. Didn't they ever paint this joint? He was in a more disgusted mood than ever.

And that terrible old snake was at his table when he got back. She told him her name was Shirley and they had been introduced several times. "Move on, bitch," he said to her.

"Ah-ah-ah," she said brightly. "I know something you don't know. And you have to ask me nice or I won't tell you."

"Get the fuck away from me."

"All right. If you don't want Daddy Wilson's address."

"Huh? What?" The TV behind her was welling up loud pictures, scraps of the late movie, and he had to sort out her words from that, groping for the lost outlines of—"Hey, yeah!" It was all coming back to him, coming with a double force. "Hey, for real? Dynamite! Whyncha say so before?"

She pouted at him. "You told me to get lost, if you remember."

"Well, tell me now, goddamit!"

"I can't, Mr. Grouchy. I don't personally know black players, but one of my girlfriends does and it's home in my apartment. Right next to the phone."

"Okay, let's hit it." He bought a fifth of Beam, took a couple of swigs and they cut out for her place in pouring rain, a fucking cloudburst. "What I'm gonna do to that big black prick," he said violently. "Him and me are gonna get to *know* each other. Lemme tell you somethin. I played some hard motherfuckers that were black. And I never seen one that had balls in the clutch. All of 'em are chickenshit in the clutch." His hurt arm hobbling at gestures, he whipped the car through sweeps of rain. "What really hacks me is, against another jig, sure they're gonna hit in a key situation. It's bread in their mouth. But not if it don't make a key difference. No way a nigger's gonna just cripple another nigger. And that's the hate you gotta have for good competition. That's why I like to go head on head with a jig. It gives me more of a hate."

He was so hot that he was making splats of sound for words. She told him to take a left. A big-ass Chrysler cut him off from the turn lane, its rear tires spurting at him. The swollen-up feeling inside of him went with it. He drew up alongside and lowered his window, bellowing, "You better watch it, asshole."

So the guy gives him the finger!

A gust of fire went up into his head. He was out of his car. Drenching sprays, long smears of color on the rain-flickering Chrysler, he was clawing at the door handle, yanking at the locked green to get at the whitish face laughing inside and the Chrysler powered away in spumes of flying water.

He hurled himself back in the Caddy and took off after it. "My God, oh please," the slit was babbling and good deal! The bastard caught a red and had to pull up. He slammed to a stop behind it jerked open his trunk and found a jack handle stooping into a run as he came around and pounced on the Chrysler slugging with the iron, plunging it in the glistening body up to his knuckles and wrestling it back out clobbering beautiful the slicky metal grunts of red smashes glass a silver hubcap rolled away splitting the whole side caving in.

The light jumped to green, the mangled car slid away from him and he gunned after it, rain blackness riddled with lights tire trails waved frantically in slips of glassy water reflections his chest was kicking and wild swaying red fog, he hurtled out into the rain again and really teed off this time, again and again and again crashes the eyesocket of a headlight gouges and trenches his blood was thundering beautiful, man, it was beautiful. At the next red he sprang off a hunching bowlegged run up onto the roof slipped off and clambered back up bashing it in going for the windshield splinters starred out over the screaming face and now he could hear the screaming better.

His elbow messed up worse soaked to the skin pants squishing to his legs breathing hard—the melted-together streaming slowed down into hunks: he was in the Caddy, the black street was empty with rain, whatshername was blubbering. His knuckles were tore all to hell . . .

The bastard had got away. Caught a yellow and coming hard forty yards behind he had to hit the brakes, bellowing in the red rain as he had to watch the fucked-up Chrysler scuttle away dripping glass and metal. "One more light," he puffed, his blood slamming. "Just one *more*, motherfucker."

"My God," she said, shuddering, "talk about weird! I don't believe it. Neither one of you would run a light!"

"That's the law," he said. He hunted the guy for a while but no dice. He had really fucked him over good, though. The feeling of it blazed sweetly in his guts. "Did I use him or not? Did you see me? I really used him." He was sopping wet and his suit was all ripped but man, it was worth it. He was feeling great. Evened up for the scratch in his Caddy and then some. He grinned into his dripping mustache and stuck out a palm for her to slap. "Lay it on me."

She patted at it with flattering awe. "Wow. You have some kind of a temper, don't you?"

"I just don't take any crap," he said. "From nobody." He laughed, rubbing at his elbow. "Did you see him take off? Like a ruptured goose. It'll be a while before *he* gives anybody the finger." Was he ever up! The old adrenalin was really flowin, the way it done in a game. You all put your hands together and yelled "Stags get it rolling!" and charged out there, man what a rush.

Whatsherass said, "Wasn't it lucky there weren't any cops around?"

Even that. Even the idea of Margie gettin on to him for breakin his word, also Le Motte. Nothing could bring him down from this beautiful high. They got to her pad and he finished off the Beam. "What the fuck?" he said at the strobe light whirling shocks of color into his eyes. A fuzzy pink dragon leered on the rug whatsherass was sloughing off her clothes and offering what a putrid old bag. "For*get* it," he said. Pretty sloshed but was he ever up, that car thing what a rush he was dizzy. Guitars clanged in sleepy dazes slithering worms of light. "Hey, look out!" he mushed. "I didn't put no moves on you."

Somehow she had his pants open and her scaly old mouth was gobblin and lickin at his meat. "Not before a game," he said, reeling to his feet and trying to work the zipper. "You're garbage. But that's not the reason. My build-up time. Even Margie don't get none build-up time." He aimed himself at the front door and banged into his own ballooning reflection. "Gotta psych up for a . . . concentrate or I don't hit good." The fuckin words were all melted together slushy with that music it sounded like a dozen-car pile-up, hey, did he ever burn that asshole beautiful rush.

"You can do anything you want to me." Pieces of ass spinnin on the wall ferris wheel round and round light goin round and round took a terrific shot right in the face shook it off. "You wanta do it to me there?" Ass joggling up to him swaying a glaze-faced doll rocking toward him. "Gotta love to hit," he mumbled. "Gotta get that super high and hit . . . the way I play my position is. My style is. Clobber everything that comes into my zone. Basically. First of all. I plug the middle and also . . . I go stormin and all-out fuckin bury the quarterback."

He wasn't sure if the words were comin out at all he might be just thinkin it. The beauty of it rose hotter and hotter inside him, he was all psyched up, he acted it out as he tried to say it, "A receiver cuts through my area, you know? And he's down. That's why I'm called 'the ax' or 'the grim reaper' or 'a green funnel a terror' that's another one. Or like that. The wall heaved over and came jolting at him. Say it's a sweep and it's formin left which I can smell it better than anybody in the game and I'm hand-fightin, I'm tearin shirts and whackin off helmets and whammo! the center is out of it, screams, groans, he took a belt from the side but he stayed on his feet face-masking him the wave of blockers was crumpling the end and the outside linebacker, oh, oh, but he had that beauti-ful shot comin across, my God, Fred, and at that split second when the ball carrier was about to turn the corner and really go, whammo! he came drivin in behind the blockers and blew him, oh, oh God, outa bounds it was beautiful gettin in a extra punch on top of it for extra measure a bloody tangle of broken teeth so you see my style . . . That's how I . . . sorry about the ass but I gotta." Sleepy one eyelash hung by a thread a lot a blood was comin from her mouth what? He was too sleepy too full of smoke leanin against a wall and workin on that fuckin zipper.

He took another shot at the door and made it this time and drove home in his sleep and went to sleep.

Next morning it was like Monday. After a game, sort of blank and all his muscles worked out. Margie was pretty pissed off. "And what hassle did you get into now?" she hollered at him. "Look at your clothes! And your hands!"

He sat on the bed in his shorts. His hands had dried blood stickin the hairs together on em. One of his knuckles felt like it was busted not countin the elbow. He shrugged: no big deal.

"Well?"

He shrugged. How the hell could he tell her; he'd lost everything except a couple of melty hunks of it, some jig and a Chrysler, oh yeah; he'd opened that Chrysler up like a can opener. And some pig tried to pick him up.

"Well, at least I didn't have to go and bail you out," she said. So it was gonna be okay after she laid some bitchin on him.

He took a shower and ate breakfast, ham and eggs and home fries and two quarts of orange juice. His knuckle was busted all right. He could still play with shots in it, though. He banged the balls around for an hour on the pool table in the rec room. Before he took off for O'Hare to catch the plane he had to give his little girls a ride on his bike. Holding them careful, soft little handfuls that looked exactly like him like in a little mirror. Round and around the block they buzzed, squealing and waving to Mommy. When they both had their turn they begged him like always to make it go up like a horsie. He said, "Okay, but just one," and popped a wheelie, chuckling as he threw out the clutch and made the bike rear up snorting for them.

Dori and Tommy were lying in bed. He was asleep and at first, ever so lightly, she ran one fingernail along his arm and down his leg. Then began stroking the still heavy flesh lying on its wet golden hair, caressing it, charging it again with blood.

He half opened his eyes and said, "Huh?"

"Ssh! Daddy and Mummy are gonna play horsie." His eyes closed. She kissed the throbbing penis, nuzzled it erect and cautiously, ever so cautiously, knelt over him and spread the urgent mouth between her legs. Sank onto him, moving her hips a little and clamping her muscles tight around it. Pushed down harder and moved sweetly, riding, riding.

Drove it deeper inside herself, hands on her waist, riding there. In the bedroom mirror she could see her naked body take the TV light and toss it sweetly. In his sleep he began instinctively to move with her and woke up with a grimace of pain.

"I'm sorry, Tommy. I don't want to hurt you. Let *me* do all of it." She moved on top of him, going blurry, and then the room whirlpooled and the lovely contractions took her faster and faster and she was there, lying on him and breathing hard, like the little girl who ran naked between the tall green rows of corn leafing over her head.

She rolled over and sighed, floating in the warm milky dreams of her body. In a minute, with a stifled grunt, Tom got out of bed and stretched his bruised arms. Then he limped off to the kitchen to get himself a Coke.

Never in her life had she seen anybody take a pounding like the one the Vikings had given him on Sunday. The team fell apart. Nobody blocked or tackled; half the time the relay man came in with a garbled play, the offense lined up wrong, and while Tommy was motioning a setback to the other side, whistles were blowing for delay of game. There were quarrels in the huddle, and Tommy kept looking helplessly to the sidelines because the Vikes knew the play. It was dreadful, offsides and fumbles on the wrong count, and all the long afternoon purple jerseys crashed in on him and he was thrown to the turf, stormed under, blind-sided, clubbed with a taped forearm by a charging end, beaten and beaten and beaten till she was in tears in front of the set.

Tommy eased into bed beside her in slow creaks. Her eyes were wet again, and all she could make out was the can of Coke glimmering on his chest. And his face: blank.

"Tommy, Tommy," she said, kissing the welts, the

hump of crushed muscle on the calf of his leg, the dark stains in the golden scrubs of hair.

She put her head on his breathing chest. Deep in the arched chapels of bone and flesh she could feel the strokes of his heart, drumming in there, and feel the blood beating out into his hurt young body, strong tides pushing all the way out into his prone feet and hands. She tasted his sweat, mineral-salty, oozing out of him like fresh sap. She breathed in his smell, the sweat smell all mixed up with the woody fragrance of his hair and his shaving lotion and his sperm.

She coiled herself around him, pulling his face down to her breasts, cupping them into his sleepy mouth with little cries. She wanted him so much it hurt till he was inside her swollen oh God beautiful her hands on his slugging buttocks taking him into herself with long pulling motions of her legs, long sucking pulls, again and again and lost, she'd let go and lost it all again, kicking out blind and lost in great sluices, delirious pours, and sinking whirling under again . . .

"Oh, Tommy," she whispered when she had groped back some of the way. "We shouldn't have."

"Unh."

"You're too banged up to move." She snuggled her butt against his panting stomach, soaking in his sweat and hers mingled together. "It's all your fault, you know," she said, flopping over to pout at him. "If you weren't so damn attractive I wouldn't be acting like this."

She was happy and *full*. His sweat. Her body felt as if it had just been rained on. "Tommy? Could I ask you a question? Sort of a personal one?"

"Unh."

"Well, just exactly how does a man *know* he's in love? I mean, for a woman it has to be different."

He hiked up on his elbows, and even in the washes of TV light she could tell he was blushing. "I don't wanta talk about it," he said, but she pestered it out of him. "Boy . . . well . . . say you see some real great chick walking down the street and, you know, you can't see them taking a crap. I mean, in your mind, you know? Then you know you're psyched out."

"I see," she said.

"Some chicks, you can't see them doing anything else except sit on a pot. I mean, they fit there best, you know?" His mouth was stumbling. "Other chicks, you can only see them floating along like that one in the Dodge commercial, in a kinda thin dress? With them I keep trying to see them taking one. Marsha's the only one I never could, so I knew I was in love."

She was spitting mad. All right, she was madly jealous, she admitted it. But to think Tom could see her like that—it was the stupidest definition of love she'd ever heard. "Now I'll tell you a love story," she snapped. "On Friday night Fred Dickie put Shirley in the hospital. And you never saw such a mess in your life. All her teeth knocked out, her nose flattened and one eye permanently screwed up. They had to put five hundred stitches in her face."

"Wow! Why would he do that?"

"Who knows? Maybe somebody took away his tire. Anyhow, it pisses me off, all the Annies and jocks, I have to do it for them. *I* had to get a hot-shot lawyer and file suit. We're gonna put it to Dickie *and* the Stags *and* the league. They're all going to bleed for it. They've never been able to stop him from tackling with his head, and we can prove brain damage in the line of duty—if we can find a brain."

What she didn't tell him was that there was something more she could do. If she wanted she could put the screws on Carson Le Motte and fix it so Mr. Hughes, not Tommy, would start against the Chargers. The Shirley deal was hush-hush, absolutely no publicity and settle out of court, but she didn't mind a little treachery one bit. If Le Motte got hard-nosed about it, why Dickie was Page One material and Whitman would keep the pot boiling.

But she couldn't do that to Tommy, not even for Chip. She was turning full circle. Her whole scheme shot to shit and she couldn't be happier. She would never do anything to hurt Tommy again. She couldn't even stay mad at him—the poor thing, already he'd fallen still beside her, staring numbly at the TV. It was so sad, all that wonderful delight he used to take in things. His top front teeth were still loose from that hit in the Giant game. They were beginning to turn gray and he wouldn't do anything about it! His whole face sagged.

"Listen to me," she said. "Are you listening? You were sharper against the Vikes. Everybody says so. The team is shot. That racial stuff finished it off. Nobody put out. Tucker was running patterns like a heart patient—"

His mouth hung open. He wasn't snakebit, nothing that simple. He had given up on himself. He just went through the motions, took his hammering bravely and stumbled on. And it was her fault. She had crossed his wires and now it was like pressing a Xerox button and the light blinking red, red every time because it was jammed inside.

"We're going out to eat," she said crisply. "I'll call Li-bary and you two can toss the ball on the way. You like that, remember?" Desperate to lift him somehow, she tugged at him, smiled up into his defeated face. "Okay?"

"Okay."

Li-bary came over, dragging one leg himself and muttering, "Man, that sixty-one is a *bear*." But they played catch down the alley, hobbling and tossing a toy football Tommy had found, a little plastic job punctured all over with holes. Warming up for a game, he would stand on the fifty-yard line flipping awesome slingshots at the left and right goal posts, and it gave him a buzz to try to get twenty yards with this goofy ball.

"That's putting something on it," she said when he began to zap it instead of just lobbing it. Li-bary made a one-handed grab. The ball came snaking back, and Tommy bounded after it like a cat. Their shouts banged in the neat garbage cans and garages behind the three-flats. This was more like it. Dori trotted after them, clapping it up hopefully.

But then he stopped again, simply quit.

She ran over to him, scared at how fallen his shoulders were. "Hey, man," Li-bary puffed worriedly.

"Please, Tommy," she urged. "All you need is five completions in a row." He walked like a zombie, walked slowly back toward his apartment. He wasn't hungry.

Li-bary gave her a lift home. He let out a sigh like a buffalo breaking wind and said he wasn't all that optimistic Tom would live out the season. "I know, I know," she said.

Maybe, oh God, maybe he *should* sit out the last four games. His running was strong, of course, but he wasn't really improving except for his footwork and timing. He was mostly just being smashed, torn into pieces, and that fat retard Simson had only one motto: root hawg or die.

But pulling Tommy—it would break his heart. He would think Coach had given up on him too. And now she didn't want to hand the team back to Chip. Even that miserable set of retreads.

Besides, Chip was dangerous. When he got it going he could carve anybody up with those short passes, and for brainy calls there was nobody close to him. Tommy might never get his spot back. She was working her way up a blind alley with Chip in her right hand and Tommy in her left.

Scrambling out of bed, she phoned George to ask his opinion. She'd forgotten. All *that* one could think about was his busted romance with Chip. He was sure worried about Chip, Dor. Chip had parted company with Jackie, but instead of moving back in with him he'd holed up in a motel out near the airport and could she, maybe . . .

"I don't know where he puts his shoes these days," she said. "It's not under my bed."

She was sitting in her cubicle at the office the next morning, up to her ass in the chewing-gum campaign. Oh hell, she'd forgotten to call layout. Weldon popped his bald face into the doorway. He seemed to be having a nervous breakdown, and where was Alfredson? She was just as confused as ever about Tommy and pissed at herself and Chip, too.

Flip a coin, then, Dori—do something. She put in a call to Le Motte. After a longish delay the secretary said he was in conference.

"Do tell," Dori said. Instantly she was wide awake with anger, sharp. "Honey, you just tell him two words, 'Fred' and 'Dickie,' you got that? Good girl. And tell him he's having lunch with Miss Frazier at Sage's East. Twelve o'clock. Ri-ight. That a girl."

But then she wandered to the glass wall overlooking North Michigan Avenue. Across the straining and slipping traffic a building was coming down. A burly yellow crane was slugging with a two-ton iron ball. The dark cornices fell, arches tottered, leaned drunkenly and crashed into scraps of snow. Yawning, she got under way again, drifting in a warm half trance. God, she stayed turned on all the time. He dissolved her cool like nobody ever could. Her body kept remembering him, naked under her clothes and dreaming, yearning for him again, dreaming and then, oh, filling with rich gluts of summer. The high priestess of the sack was just one of the females now.

Herb Fisher rang her at ten o'clock. Mr. Magnificent Seven himself was in town hustling for a cigarette company.

"No can do," she said. "Not free tonight."

"Hell with that noise. Late-date the bastard."

"I'm tied up. I got sixty thousand hours of homework to do on that gum campaign."

IBM typewriters hummed and popped, phones jarred and she drifted past her cubicle into the john. Her eyes were dry and burning in the mirror. The surface drew her, drew her toward her nervous, scrutinizing face. "Mirror, mirror on the wall," she said crazily. "Who's the fairest of them all? Me or Marsha? Careful now, because I don't mind seven more years of bad luck at all."

She was feeling very spaced. She had a thirteen-aspirin headache and her forehead was on fire, but when she took her temperature the shining vein turned to ice at some ridiculous number like 91.

Still, she put Le Motte away in less than three hors d'oeuvres. She'd kind of hoped he would tell her to kiss his fanny when she said, "Much as I hate to snitch, Carsie . . ." And he did call her a bitch, a double-crossing, blackmailing Judas bitch.

"Let's just say"—she grinned— "I've got you by the seedless grapes and I'm taking an extra squeeze."

"Well, I can't do it," he informed her. "I can't *make* Gabe start Hughes! The coaching domain is absolutely and one hundred percent in his area."

"Fiddle dee-dee. You tell Fatass he goes along with this or his precious All-Pro Dickie goes bye-bye. Rentzel had to be traded for a little *faux pas* like exposing himself, remember?"

As she was standing up in the booth he waggled his exquisitely clipped head in admiration. "You're a real stabber," he said. "I wish I had you on my team."

"Couldn't make that team," she said. "I'm not hung that good." She went gliding away, but outside she collapsed into a tripping run for the nearest shop. Escaping from her headache into a shimmery maze of furs and scents, faceless mannequins, patterns, fabrics.

She spent more time buying Tommy a shirt than she had on saving his life.

If she was saving his life. There was more to it than keeping him from getting killed. She had to be sure, and her mind was a scramble, a little girl's junk drawer. But way down at the bottom of it, razor-edged and dark and terrible, was something she *was* sure of. There was a hole, a fatal hole in Tommy's quarterbacking. Some one vital piece was missing.

It was up to her to find it, too, because Two-Ton and his brain trust weren't even looking.

And next season would be too late to find it, next week might be too late, even tomorrow. . . . Right about now Simson was taking the ball away from him . . . with poor Tommy already broken. She had fucked up good, getting him benched before finding out. He might be so completely dead that he couldn't be brought back even if she had the missing piece.

There was one, just one place to get it—maybe—if she could get the jelly out of her spine and do her thing. It just killed her to give up even a minute with Tommy, but when he called she told him not to pick her up.

"Okay."

It made a bruise on her heart, the slack hopeless tone of his voice.

"Hey there," she said. "Show a little life. The world hasn't come to an end. It just looks that way."

There was no answer.

"I think I know what you're doing wrong," she lied desperately. "But I want to check it out. I should be at your place by nine."

Wrong again. It was after midnight when she draggled into his bedroom, a complete and total mess. He was asleep with the TV on. She woke him up and let go against his naked chest, sobbing, "You don't know. This is so silly, crying like this when I made out—I did, honey, for real! But it was so horrible, all of it!" He sank back on the bed, bowed and cheerless, pushing at his straw hair. He wouldn't let her turn off the TV. Kneeling between his knees, she blubbered, "You don't believe me, but we got it knocked!" It was insane. She was weeping the magic words like a dirge, the secret that would break the spell and save her dear golden boy. "You know your problem about looking downfield? Unitas had the same hangup when he first started. Brad told me. Look, you can't just look for a receiver—this is so crazy, I can't stop crying. Look, say you're going to run a flag pattern—"

He sat there, limp, castrated.

"You're not even listening!" She wanted to shake him and could only put her sopping face against his legs. "Just trust me. You've got a hot future, kid! Tommy, I made those assholes hire Will Bradberry to work with you—Brad's an alky but he was a great quarterback and —please hold me, will you, and I'll be all right in a second, I promise." Trembling all over, she folded her arms around him. "You know," she sniffled, "I lucked onto Brad afterwards. I'm not smart enough any more to have thought of him myself. I'm missing everything. I just . . . love you."

His smashed young body went back on the bed. His eyes closed.

"Go to sleep. That's right, poor baby." She couldn't stop trembling.

He was snoring on his side. With all her clothes on she crept in next to him, into the warm streams of his breath, shivering with her hideous victory. She had to make Tommy a winner, a champ, another Namath, but it was so completely shitty having to push success on that barrel of guts and his go-go general manager. Having to force them to be winners too. That would melt and go away, though, like a couple of frozen dog turds on the sidewalk.

Chip, never. He was frozen inside her, his eyes going darker when he caught sight of her. Half the team had been piled around him in the Nile Room of the motel, roaring and sweating and slopping down drinks to whoop up his return. "Dori! Hey, Dor, come on have a drink," they all gurgled. Except Chip. "The airport," he said, "is two miles thataway."

"I thought I'd join the ball," she said. "I knew you'd be having one."

Mr. Supercool looked up at her from his drunken menagerie. "Scuse us," he said. "Got to see if her foot fits this glass slipper." Carrying his glass of Scotch, he took her off to a potted cactus out of range. "Nope," he said. "You got round heels but the toes don't fit. Back to your cinders."

"What the hell!" she blustered. "I got your spot back for you—that's right, *I* did it, and I don't even rate a drink. What the hell gives?"

The way he smiled at her. "Well, well, so you didn't cop out after all. You really and truly got it for me."

She couldn't look at him. She told him about Shirley, Le Motte, the whole bit, and he only smirked.

"I said, 'For *me*.' But let it ride. Bless your little heart anyway."

"Well Jee-zuz," she said, but her heart was sliding sideways with guilt and shame. And amazement at herself. Do her thing with this one, huh? Big hairy joke. She'd planned to get him feeling obligated and, when he was thoroughly sloshed, finesse it out of him. But Dragon Lady, super-spy and double agent, CIA girl for twenty jocks, had lost that quick step upstairs.

His face was contemptuous. "Okay, Dori, spit it out. What are you after?"

Her mind flared and went black. "Nothing, Chip. A drink to celebrate is all. But if you want to be an asshole about it . . ." She made a fake of leaving, actually wheeled and took a couple of steps. And had to come back, her face smeared red with humiliation, while he laughed at her.

Somebody shouted, "Come on back, you-all. If you wanna screw we'll close our eyes."

Chip waved them down. "Take your time," he said to her. "I'll just relax here and watch that evening sun go down."

"It's been down for hours, Chip."

"Ah, that explains it." He was having a real cool blast for himself. God, God, what a dunce she was. Of course, he *had* to hate her for switching to the man who'd taken his spot away, and the idea that she'd pulled the string for *him*—she must have been thinking with her snatch to believe he'd buy that one.

"Well?"

Finally, in a horror of shame she had to blurt it out. "Okay, don't believe me. But it's your job and . . . just out of curiosity, what *was* the problem with Grover? It wasn't only inexperience and"—she swallowed and said it—"stupidity."

It just killed her. He began to cackle and cough at the same time. "That's better," he said. "You know, it could be motivation. Have you tried throwing him pieces of sugar? Not funny, huh? Let me see, he *does* have some technical problems. Like he stinks. Like I wouldn't choose him for a game of recess football."

She had betrayed Chip, but he'd gotten it all back and more. He'd done it all to her, and now he would tell her to screw off, cunt. Split. Take a flying fuck at the moon. Instead, seeing right into her, he said, "Aw, what the hell. Say 'please.' "

"Please."

"Say 'pretty please.' "

"Oh God! Pretty please."

"We'll skip the part with sugar on it. All rightie, let's see how I can put it so a well-informed slut can get it. Say you're a quarterback and you come up to the line of scrimmage. You're working either against a zone or a man-to-man, okay? Course there are different types of zone, but time does not permit. Anyhow, whatever type it is, there are seven zones to cover, short and deep. And let's say on this particular play your life depends—and it always does—on knowing whether you're going against a strong-side or a weak-side zone. What's your key? Now those dirty bastards *will* mask their keys and they *will* shift their defense, so you have to audible off to another play. But let's keep it simple. What is your key? Aha! The middle linebacker, you say to yourself. That's pretty brilliant for a whore. So, along with seven hundred and fourteen other things you keep an eye on that middle linebacker. If he goes away from Jaworski, your tight end, then you're working against a strong-side zone. Maybe. Depending on what the strong-side safety does. Are there any questions? No? Then ting-a-ling, class is dismissed. Bartender, I'll take another hit of that Scotch."

She was left behind, groping. "Wait!"

"Ta-ta. It's been tepid, dearie, real tepid." Turning away, he paused to smirk at her. "Now you figure real hard on that and when you get the answer you run straight to Grover with it." Then he strolled back to his guzzling bodies, his glass raised in a toast to himself.

She was destroyed. Why had he even told her? What was going on?

A fifty-pound arm wrapped her in. Swaying above her was the plushy stunned face of a scout for the Dolphins, Mike Farmer. She was looking pretty tired and could he give her a lift? Her eyes were sandy and she shivered beside him in the car grinding back into the city through the snow.

The type of coverage . . . strong-side versus weak-side zones . . . keys . . . Her old buddy had given her the bare minimum of clues and her mind was blank; it was between channels. All she wanted was to be with Tom. Muddy and desperate, she kept trying. Keys! You had to read the coverage, what type, to know what receiver was the best bet—and when! That's why Tommy was so help-less! (She was sure she had it, but why was that cold face inside her gloating? With a feeling almost of doom she bumbled on.) Tommy couldn't read, and if they switched defenses the play sent in to him might be a total dud and the poor thing ended up throwing into a crowd or run-ning for his life. He could only audible against a blitz. Those fuckers! In the bad old days Lowry had fooled around with his charts and Chip had gone out there and done what he goddam pleased. So when the big shuffle came, those morons had simply handed Tom a playbook and said, "Hit it, boy."

"*A* for the course," she could hear Chip sneer, "for you. When does Nature Boy sign up?"

She had begun to shudder so violently that Mike had turned up the heater. "No, no, I'm not cold," she said. "My goddam head's no good." Not to have seen why Chip had given her clues and even encouraged her to work on them! He was going to break her fucking heart. Break it every day of her life with the magic key that *wouldn't* open the door, the skill Tommy couldn't learn.

And she was so muddled and forlorn that if Mike hadn't stopped off at Freyr's and picked up Brad, she would never have known what to do.

She turned over and crooned to the slack, sleeping face, "Tommy, he blew it. You *can* learn how to read. Chip can take the knocks while Brad teaches you. That's what Chip didn't figure on, a quarterback coach. We've done it, Tommy, and I love you, I love you."

She breathed into the wet grassy hollow of his armpit. Timidly she just touched his wheat-glimmery skin. Flung down on his back in his sleep, he sighed and his penis came throbbing up from the rough gold fleeces at its base, erect, monumental in the dim light. She threw off her clothes and knelt at the foot of the bed. "You'll make it, you'll make it, Tommy, we've done it."

"Oh say can you see
   By the dawn's early light . . ."

A pop vocalist in a mink jacket
was making Sloppy Joes of our
national anthem to start the San Diego
game. It was cold and the pale weak
sun kept disappearing behind the grim
clouds. The Stars and Stripes went up,
snapping heavily. Huge, chunked out
with pads and equipment, the players
stood in a long wind-roughed line with
their helmets under their left arms.

Chip coughed. His cold sleepless
eyes rejected the braying band and the
pompom girls, Sammy Stag with one
plastic paw over his heart. The half-
empty stands jutting up all around
had the look of gigantic picked
carcasses. The pillars on top were the
gnawed bones of a rib cage. Fine,
nobody up there at all would be finer.
His guts were squeezing with pre-
game pressure. Okay, you lived with

it. But slippery Carson Le Motte, his announcement to the press: "We've had a good look at Grover. Now we think it's time to give Hughes an opportunity to prove himself."

Prove himself! How many times did it fucking take?

And prove himself with what? This raggedy-ass bunch of derelicts. Daddy Wilson was out with a pulled hamstring, 57 Flavors and Toof were out, and the rest of them—they were packaged up real nice, like bad meat in a supermarket. Under those fresh clean uniforms they were all screwed up: a groin sprain, a broken wrist, a bruised kidney, you name it. He'd gotten the team back all right, a hospital ward in uniform. *With* a record of one-and-nine for the season. *And* the habit of losing. *And* split right down the middle between niggers and Anglo-Saxon heroes.

His lick at the lollipop. Thanks loads, Dori. All he had to do was pull this garbage together and be so super sensational that Biggie couldn't *not* start him over his muscular pet, ever. Mr. Meat was stationed in the center of the line, between the offense and defense, his cap held fervently over one tit. Biggie had a very severe case of Woody Hayes mind, where God, the flag and winning were all the same thing, and today he had to be putting something extra in his prayer: "Lord, we can't win with Hughes. Leave the little pisser break a leg, Lord. In the first quarter. How about it?"

> "And the rockets' red glare
> The bombs bursting in air . . ."

The self-loving voice screamed at the high notes, in a drizzle of pious falsettos from the stands. God*dam*. In the lumpy row of defensive players he could see George's busted face: in a fucking trance. He was going to perform miracles for his buddy today, and piss on that. The big goon had put his favorite talisman, a silver dollar tie clip, and a home-made sign, "Good Luck," in Chip's locker. Sick at heart he'd told him, "Get that crap out of here, George."

Everything was balls up. Why the hell couldn't Whitman stick to writing prose poems instead of going in for prophecy? Predicting in his column a win over the Chargers with Earl Hughes back at the controls! The Chargers were *bad* this year. They were leading their division by two full games and they had a brute of a pass rush, led by George King (or, as the hot dog preferred to be called, "The King"). Lovely, just beautiful. Go out there and walk on water, Chipper.

The band strutted off and the team huddled. The kickoff unit scattered out on the field in a hailstorm of boos. Just to make the impossible really hard, they'd lost the toss of the coin and he'd be working against a twenty-five-mile-an-hour wind off the lake in the first quarter. Man, he didn't have a thing going for him, nothing at all. Trying to psych himself up, he blew on his hands and snapped his fingers, crap shooter style. And *nada*. His mind was a scramble of dark equations. This wasn't a football game; it was a public execution.

The Chargers teed it up. Rows of helmeted men smashed together and a sub ran it all the way out to the seven-yard line.

Chip felt the sick brown water in his bowels back up into his stomach.

Moving out with the offense, he was aware of a splash of cheers in the booing. Yeah, sure, they were for him but mostly against Grover. Man, he could not make it. He was fucked. Gabe hadn't even given him a chance to run through his stuff in practice. They'd stayed with the Neanderthal game plan, 70 percent on the ground. Having commanded this from on high, Biggie had retired to himself alone. He'd turned the offense entirely over to Ellis and told the spotters upstairs not to bother him during the game.

It was strictly Mr. Hughes's wide river to cross and Mr. Hughes's stove-in canoe. The caged, steaming faces bunched above him. Against this wind even a super arm, a Namath, would start with a handoff into the line, just to get the blood and adrenalin pumping, and then go with the run and dumps to a man coming out of the backfield, good safe stuff.

In an icy fury he let it all hang out. He called an 84-X-slant out—a pass with Tuck as the primary receiver. "Shorts," he said, "get on your horse if it doesn't go."

"You somethin else, baby," Tucker puffed down at him. "You the best."

Chip's eyes were dark cuts. They broke from the huddle, trotting with their cold black shadows. Crouching behind the Rook, rasping out the signals, he looked over the deadly Charger double zone. The outside linebacker was cheating over to help the cornerback with Tucker. A slant would be intercepted and run into the end zone. His asshole was wincing. Damn, that first hit, waiting for it was fucking agony.

"Hut!" He back-pedaled like mad. King and the other end came grinding and crunching in, pinching to keep him in the pocket. The other people fired straight in at him, clashing forearms and wrestling, plunging and heaving and plunging again and again in spine-wrenching matchups. Grunts and farts, the smacks of pads and helmets, windy yells of "Pass! Pass!" He squirted away as they burst in on him, popeyed and shouting. Dodging artfully, a small cold dancer looking downfield.

Everybody was covered. He had to play Gingerbread Man with the pass rushers in the end zone while his receivers ran busted patterns. Tuck pulled up, then went flying straight down the sideline, while Bird, on the other side, running a stop-and-go, stopped and came back toward the play, and Shorty slid off into the flat, waited to get loose and took off, chugging toward the middle. Skittering around in the panting and flailing monsters, Chip pump-faked at Jay, shallow, tore loose from a grab and dipped under a windmill arm. King loomed on his left, a tower, zigzags of lightning flashing on his helmet. And it all dissolved in a crash of light as he threw his knuckler, his Fran Tarkenton flutterball, right into the teeth of the wind.

He was leaning back on the bench, slack. His eyes were jellies floating in blood. Hold still, man, did you ever get mangled, you okay? you look horrible like a car wreck somebody was crying it was Shorty I blew it I blew it, hands were working on him his neck was a numb space between his shoulders and his head, a salty taste he could see now, a blood-soaked towel, but he couldn't swallow.

"You're done for today," Daisy said. "This needs fifteen stitches."

"Fuck yourself," Chip croaked. "Tape it shut. Is it taped?"

"Yeah, but it won't take a hit. You won't last another set a downs."

Pushing him off, Chip struggled and sat up. Gabe mustn't have an excuse to pull him. Out of focus, everything. Trying to swallow. Voices. Swimmy in the head, but he got the picture: he'd been whipsawed on the throw, hit high from one side and low coming the other way. Then in the pile-up they'd just about popped his head off with a knee in the neck and clawed his forehead wide open. A real gang shag. Shorty had caught the pass and made it to mid-field but had the ball punched away from him on the hit.

"Forget it," Chip said to him in a dry whisper. His jersey was sticky-wet with blood chilling into a cold mat on his chest. Another storm of boos. A trample of players moving out. "Who worked me over?" he whispered.

"King. King put the shit on you."

He nodded. Rubbing his blanked-out neck. A 3 on the board for the Chargers. Behind him the slap of a football being caught over and over—Grover was warming up! Scared, he creaked around to look at Ellis and Gabe. Starting today was a rip-off but, damn it, it was his game.

Hey, no sweat! Ellis was on the phone and Gabe was standing with his hands in his pockets and a "supper's on" expression on his chubby face. Gabe was not about to yank him. He was waiting for the good Lord to finish answering that prayer. It was obvious all the way up in the bleachers that his quarterback was on funny street and just about defenseless. One more good shot and Mr. Hughes would be long gone. What a stand-out prick he was, but for once it was a help.

A cold flare of hate took Chip onto his feet. This time the kickoff went hopping through the end zone. He shuffled onto the field with the offense, massaging and stretching his neck. Then he heard a snuffling laugh: "Hey, you back fo some mo pancakes? Hey, sissy shit?"

The King. Bone-cracking hands loitering around his knees, laughs steaming through the bars of his helmet.

Chip set colder and harder. He owed Mr. King something. His legs steadied, his head cleared into ways and means. There were all sorts in this league. Some did it for money and some made it into an ego trip, putting the other man down. But for a whole bunch of the cats, they had to let that old aggression out somehow and here it was, a chance to get big money and glory for what they'd do in a tavern anyhow or in an alley with a base-ball bat. They loved to cripple, they got a big rush off it. The King was this breed something special. Mr. Terror, with the bloody fingernails.

However, he hadn't met The Slasher yet. Batman could be nobody to fuck with too.

Kneeling in the huddle, he called a turnout and rasped, "Leave The King in. Open the gates." And added sardonically, "You couldn't keep him out anyhow."

At the snap King came thundering on an outside route, lunging and slamming, snatching people out of his way. Chip lost him with a fake, rolling away and not throwing, not throwing, not even looking, setting him up. King wheeled around like an armored horseman and came charging down on him. Flick, at the last split second, Chip sailed the ball out of bounds in the general vicinity of a receiver and went down flat on his back, slashing the legs out from under King. King belly-flopped in the air. As he whomped onto the turf Chip caught one of his size-fifteen shoes by the heel and the toe and followed it up, then hurled himself back down, twisting the leg and driving with everything he had. The sweet crack of tendons. A tortured howl. The whistle tweeting and whammo! he got some assistance: the Chargers' middle linebacker, hitting late on the play, landed on his back like a sack full of bowling balls. King screamed as the whole network of tendons came ripping out of their sockets in the bone. He screamed and screamed on his back, kicking in agony with one leg.

"Well, shithead," Chip said, looking down at him with a pink grin, "that about wraps you up. No doctor is gonna fix that knee."

Deliberately, he spit on the stretching and groaning face.

The penalty flag had gone down, of course. Officials had come dashing in, bumped by oblivious walking bulks. But a quarterback bulldogging a pass rusher was a first, a complete never-before and never-again, and it had all happened so fast, in one somersaulting motion. Even the linebacker had missed it, diving in. What everybody caught was the cheap shot after the play and the officials stepped off fifteen yards against the Chargers.

After a couple of minutes on the turf King went crutching off, hanging onto the shoulders of two trainers. His brawny face was clay-white with pain. Every step forward dragged a sob out of him.

"Motherfucker!" the linebacker shouted at Chip. "It's your turn comin."

"Next play, baby?" Chip croaked. It didn't matter that he was in a red fog of blood oozing through the tape; he was *there* now. His neck was hurting like a bastard too, but the knots were all untied and a bitter gray fire was blazing in him, zero at the core.

Dumb as they made 'em, the linebacker came storming and Chip caught him wrong with a quickie into his vacated zone. The play was whistled dead. Players began getting up and starting downfield—except for the maddened linebacker. While everybody in the house watched he kept driving toward Chip, who swerved abruptly and stopped, seeping blood into his smile, and twitch! left him grabbing air and sprawling, faked completely out of his jock strap. "Again, baby?" Chip said.

Death, Pestilence and Earl Hughes, they came riding. In five slashing plays he put a TD on the scoreboard. Grim and bloody he walked through the showering cheers. "Tape it again," he told Daisy. "Just shut up and do it." He was in a kind of crazy high, ice cold and vicious, hating everybody and everything. Simson gave him both rumps. Chip swilled a mouthful of blood and water on the turf and grinned. "Not impressed, huh?"

They kicked off and the defense rumbled out there. And man they rose up; they played like there was an oil refinery on fire behind them. "Good D! Good D!" the offense yelled, flapping in their green capes on the sidelines.

The Chargers had to punt and the offense ran onto the field, clapping and stamping and talking it up. Forget the race stuff, forget the nine losses, forget everything and get 'em. They wanted to *go*. Chip had seen a team smoke up like this a hundred times. His own head froze harder. When Lips barked, "Let's get it *on*," Chip called for a difficult trap and said, "Let's see it, prick." Lips showed him; he exploded from the side into the sucker, and Shorty, butting like a billy goat and shaking tackles, picked up eight.

Lips looked at Chip for a nice word.

Unmoved, shut into himself, Chip took them all the way in a second time, going five for five in the air, while the rundown old temple filled with cheers and the scoreboard flashed "GO! GO! GO!" and the horns honked for him. The killing shot, on third and long, he zipped *to one side* of a rusher jumping down at him out of the sky. And was flattened, pinned down and slugged. A grunting hairy face in a cage dissolved in blood rolling deep waves and breakers up on his feet. The scoreboard was a red fountain in the winter sky. Tugging at his chin strap and wiping his eyes, he groped through the inevitable pats and hugs doin a job baby sooty whiskers bubbling sweat you okay? Tucker was crying. Shorty said, You're indomital. Daisy lashed tape over the long wet red slit in his forehead. And he sat, cold with rage, in the warm spouts and gushes from the devotees in their blankets and mufflers, ear flaps, parkas, mittens.

"Did you get there?" he croaked savagely. "Did I get it off for you? Really and truly? I'm glad."

Yells releasing and releasing, tiers of delirious customers contracting and emptying it all out in steams of hoarse praise.

Taped back together, he put it to the Chargers again, giving them his sidle-up-to-them-and-open-an-artery offense. Double-hook patterns, a play-action to freeze the linebackers, sleight-of-hand draws, moving it around all the time, breaks in the cadence to blunt the defensive thrust, audibles, eye fakes, the entire repertory.

Super Mouse was having some kind of a game. Along with the skills and brains—and he was astute, man, canny —he was having one of those days. His body was as good as his mind, and he saw (through a haze of blood) more things, anticipated better, reacted better, moved better and read better, finding the seams in that double zone and drilling the ball in there. And every time he put it up he could feel it was right on the money, all hands and catch at the end of the throw even as he triggered it. Hit and spun down, heaped under, buried, he knew the roar for a completion was coming. It had to *be*.

And did the guys ever love him. Lungs seared with cold, the skin on their hands numb and torn, snot dribbling out of their noses, they leaned down to him in the huddle, hawking and blowing: "Doin it all, Chip baby!" "Beautiful!" They fretted about his leaking forehead, they pawed at his helmet, they tried to slap hands with him.

And it only made him shrink deeper into himself, more and more wintry, alone. It was as if there were glass or thin ice collecting around him. Sure, they loved him. And they'd love a child-raping, bank-robbing runaway preacher if he could win for them. "Never seen you this good," they puffed. "Man, you sorcerin today. Like you a witch doctor."

"It's talent," he said curtly. "It's ability, man."

Ferocious, he preferred Gabe Simson to this crap. The old bonfire was burning in Fats and he was stomping and bawling on the sidelines, his face a swollen red glare. After the third TD he actually came over to see if the trainers could keep Hughes in one piece.

Chip looked a frosty hole in him. "I know I can't win your heart," he said, "but maybe I can show you a good time."

It was George that got to him. He was playing the run like there was an open elevator shaft behind him and pass rushing like a green cyclone. Squatting on the crumpled quarterback, timidly, hopefully, he peeked over at Chip on the bench, offering it to him.

Shaking and sick, Chip put his face in a towel.

There was time for one more pop at them in the first half. On the first play from scrimmage the Chargers blitzed and he butchered them with a screen. Cheers poured over him. "That grabbed you, huh?" he said. But he caught himself expanding in the crowd reaction, larger and larger, Mr. In-There, Mr. Success.

Just what they were doing, scattered up in the seats and from coast to coast at the tube. It was all a fucking House of Mirrors at Coney Island.

Sourly he began to announce the proceedings on TV. "The gallant little scrapper is dropping back to pass . . . He's gonna be sacked! No, he gets it away and it's complete! This is fantastic! What a super-demonstration of raw courage and ability under fire. Here's a man that's a real credit to the game." (He was Howard Cosell now, running off at the mouth.) "What these fans don't know is that Chip Hughes is coming off a severe case of the clap, and yet today the man is invincible!"

Only once was there a screw-up, and it was nothing much. Lips, who had been handling his man all day, doing what he wanted when he wanted to, got careless and let him through. "Look out!" he hollered to Chip. Too late. He was really sponged up. Tottering to his feet, he went over to Lips, cursing in dry squeaks, and kicked him—in full view of both teams, the fans and the entire country.

"Hey!" Lips yelped, clutching his barrel leg. "Jesus, Chip."

Otherwise, it was Glory Road for Super Mouse. He stuck it in their eye, he proved it all. Limping off at half time, he was 19 for 22, for 297 yards and four TDs. Biggie would have to start him until he was on Social Security. They streamed into the locker room, hair soaked, sweaty faces cradled in great rocking shoulder pads. Scowling impatiently, he wrenched away from their joyful cuffs toward the training room for another patch job.

There was a commotion somewhere in front of him, a high terrified whinnying, shouts. Six or seven players were thrashing back and forth. Swollen shadows collided in the narrow aisle. Jammed and pushed backward, Chip snarled, "Goddamit, if you wanta fight go out in the street." Helmets and pads surged in thick gusts of violence. George was bellowing and his taped paws were closed on somebody's throat. Five or six players were hauling at him, but he had Lips like a boa constrictor with his brute hands, tightening, crushing in. "I told you," he panted. Lips was twisting and kicking more and more feebly. "I warned you, didn't I?"

He was torn away finally. The coaches, flaying right and left, elbowed in. Lips was down on his hands and knees, gagging, coughing greenish slops. One of his shoulder pads hung out like a broken wing from his jersey.

Cleats gnashed on cement. Heaving himself loose and swinging his long arms taped into clubs, bludgeoning, uprooting players and coaches both and hurling them aside, George drove in on Lips to finish him off.

"George!" Chip said harshly.

George stopped, like a bear jerked by an iron chain.

"I told him," George yammered, his sodden jersey twisted, his arms draggling tape and elbow pads. "I warned him I was watchin . . . all the time. I told him, and he opened the gates on you. I seen it."

"Do me a favor, will you, George?"

"Sure, Chip! Anything, anything atall."

"Good. Don't do me any favors."

The tiny red eyes blinked, the grizzled snout squeezed in welts of sweat. Then he got it and a small noise came out of him, a cry out of his blind lurching chest, and he grabbed at his crotch, pissing all over himself.

It was more than Chip could handle. That dumb pitiful sacrifice, betraying all his most sacred principles for nothing, when it was too late—Chip felt as if his head had frozen solid and come clean off the painful throbbing in his throat. It seemed to hang by itself in a cold abstract fury.

When they trotted back onto the field the pre-Christmas half-time show was ending. The band, spread out in the wide zigzags of an enormous pine tree, was tooting and thumping and the floats were going off. Plastic creatures fifty feet high, fleshed out with gas, riding on trucks wearing tinsel skirts: jolly St. Nick wallowing a toy smile in the wind, elves and reindeer, a sexy crew of Santa's helpers waving from a hill of Styrofoam snow. A hodgepodge of cartoons and mummers winding out of old legends toward the parking lot. Old Man Winter brought up the rear, yawing and balancing, tipping, losing gas and drooping his gaudy bags and sacks to one side as he was rolled away to the racket of "Silver bells," blah, blah, "soon it will be Christmas Day."

Shit.

On the first play from scrimmage Chip put the ball right to the Charger cornerback—with Bird wide open and flagging his hand behind him.

The cornerback was so flabbergasted he let it skid off his hands.

Chip came right back to him. As if to say, "Look here, Number 20, I'm putting it right in your guts. It's gonna be embarrassing if you keep dropping them."

There was no hysteria about this, no sudden crazy impulse. George had only put the last nail in. This was the most conscious act of his life; this was something he had been building to ever since he'd crept onto the sun-whipped playground with his new Wilson basketball. He'd had it with faking he was a jock and raising it from the dead for CBS and all the rest of it. Even with the great things, the spit-on-a-griddle moves and the impossible whirling runs, the dazzling catches tumbling over and over and the gory magnificent courage, hitting and hitting in a blood-splattered ecstasy of pain and effort.

The next time out he fumbled the ball away—in cold blood, as methodically as breaking a mirror and crushing the splinters under his heel. Sighs came out of the cold stands, murmurs, boos. Gabe was screaming at him from the sideline. "Oops," Chip said, serving up another interception.

The ragged gray sun came out of the clouds. Bright green shadows sprang out of the players and he threw his very best dying duck into a crowd of white jerseys. Men and shadows swept past him in the pale sunshine.

Eventually, with San Diego ahead and pulling away, Gabe had to yank him.

"You cocksucker," he raved. "What went wrong?"

Chip had been creamed on the last pass and his face was a mask trickling with blood. "The sun was in my eyes, Coach."

"Get outa my sight," Gabe gibbered at him. "Choke! Loser! You nickel-arm cocksucker!"

In a snowstorm of boos Chip walked to the row of hooded players on the bench and dropped, shrouding his head in a towel. Darkness. One of the trainers led him to the locker room, pelted like a scapegoat with boos and catcalls, beer cans, programs. He didn't bother to give them the Hughes salute. He was the man of ice, the man of glass reflecting nothing.

Dori was cooking up a *bear* of a post-game meal for Tom. Naked in a hostess apron, she was stirring the chunks of rump steak bubbling in onions, peppers and tomatoes. Glory and hallelujah, the dead look wasn't quite so dead on Tommy's face; he had *one* of his balls back again anyway, and Brad had actually said to her, "He's comin along in practice. Could be we're gonna fill our straight."

Thank the lord Chip had gone cold in the second half.

Gallop-a-gallop, she mashed the potatoes, filling her lungs with the butter and hot milk smell breathing up to her face. Her arm churned warm little tides of motion into her breasts. On her apron was a bib with a lacy trim that scratched at her nipples, swelling them with dizzy blood till they were tight little buds. Gallop-a-gallop, the dangling strings whipped at her butt and the ruffles of the apron plucked at the fur between her thighs.

The front door rattled. She ran madly through the living room and flew up into his arms. "Welcome home, hero!"

"Hey what?" He set her down with a red frown. She was hurt, then flustered when she saw Brad behind him, sporting a new coach's cap and windbreaker. "Oh Lord, it's the preacher," she groaned. And she'd never seen a preacher that didn't stay for supper. Embarrassed or not, she had to run him off.

For a start she pirouetted into the bedroom, tossing her rosy behind at him. Then came out in a pair of slacks and a sketchy top and smiled. "Excuse my chef outfit, Brad. I cook better in the nude."

"Hey." Tom blushed. Ordinarily Brad would have lit out for points south at that, and then in the kitchen Tommy would kneel over her, his erect flesh dripping light, and she would lie sprung open to him on the floor . . . She blinked. Brad was still sitting there. His lean, creased-in face was the color of the wattle ears sprouting out of it, but for some reason he was hanging tough.

"I don't suppose you'll stay for supper, Brad," she said.

"Much obliged."

Then he really shook her up: He turned down a drink! "Much obliged, though."

When she'd regrouped a little she noticed that both of them were only half watching the Forty-Niner game from the coast. And they were fidgeting and looking at each other like a couple of kids who were up to something.

"Well, let's eat," she said, "so we can get started on the strip poker."

"Coach says he won't play Hughes no more," Tom burst out. "You should've saw him, Dor. It's not fair. He was super great for two quarters, but Coach—"

"He was shittin fire, for a fact," Brad echoed.

"So," she said, "what? Gabe is three hundred and twenty pounds of no problem at all. He pushed once to keep his darling Dickie and he'll push again. Leave it to me."

"You should've saw him! Was he ever teed off! Mr. Bradberry and me really got to hit it to be ready for the Packers." He didn't need any more help, thanks. "What we're gonna do is, he's gonna move in. You know, live with me so we can work day and night." He was padding back and forth, his big muscle-filled arms working, mounding up his shoulders. "We can't do it gradual over the winter, so it's like a, you know, a crash campaign."

"Hang on," she said. "Will you hang on just a second? There's *no way* you can get ready, baby. You'll just bust yourself up for nothing. Brad?"

"It's a forty-acre field and only one mule," Brad agreed. "All's we can do is git the plow in the ground and have a go at 'er."

"But it's stupid! You can sit out the last three games and take your time!"

It was maddening! They'd thought up this gorgeous plan all by themselves and they were as thrilled with it as a couple of Hottentots with a hubcap.

She sighed. "Okay, guys, have fun. Tom, you *can* work me into your schedule, I hope? While you're resting your eyes or something? Lifting weights?"

Everything jumbled, fell together and sucked away into the babbling television screen. The Forty-Niners punted and new model cars, wide-shouldered and shimmering, jumped out of the light. "Appreciate," she said numbly. "Appreciate."

He'd thought she understood! Him and Mr. Bradberry didn't have a minute to relax; it was a crash campaign, and wow! If it hadn't been for her, and so forth, and he sure appreciated it, Dor. The TV rapped away and Brad was saying something in his high buzzing voice, something about a deal; he was giving up likker, and the kid—no offense, Dori—he was laying off of tail. And yeah, Tommy said, it's our concentration, Dor.

"No offense," Brad said again.

"No offense, huh?" She lit into him. "Why you goddam hillbilly alcoholic, who do you think got you this job?"

"Hey, come on," Tom said. "Don't be mad, Dor. Let's grub up."

"And right afterwards I'm supposed to leave, right? So you two can hit some films, right?" The sweet fires flamed sick inside her, and she told him to eat it himself, goddamit. Weeping with anger, with pure fury, she threw on a coat and her shoes and banged out.

A red stoplight burned through the falling snow. The drugstore was a labyrinth of red paper bricks, tinsel glitters, Santa Claus beaming at her over the gun barrel eye of a camera. She found a phone, but Le Motte was out and so was Simson, probably eating a couple of sheep to calm his sorrows.

Tomorrow, then. She was damned if Brad and Tommy were going to hatch a plan that cut her out. The headlights raked through the snow-filling darkness. She went up the stairs to her apartment so goddam mad—and there was Chip, comfortably smoking a cigar, sitting by her door. A band of tape went all the way around his head.

"You!" she said and all her rage exploded on him. "How the hell did you get in?"

He smirked. "With man's oldest tool."

"Very funny. You asshole, you sonofabitch!"

"Innuendoes," he said. "Speak your mind straight out."

"Oh you—you—I got it! I see it now. You *made* them throw Grover in there."

"Is it mad its pretty boy got chucked into the trenches? I'm sorry about that."

"Like hell you are," she said. "What are you doing? Stop it!"

A door opened, steps thudded on the stairs and Chip was taking off his coat and kneeling with it flung out in front of her! "I didn't mean any harm. Please forgive me. No?" Off came his shirt and tie, his undershirt, exposing a chest the color of a corpse with bruises. He threw out his arms. "Look how sorry I am. Listen, I beg you. I can explain."

"You crazy asshole!" Swatting at him with her purse, she told the wide-eyed neighbors, "He's just drunk. I'll take care of it." Chip made sniveling noises. "You complete nut," she fumed, "stop it! Get up!"

"Well, I like that. A guy lays a nice apology on you and this is what he gets." Damn it, she hated his guts, but she couldn't help being a little charmed by the screwball. Off came his pants, his shoes and socks. Down to a cigar and jock strap, he went to his knees again and, twirling a sock on his finger, sniffled, "Please! Is this enough? Okay, both socks, but you have a hard heart."

The people from upstairs said they were calling the police. Their dog was barking.

She said, "Please do! Get this kook out of here."

Now Florence came wheezing into the mess. Slicing a wink at her, Chip said, "Hey, Gramma, you're just in time for the grand finale. Ladies and gentlemen, here it is, the one and only Little Fooler, author of destruction both here and in foreign lands!" Humming and puffing on his cigar, he twitched his jock strap down, down, from his pudgy quarterback gut.

Shaking her blond curls, Flo squawked, "I wouldn't look at that thing for a ten-dollar bill."

Dori panicked and grabbed him. "Don't call the cops," she yelled up the stairs and got the door open. Under her breath she said, "You're gonna get me kicked out of this place."

He solemnly kneed his way inside, leaving her to scoop up the clothes. And then she saw his luggage piled in the shadows. "What the hell are the suitcases supposed to mean?"

"They mean I love you? I'm an orphan? The motel and me are pfft?"

"Well, you're moving on, buster. Find yourself another insane asylum." She flopped his clothes at him.

Ignoring the hint, he poured himself a Scotch on the rocks. "None for you? Good."

"Okay, you asshole, explain. You got your damn chance to start and you blew that game on purpose. I should have known it when you started throwing interceptions. Go ahead, tell me it wasn't to wreck Tommy before Brad could do a job with him."

"It wasn't to wreck Tommy before Brad could do a job with him." He dipped his glass to her and tossed it off. His grin was a needle. "I'm hanging it up, Doris Nell. There are other things in life."

The blood drained out of her head, but she said, "Don't give me that."

"Okay," he said, "name your flavor. Press conference? Business letter? A note tied to a rock? Not enough style, you're right." He went to the phone and dialed Information. "What's the number of Western Union?"

She snatched the phone from him and slammed it down, feeling the room go gray around her. His eyes under the crown of tape—he meant it. "My, my, you're right again," he said. "Surprise 'em, that's the stroke. Tuesday morning show up missing."

She sank down, trembling. If Chip took himself out of it there was nothing she could do to keep Tommy, nothing. She pleaded with him to stick out the season at least. Oh God, if only she hadn't gotten Brad hired. "You can't do this," she quavered. "Why?"

"An owl bit me?" he suggested. "It's just too bad Olson is healed and can back up Grover. Otherwise they'd have to activate Brad."

She kept protesting that he couldn't quit and what about all the money he owed the club, but she knew that grin. There was no way he was going to change his mind. "I always wanted to be a rodeo rider," he said. "All I need is a horse—or a Cadillac. I'll be a guru. Dye myself brown, hire a chauffeur and give Yoga lessons from coast to coast."

He came bumping in with his bags, put on his pajamas and made up the sofa. "But first I got a matter to settle with old Fats."

She was helpless. The color leached out of the "Green Nude in a Mirror," leaving a gray architecture for the fruity sections of flesh. She gasped, "Go live someplace where you're wanted. Live with George, why don't you? You're married to him, not Martha."

"It can never be. He's a poor housekeeper."

"Where's your pride?" she said, but he only smiled and said, "Where's some coat hangers, goddamit?"

She was too exhausted, too emotionally beaten to fight him any more, or even to care much. She just wanted Tommy. Her only hope was to get him to change his mind about seeing her.

"Please can I talk with him?" she implored Brad on the phone. "Just once, Brad, face to face."

"Cain't do it, Dor."

"Just five minutes, Brad? Give me a break—wait! Don't hang up! All right, on the phone, then."

"Sorry, we got to git it now."

The line clicked dead, and when she rang back and then back again, there was only a hopeless burring at the silence. "Tough," Chip said from the sofa. She told him to screw himself. Somehow she had to get past Brad, who was acting like a goddam dragon sitting on a goddam hoard of gold. Phone calls, letters, cards, a tortured message sent through Poppo: nothing worked.

Cold streets and darkness riddled with lights. She waylaid them in the foyer of his apartment building. "Don't do it," she said, the words she'd prepared melting into tears. "I love you."

Bleary shapes boomed to each other, a big hand

landed on her shoulder and the door closed. Brad was facing her by the blank-glittering mailboxes. There was something reptilian, narrow and unblinking, about him. "I sure am sorry," he said to everything.

"Ten minutes. Just give me ten minutes alone with him." He took her wet hand off his arm. "At least," she begged, "tell me how he's doing. At least tell me that."

Brad shrugged. "It's one cat and a barnful of mice."

Something seemed to fold up smaller inside her and go still.

She drove home and the phone rang. It was Tommy! And did she want to meet him at the airport a half hour before the team took off for Green Bay? She was saved. Her head was going around and around and she was slipping out of herself like the string of a kite slipping away and up, flying in windy lifts . . .

"Hi," he said, swinging off the escalator with his bag. Her heart was jerking. He was striding in a window full of sunshine. Out there tubby fuel trucks hooked up to the feeding planes, baggage trucks puttered around like toy trains, and the tail of a jet moved across the window like a sliding wall.

"I'm getting like flashes, you know? Like out of nowhere sometimes I read the coverage and what man to go to." The words fluttered in the warm wind of his breath, swirled and flew away into the hubbub, arrivals, departures. "Only it still takes too long, you know? Because I have to think. What it's gotta be is a reactionary thing. You know, instinctive like. So in a kind a way, what I gotta do is turn into a animal."

"Please," she said in a scratchy whisper. "I helped you, didn't I?"

"You know it!" he said, blowing out his breath. "Man, my ass was dead without you."

"Then let me see you. I won't be any trouble."

"You *are* seein me," he said, looking puzzled. "Right now."

"And I can see you other times? I'll be good, Tommy, I promise. I'll go home the minute you say."

He was blinking at her. Hey, what was the deal? He'd told her it was a crash campaign, didn't he? Today was only because she'd asked to see him once, face to face. His beautiful innocent mouth was open.

She said, "Okay, it'll about kill me, but I guess I can hold out till the season is over."

But the crash campaign was just starting, it seemed. The only time Mr. Bradberry was giving him off was three weeks for a honeymoon. He told her he was getting married and everything, didn't he? On Christmas Eve.

"I'm out in the cold, huh?"

"Aw, hey, you got your pick of guys, and honest, I don't have time even to lift weights half the time any more."

Like that. He had shucked her off like that, practically without knowing it. He had the innocent ruthlessness of a child. His hair was a golden pelt around his eager face, and bein a quarterback, Dor, you know what it's like? It's just like drivin a car, no lie! You got to watch out for a dozen things at once and react before you know it. . . .

In a moment of happy inspiration, Carson Le Motte had put up a promotional balloon at the stadium. It sailed the autumn sky above the row of cement columns, a green-and-gold vinyl football twenty-five feet long. STAGS, it said on both sides, straining on its long rope, swaying and wallowing this way and that as the wind took it.

On the Monday morning after the Green Bay game it was gone.

Shortly after noon Coach Gabe Simson was taking a snooze in his cubicle. He heard a whoosh of compressed air and felt himself pinned against his desk. The projector and screen tumbled in bulges of green-and-gold rubber vinyl, the golf clubs slid out of their bag. The Egyptian dancer went from exotic to obscene and back to exotic in the growing bellies that took shape around him. "What the fuck!" he roared, shoving it away, fighting it off. Whomp! it took shape and lifted him off his feet, up, up, shouldering him and the projector screen against the wall over the desk. He heard a cackle in the rushing air: "How's that for size, Two-Ton?" Cursing, he grappled with the oncoming rounds that pressed him tighter, tighter, squashed him against the leaning plywood wall.

"What the hell?" he choked in a voice squeezing out. "What the motherfucking hell?"

"It's on the principle of a tube of toothpaste, Fats." Chip's voice came chuckling over the bumping and cracking of plywood. "I just wanted to see what you had for lunch."

Dori was in a motel near the airport with a quart of Beefeater. She was cold, trembling all over. Hunched in a blanket, she choked down hot mouthfuls right from the bottle. The burning poured out from her stomach, out into her breasts. Gagging and shuddering on the bed, she kept swallowing till the shock and the hurt stayed on the surface, widening in scummy rings on deeper and deeper pools of emptiness.

Came to, woozily counted the bottles. There were two empty ones and one half full. This was some kind of bad trip. She straggled her arm over to the phone and called the desk. It was Monday and the Stags had lost 20 to 6. She got an outside line and phoned the office: "Tell Weldon I'm not coming in. Tell him anything. I can't find my underwear or something."

But the switchboard girl said, "Just a moment, please. Mr. Weldon wants to talk to you." In a second the bastard came on screaming about the gum promo on radio. "Don't bother to come in for your check," he said. "We'll mail it."

She was fired, sacked. Weldon couldn't do that; she did three times the work that little . . .

Staggering to the sink, she drank water until she was waterlogged, then she was falling, only it was upward. She couldn't believe it. Dumped again, first by a hick from Nebraska and now by that asshole Weldon. She hiccupped in the darkness. She was thirsty again, and she sloshed down the stale water from the carton of melted ice cubes, alternating with more sips of Beefeater.

Somebody was knocking. "Hold on," she said. There was a meek thunderhead rimmed with light in the doorway. It was Fuzzy, 290 pounds of ex-lineman with a brand-new crop of hair on his face. "Hey, Dor! Hey! Whatta you think of my mustache?"

She scraped up one eyelid. "Fine, Fuzzy, just fine. What you doing here?"

A surprised gap opened in the hair. "*You* called *me*, 'member? You said come get you, so I caught a cab and here I am."

"I did? I must've come to for a minute." Her head

was filled with crowd noise. "Coffee. Get me some while I . . ."

Fuzzy wanted to know what she was doing here herself.

"Tryin to find Kokomo, Indiana." But suddenly she began to cry.

"Aw, don't do that," he said and her shoulder was thumped. "Jesus, Dor, I never seen you in this bad of a—"

"No use. I'm shot." More and more tears ran out of her and she was bawling helplessly. She was made to sit up after a while and blow her nose like a good girl. "Fuzz," she said, "I've never broke down before . . . spilled my guts to anybody, right?"

"Never," he said, holding her up. "Not to my knowledge."

"Gotta tell somebody—you're my friend, right?"

"Right."

She hiccupped. "This you'll never believe in a million years, never, but it happened. I was dumped by a redneck. I was fired too, but the worst part is I was dumped! Me!"

"Bullshit! Nobody would do that to you."

"It's true. I was kissed off, just like that. I can't take it, Fuzz. I was hung up on the sonofabitch too, hung up bad."

She was squeezed in a bear hug that like to broke two of her ribs. "You gotta get past it, that's all."

"Can't. Please don't tell anybody, Fuzz. . . . In a nightclub, the MC introduces me as Miss National League, and now . . . I can't take it." Swallowing salty flows, she stretched up to blob a kiss in the festoons of hair. He hovered over her, nuzzling. She must have still been

drunk because when she reached behind herself to un-
hook her bra her hands didn't shake at all.

He was astonished. "Dori! You sure?"

"Sure, what the hell." She gave a wriggle, then
smacked her lips into his bashful convulsions. He surged
and whomped his bulk timidly, huffing and puffing on
her like a worried walrus. "Am I too heavy?" he asked.

"No problem, Fuzz."

Proud in his sweat and blubber, he kept coming up
to the old line of scrimmage. Then they drove into the
city. She wouldn't go into Freyr's with him, though, because absolutely everybody in there would know.

In a downstairs pub off Rush Street she started off
on Stingers and went on to anything that was bought for
her. A dope with bulge eyes, a fleshy nose and mouth, all
crowded together in a miniature face, was trying to make
her. They were on the way to his hotel room before he
could spit it out: He had a buddy and . . .

"Why the hell not?" she said. "How about your
three cousins from Kokomo, too?" Everything floated
around. The ceiling light was a big chromium eye; it was
the sun rolling away into a deep dark hole. She opened
her eyes. Some jagoff was watching in his underwear. "I
think he's interested," she said, pumping away. "He's got
his dong out." Her eyes were drowning in light. She saw
a face in close-up, familiar.

"You still think you got something between your
legs worth a million bucks? It ain't worth forty cents."

A lot of faces now. A slouching hairy gut and
butcher-boy rumps swinging around and exploding at
her: ka-r-r-rump! Guffaws, a shower of spit in her face.
A weird jabber hopped on top of her, "Ooh-ah, ooh-ah,"
crushing down and pumping. Smeary voices. "Did you

score last night?" and a lofty "Does a bear shit in the forest?" Gleeful howls. "I didn't know you could read *words,* asshole." "No, hey, listen. This is a real mind-blower. This guy is a scuba diver, see, and they ball under water so much he can't come anywhere else." The faces changed with the game on television. There was a fight, smashes, incoherent gurgles. An all-new Ford spewing dust gunned past the Sphinx for thirty yards and a first down, faces swapped with spurt after spurt of sperm, sweaty discharges, juices swashing together. Exhausted. "Go! Go! Go!" Writhing like a snake with a broken back. A flash bulb scorched her eyes. Somebody was on his knees vomiting. They threw a blanket over him so they wouldn't have to look. "Schlitz," said the bells. The TV shouted excitedly and somebody crowed, "Hey! look who's on the bottom of the pile-up. It's Shirley!"

"Nah, it's Dori."

She must have gone for a walk to clear her head. Buckingham fountain was boarded up, a little dry roof in the snowy park. A black horseman came galloping out of a gash in the earth. All the snowflakes were falling up into the light.

She'd lost track of her car, so she took a cab to the Green Knight. "What're you crying for?" the boob on the next stool asked her.

"I can't find Kokomo," she told him. "I know it's around here somewhere." She flopped wildly underneath somebody. Then the bottom dropped out again and she was freezing in thick hot mush. The jerk beside her on the bed was watching the Stag game on TV. It must be Sunday. "Come on, slugger," she said, "it's your turn at bat."

"Hold on, look! Hey, look at that! The kid's great!"

Dizzily she saw Tommy get belted three times but stay on his feet, looking downfield all the time and, zip, hit the secondary receiver for twenty-five yards. That super body had finally been programmed and he had it all; he would be another Unitas.

"So fucking what," she mumbled, dragging at the guy. He didn't want to fuck while the game was on, but she pulled him on top of her, spreading her legs to get it in and driving her hips up at him, dizzy, falling. The room whirlpooled and she was falling, falling (the vertical hold had slipped and the screen was spinning, rolling out a fiery wheel of plays and pizzas, dancing cans of deodorant spray, complete for 26 yards and another first down, the upset of the year, new dynasty, he planted and threw), falling up into the swallowing light.

She came draggling into her apartment and collapsed in a chair. Her mouth was a dry crack. She couldn't keep her hands still. "God," she said, "God, my head's coming off."

"It came off about six weeks ago," Chip said.

The bastard was lying in state on the couch, sipping at the ten-o'clock news.

"Please fuck yourself." Wretchedly she stared at her purse. The lovely fawn-colored suede was all smudged and the clasp was broken. It was too much effort to push the red tangles of hair out of her eyes.

"Mind telling me the highlights? I lead a very sheltered life these days."

Sick rage jerked her to her feet. In a whispering screech she said, "Okay, I've been paying my fucking dues in the gutter for trying to save your lily-white ass. For the umpteenth time."

"Do tell. And here I thought you fell for a big Nebraska dong and—"

"Which beats some measurements around here, buster!"

"I do have my limitations," he agreed serenely. "But to continue. When he took back his ring, you—"

"That's none of your goddam business!" Her hands went up to the throbbing in her head. "You cop-out sonofabitch! You're incredible! Quitting football when you had it made. You're not half a man. You're a gutless quitter!"

She had to sit down, weak, shaking.

"Gabe Simson already told me that. Anything else?"

"You're goddam right there's plenty else. You're a little stuck-up asshole with a kooky act. And talk about cutthroat. What you did to me—"

"When you tried to pump me for Grover? That *was* enjoyable, I admit."

"At least I'm human," she croaked at him. "You little prick! You don't give a shit for anybody. You never have!"

As cheerful as ever he said, "I got my doubts about you too. You think love is nine inches long."

"Die!" she gasped. "Just die, will you? You heartless bastard. Why'd you waste half your lousy life playing football? You never gave a shit about it. You're so much into being a celebrity and a weirdo mental giant! But being a football player is a little too much for you to handle!" She was still drunk, struggling to get the sticky words out of her mouth. "You remember that night?

When you blew in here and told me your sad, sad story how you were tired of faking all those years and there was something missing? And laid there with your soft dick, pitying yourself? I'll tell you what's missing, buster. I'll tell you what your problem is. It's not just that you're not a jock, you're not even human!"

"Is that so bad?"

She slumped back. Fucked up and fired, her life unraveling, she picked at the cigarette hole burned in her skirt. And amazingly, he was giving her a glass of water and she was sucking it down like a child.

"You never lost a game before, did you?" he said to her. "I know how it feels, kid. I'm an expert at that."

She didn't answer. She felt him lift her to her feet. Feebly she elbowed at him, but he said, "You're wanted in the other room." He carried her into the bedroom and, standing her up, began to unzip and peel off her damaged clothes.

"Cut it out!" she said.

He only grinned. "Just think of it as a new kind of striptease." He put her under the covers.

"Leave me alone, you bastard," she said. "I wouldn't screw you—"

"Why, how you talk! I'm a Baptist, remember?"

It was astonishing. And slowly, in the awful fatigue and emptiness, the feeling that had always been there between them, even in hate, even in bitterness, even while she was so hung up on Tommy—it came back clear and sweet, like the delicate touch of silver on the thinnest glass. Not passion, maybe nothing anybody would call love, but chiming delicately, delicately.

A grin had twitched at her face. But it died as it started and she said, "I'm so tired. A twenty-eight-year-old ex-advertising pro, ex-big deal, and perpetual hick that's lost every bit of respect she ever wrung out of anybody."

"That's openers," he told her. "Look at me—I'm a thirty-one-year-old plaything of destiny that's lost one wife, two gorgeous kids and all my respect for the play-action pass."

"Neither one of us is any flaming success, are we?"

"Not likely. But there's no harm in your having forty hours of sleep and then some of my extra specially burnt bacon." Holding her head up, he sponged off her face with a washcloth and smoothed back her hair.

"Put your arms around me, Chip. I'm cold."

"My normal temperature is forty-two-point-six degrees, but okay, here goes." And he held her until she stopped trembling. "I'll get you a blanket," he said.

"And a thumb?" she tried to joke. "You got a thumb you can spare?"

Grinning, he said, "All right, only I seem to remember a young man in your past who was all thumbs."

"Oh, don't tease me, Chip," she wailed. "I'm so tired. And I can't sleep. I can't—"

"Ssh!" he said. "Don't sleep. I want you to listen to this six-hour bedtime story that was banned out of *Grimm's Fairy Tales*. Once upon a time there was a fairy godmother that lost her wand. . . ."

And what about the Chipper, author of the 75-yard quarterback sneak and other smash hits? As on so many mornings lately, he tucked a notebook under his arm and headed for the old game refuge, where he could rest his overtaxed nerves.

The same grubby friends were waiting in the toilet

off the entrance lobby of the public library. Bumping each other, they surrounded him, unshaved and reeking, coughing, their bloodshot eyes watering with affection. One of them unscrewed the cap of a pint of California muscatel and offered him the first belt. He sniffed the sweetish chemical odor, faked a sip and passed the bottle around. "Dee-licious," he pronounced. "I believe it's the hydrochloric acid that does it." Worn hands still blue from the cold grabbed for the bottle. "Way to go, Gabby," he said. "Since you busted that set of teeth, you don't spill half so much."

Grandly he lit up one of his little cigars and, after a couple of deep soulful drags, gave butts on it all around. Then he said, "Phil boy, I'll trouble you for the borrow of that baton." The old geezer, his coat held together with a safety pin, handed over his cane, and Chip led the way into the vast intimidating hush of the Reading Room. Past tiers and tiers of reference books, bound volumes of periodicals, encyclopedias. The lamps were small cups of light over the almost deserted tables.

As they straggled by, the guard, grim in his cop's uniform, gave each of them "the look": just put your head down, just close your eyes for one second, bum, and out you go.

Chip whispered to him, "Fine morning, ain't it?" They pulled out tomes at random and sat down to fake through the endless day with articles on the Boer War, the rise of Xerxes in a German encyclopedia, anything at all, blinking and blinking, fighting to keep their eyes open in the soft rustling warmth.

Chip picked up where he'd left off in *Prosser on Torts*, Third Edition. It was a whole new game, another board and a different set of chessmen. Once an hour he took off for a minute at one of the immense windows overlooking Michigan Avenue. The old hag who scattered bread crumbs to the pigeons had gone. The shabby gray birds swirled in the wind and settled on the pattern of walls and ledges in the snow-covered park.

Coming back to his place, he saw Charlie's ragged head sink toward his book. Quickly he snatched up the stinking clutch of old clothes and flesh. The guard, grudgingly, went back to his post by the door. "Thanks, Chip, thanks a million," Charlie snuffled. "Hey, what's the deal, huh? You're really readin that stuff. What you doin time here for?"

"Ssh! Man, it's *brisk* out there."

"Come off it. You got a room."

Chip shrugged. "Well, what with inflation and everything, I figure I better handle my own bankruptcy and divorce cases."

But Charlie's eyes were drifting and closing. "I can't make it till noon, Chip."

"Okay, let's take ten." He gave the signal, patting a loaded pocket in his elegant sports coat, and from all around dingy men shot up eagerly, coming. Along the ranks of books they went, a shambling procession led by a dapper little man, ex-scrambling quarterback, ex-Super Mouse, ex-bullfighter magician, ex- a lot of things, strolling away to the can with his team.

About the Author

Bernard Brunner was born in St. Paul, Minnesota, in 1923, the first of eleven children. Of his youth and education he writes: "Having helped my father to fail as a chicken farmer, I assisted my family through the Depression by caddying, stealing coal, gambling and hustling pool.

"I went to Bishop Cretin High School, a military academy two blocks away—and sixty-three degrees down the social scale—from St. Paul Military Academy, where F. Scott Fitzgerald was taught what little he knew. During World War II, by keeping my latrine spotless, I rose to the rank of Pfc. in forty months.

"The rest has been a Ph.D at the University of Chicago, current teaching at De Paul University, and a lot of writing. I am married and have one son, now at the University of Chicago, majoring in psychology. My only hobby is losing to him and his friends at chess."

Brunner is the author of three previous novels, *The Face of Night*, dealing with narcotics, *Uranium!* on the uranium boom in the fifties, and *The Golden Children*, on interracial marriage. *The Face of Night* has been made into a movie, "Hangup."